SHADOW OF A LIE

DS TONY HEATON'S COLD CASES

STEVE HIGGS

SHADOW OF A LIE
DS TONY HEATON'S COLD CASES

Book 1
Steve Higgs

Text Copyright © 2024 Steven J Higgs

Publisher: Steve Higgs

The right of Steve Higgs to be identified as author of the Work has been asserted by him in accordance with the Copyright, Designs and Patents Act 1988

All rights reserved.

The book is copyright material and must not be copied, reproduced, transferred, distributed, leased, licensed or publicly performed or used in any way except as specifically permitted in writing by the publishers, as allowed under the terms and conditions under which it was purchased or as strictly permitted by applicable copyright law. Any unauthorised distribution or use of this text may be a direct infringement of the author's and publisher's rights and those responsible may be liable in law accordingly.

'Shadow of a Lie' is a work of fiction. Names, characters, businesses, organisations, places, events and incidents either are the product of the author's imagination or are used fictitiously. Any resemblance to actual persons, living or dead, events or locations is entirely coincidental.

PROLOGUE – JUNE 1993

HE STOOD OVER THE BODY, HIS PULSE JACKED ABOUT AS high as it had ever been. The easy part was done, now he had to get away with it.

Get away with murder.

They would call the attack frenzied, he knew that much, and they would be right. Bruce Denton's attempts to escape or deflect the blows stopped more than a minute before his killer ceased swinging the old cricket bat he held.

Placing his hands on his knees as he sucked in gasping lungfuls of air, the killer was careful not to touch the walls with his body. There was blood on the protective outer layer he wore; transferring it could leave behind a smear that might tell the police ... something and the safe play was to leave nothing behind at all. Hence the protective outer layer.

Complete with gloves, overshoes, mask, and a hood, his DNA would go with him.

The body twitched, jolting Bruce's killer to once again raise the blunt weapon he employed for the grisly task. Holding it aloft, he prepared to deliver yet another blow only to lower it again a few seconds later content the victim's life had expired.

Another convulsion racked Bruce's body, confirming his killer was witnessing nothing more than cadaveric spasms. Not that he'd seen them before, not in person, but he knew what they were.

Looking around, the face behind his mask showed no trace of emotion. The murder had been necessary, at least that was what he told himself. It was his first and would be his last. Until a month ago, he would never have thought he was capable of such an act.

However, it turned out that all he needed was the right motivation.

The bat was going with him – leave no clues – as was the plastic coverall he wore. They would vanish, never to be found even if the police figured out the connection and came snooping. He very much doubted that would happen, but caution was his ally and he embraced it with both arms.

The body continued to twitch, the early signs of rigor mortis setting in. Soon Bruce Denton would be still and ever more would remain that way. He had paid for his sins and would never sin again. Acknowledging that fact brought a hint of a smile to his killer's lips.

Turning around, the killer walked away, taking care to avoid the spreading blood and the droplets on the tile floor in the kitchen where the attack began. At the backdoor, he took care to use two fingers free of his victim's blood to push the handle down and performed the same again on the outside to shut it soundlessly.

Waking the neighbours with the attack had formed his biggest worry. Weeks of planning and observation to learn the routines, not only of his victim but those living around him, provided a confidence level he needed before

Shadow of a Lie

proceeding, but there were elements outside of his control.

Leaving the house behind, the killer allowed himself a small congratulation on a plan well executed.

The plan had always been to find Bruce in his bed and deliver the first blow before he was even awake. It should have been easy to achieve, yet something had pulled the victim from his bed at three o'clock in the morning.

Barely had his killer made it into the kitchen before he heard the man's footsteps on the stairs. It was a good thing he did, or the perfectly planned murder could have gone terribly awry. The hood of his plastic coverall rustled continually, filling his ears with noise while Bruce descended the stairs barefoot, his passage revealed only when a step creaked.

Whether Bruce wanted a glass of water or a late-night snack, the killer would never know. Trapped in the kitchen with his intended victim heading his way, he was forced to improvise. Mercifully, Bruce was paying no attention in his sleepy state and failed to notice the killer hiding in the gap next to the refrigerator until it was too late.

Using an alleyway that ran behind the rear gardens of the houses, the killer slipped away, heading back to his car, but pausing to strip his gear before he got there. The overalls, the gloves, mask, and over boots all went into a black plastic sack. They would be incinerated; the only safe way to ensure they could never be found, and the ashes would be removed and scattered far away. The bat would likewise be burned, reduced to nothing so the victim's DNA, now embedded in the wood along with the killer's DNA from handling it in the past, would be obliterated.

How long until someone found the body? That was a key question. He thought it likely a day or more would pass. It was early on Saturday morning a week before the summer solstice. The first tendrils of sun were beginning to lighten the horizon to the east. Within an hour the land would be drenched in golden sunlight and by then the killer needed to be tucked up safely in bed pretending he'd never left.

Once again, he perceived no danger in that element of the crime. The risk-loaded elements were behind him, now all he needed to do was wait for Monday when Bruce would fail to show up for work. Someone would call and get no answer. They would call again and eventually become curious. The killer doubted the body would be found on Monday. Tuesday perhaps if someone from his work came by the house and peered through the letterbox.

The curtains at Bruce's house were closed to stop people peering in and had the murder gone to plan, the body would have been in his bed and impossible to see until someone entered his abode. Now though, if someone were to peer through the letterbox, they would see the blood on the walls and the victim's body lying at the end of the hallway linking the front door to the kitchen/dining room at the back. They would also know from the smell. At this time of year, flies would be laying eggs in the cadaver before the sun had time to set again.

There was nothing he could do to stop the body being found. Attempting to remove it would only increase the likelihood of being caught.

So he was ready for it to be found and had a plan for when it was.

A plan for how he was going to get away with murder.

CHAPTER 1

THIRTY YEARS AFTER BRUCE DENTON'S
MURDER

I PARKED MY TRUSTY, YET ANCIENT, VAUXHALL ASTRA estate and locked it using the key since the central locking had long since given up the ghost. I had to dash across the carpark, my bag above my head to avoid the steady drizzle falling. However, the weather laughed at my attempts to stay dry by placing a sizeable puddle in my path. Misjudging it in my haste, I absorbed several pints of cold, dirty water with my socks and the lowest inch of my trousers. Fantastic.

Had I arrived earlier, or as others might say 'on time', I would not find myself relegated to the back of the carpark and the last remaining spot. However, my motivation for keeping to the clock abandoned me years ago along with most of my effort, and with less than eight weeks to go until my mandatory retirement, it honestly felt like they were lucky I turned up at all.

"Late again, Tony," observed Doris, wandering down the corridor ahead of me when I came in. She had a steaming mug of tea in her right hand and a packet of biscuits in the other. She didn't care if I was late or not, her remark intended only as banter.

Somewhere deep into her sixties, Doris is as skinny as a soup chicken and is one of those really annoying people who can eat whatever they want without getting fat. Five feet four inches tall, with straight blonde hair that is mostly grey or white now, I could recall how attractive I found her when we first met. More than a decade my senior, she was a woman who could turn heads and did. Less so now, but time gets us all in the end.

I diffused her by opting to grin like a cheeky scamp.

At the top of the stairs, I poked my head around the corner to check the superintendent's door. It was open. Sucking on my top lip, I tried to get the attention of Gavin Dobbs, the other detective at the nick.

We work out of Herne Bay's police station, a run-down building with decrepit toilets and no budget to fix them. I started here more than thirty years ago and it's still the same interior paint though they went to the effort of updating the building's exterior – wouldn't want the public to think we were strapped for cash now, would we?

One street back from the seafront in this sleepy seaside town where nothing much ever happens, my lack of effort goes largely unnoticed. By everyone but my boss, that is.

Gavin looked up the third time I hissed at him. Sitting at his desk and engrossed by whatever report he was typing, Gavin did a double take when he realised he wasn't imagining someone quietly calling his name.

His understanding was instant, a knowing nod assuring me that he knew what I wanted. Craning his neck to check what Superintendent Charters was doing, he kept his eyes on the boss's office door when he gave me the thumbs up.

Trying to make it look casual, I hurried to my desk, slid my bag beneath it and stabbed the power button to light up my computer. *Oh, I've been here the whole time, boss.*

Continuing the act, I made sure to open several

Shadow of a Lie

searches and brought up the paperwork I should have submitted yesterday to accompany the shoplifting case I closed more than a week ago. Confident my day would drift by much the same as all the others in recent months – no one really cared what I did any longer – I was shocked to hear the superintendent calling my name.

I looked up, one eyebrow raised in question to find him out of his office and looking straight at me.

"Briefing room if you please, Tony. You've been assigned to a task force and your new partner is here. The two of you have some cases to solve."

"Don't be daft," I laughed, genuinely convinced he was pulling my leg though he wasn't known for possessing a sense of humour.

Rather than respond, the station's senior officer narrowed his eyes, waiting for me to curb my attitude and apologise for addressing him in such a manner. He stood little chance of that happening.

"I've got less than eight weeks left," I pointed out, continuing to ignore the disparity in rank. I mean, what could he possibly do to me other than what he was already proposing? "Giving me new cases is a poor strategy and you know it. Give them to Dobbs."

"Yeah, I'll take 'em, boss." Detective Sergeant Gavin Dobbs piped up from across the room.

Superintendent Charters acted as though Dobbs hadn't spoken, his gaze fixed firmly on my face. A small tic twitched next to his left eye, a sure sign he was weighing up chewing me out in front of everyone in the open-plan office. Nature made him both tall and barrel-chested. He towered over me, his bushy, black eyebrows acting like quotation marks around his annoyed expression.

To head him off, I said, "Boss," in a tone that wasn't exactly respectful and supplicant, but was several steps down from the aggressive challenge I started with. Mostly, it was a question: had he really thought this through?

Pursing his lips, the tic by his left eye refusing to settle, the superintendent growled, "I'll say it again, shall I? Clear your desk, DS Heaton, I have work for you. I'm afraid those detective skills of yours won't be going to pasture just yet. Head down to the briefing room."

A frown pinched my face, my eyebrows meeting in the middle as I tried to make sense of what was happening. You don't give fresh cases to a guy going out the door in a few weeks. You have him help others, tidy things up, deal with minor infractions and stuff. What kind of case was the boss proposing to give me? Something I could put to rest inside a few weeks, clearly, but even so, as a team we were not that busy and there were other guys, guys like Dobbs, who wanted the work.

Why give it to me?

"I don't see you moving, detective sergeant." The superintendent was yet to shift from where he stood looking down at me.

"I can take the case, boss," Dobbs tried again, his cheery and keen demeanour that of a Labrador puppy – eager to please, but clumsy. "Is it something juicy?"

Still unwilling to look his way, the boss said, "You are assigned to the Larson fraud investigation, are you not, Dobbs?"

"Yes, boss, I ..." Too dumb to see he was on the back foot and ought to be retreating, Dobbs would have continued speaking had the superintendent not shot him down.

"Then I suggest you get on with it, man!" the super spat, uncharacteristically raising his voice.

I knew why the outburst came. He didn't like coming onto the office floor and he hated being challenged. In his

Shadow of a Lie

mind his decisions were final and should never be questioned. I had never agreed with that policy, and it didn't help that I was his boss when he started. It gave me a position of latent authority that existed somewhere deep inside the superintendent's head. Somehow, he would always be Bobby Charters, the kid who wet his pants the first time he got into a scrape with a hardened criminal.

No one else in the station had been here long enough to remember that. Only me, and I was soon to leave.

Accepting defeat before things escalated, I asked around a sigh, "What's the job?" I figured we had a body in suspicious circumstances, a suicide most likely, but one that came without a note and would therefore require investigation. Or it was a burglary with property destruction on the side. I wagered myself a pork pie that it would be one or the other, a habit I developed long ago to keep myself entertained in what proved to be an unrewarding career.

With something akin to a grin, the super started walking toward the door. Over his shoulder, and with a definite chuckle in his voice, he said, "Multiple murders, Detective Sergeant Heaton. Multiple murders."

My eyebrows bolted for my hairline, expressing their surprise while the rest of me was still trying to catch up.

Dobbs mouthed, "Multiple murders?" his words capturing the confusion passing through the entire room as everyone looked about at their colleagues, each asking if the person across from them had any idea what the superintendent was talking about.

This is Herne Bay, a sleepy nowhere destination in the southeast corner of England. We don't get murders, let alone a slaughterhouse full of them. How could there be multiple murders and none of us knew anything about it?

Rising to my feet, I said, "Sir?"

Naturally, I wanted to know what was going on. He

said the words 'multiple murders' with a chuckle and seemed to want to give the case to a man with less than two months to serve. There was something he knew that he thought it amusing not to share.

Pausing in the doorway that led to his office and the stairs to go down to reception, the custody centre, and the briefing room, Superintendent Charters turned around. I think he planned to say something cryptic, but seeing the concerned faces staring back at him, he relented.

"A national audit of unsolved murders took place earlier this year. The results were announced a week ago."

I glanced at the old, cardboard case file tucked under a pile of paper at the end of my desk, a stab of guilt making my heart pound for a second.

Around the room, my colleagues were again exchanging looks: did anyone know about the survey?

"Kent scored second to last," the superintendent continued at a volume intended to make sure everyone heard. "Only Northumberland rated lower. Consequently, the Chief Constable for Kent has deemed it necessary to deploy a task force to tackle a slew of what you would all like to call 'cold cases'." He stopped speaking to shoot a meaningful look in my direction. "I'm sure, DS Heaton, you can imagine why I picked you for this task."

A rush of blood sounded like a claxon inside my head, my brain filling with conflicting emotions, thoughts, and ... memories.

I missed what the superintendent said next, but he was going out the door and it was clear he expected me to follow. The door swung shut to muffle the sound of his footsteps on the stairs, but I heard them all the same.

My whole body numb like I'd been sedated, I gripped the edge of the ratty, cardboard folder. Tugging it out from

Shadow of a Lie

under a pile of loosely stacked papers I'd been happily ignoring for weeks, my heart thudded in my chest.

"This is great news, Tony," said Gavin, the eternal optimism of youth rising to the surface once again. "You've been trying to solve that thing forever. Maybe some fresh eyes will help."

CHAPTER 2

I COULD HAVE TOLD GAVIN THAT FRESH EYES WERE THE last thing the case needed. I wanted to scream that there was no way I was turning it over to a task force of detectives I didn't know. Not that I would get a choice in the matter, not if the chief constable wanted it to be investigated.

My hand trembled slightly when I lifted the case file from the surface of my desk. It had a coffee ring on the front cover and various other marks where the passage of time had eroded the pristine look it possessed when my fingers first touched it.

The file number was written in my hand, as were most of the notes inside. I didn't need to open the folder to review the contents; I could probably recite them.

Bruce Denton. Thirty-one years of age. A schoolteacher by profession. Brutally bludgeoned to death in his own house. That was thirty-years ago. Thirty years. The passage of time resounded like a gong inside my head.

Pushing painful memories from my mind, I dropped the file into my drawer and locked it. Everyone in the office

Shadow of a Lie

was looking my way though most were pretending not to. They all knew about the case. They all knew what happened and what it did to me ... to my career. They all knew how all it took was the very mention of the victim's name to send me into a spiral of depression that could last hours or days. Bruce Denton was a trigger for mental ill health and likely always would be.

Taking my notebook, I left the office without another word, descending the stairs two at a time as if acting unphased would cover how thrown I felt.

Arriving on the ground floor, I heard the superintendent's voice drifting out from the briefing room. He was talking about me, so without the slightest soupçon of shame, I chose to pause outside the door to listen.

"What do you know about DS Heaton?" he posed the question to someone unseen.

"Nothing, Sir, other than he is close to retirement. My boss, DCI Harris, told me Heaton was known as a talented detective, that he used to be requested by senior investigating officers across the county because of his ability to read suspects and close cases."

The voice was young, in line with my expectations. It was also male, but beyond the accent which bore a London twang, I could determine little about its owner.

Superintendent Charters gave a small snort which could have meant anything, but followed it up with his summation of my abilities.

"Yes, that may be true, but I'm afraid DS Heaton is no longer the detective he used to be."

I gritted my teeth.

"While it may be true that he has an uncanny sense of ... shall we call it 'smell' for unpicking the subtext of what suspects are really saying, what they are trying hard to keep secret, over the last decade or so DS Heaton's attitude toward work and his level of commitment to taking down criminals has become less than exemplary."

I knew this was true, but it spoke volumes about my boss that he would tell my new partner what to expect before he'd even met me. Talk about setting someone up.

"You will find he has a chip on his shoulder too. DS Heaton views senior officers such as myself as nothing more than incompetent brown nosers who advanced only because we are prepared to play a political game. However, were it not for his downfall, he would likely be my boss by now."

"His downfall, Sir?" the other man in the room voiced a question. "Is that to do with Bruce Denton?"

"Yes."

I wanted to shove my way into the room so Charters would have to shut his mouth, but morbid curiosity made me wait to hear what he would say next.

"Heaton lost the one piece of evidence that might have brought Bruce Denton's killer to justice. It was pure incompetence; nothing more or less. He will tell you his boss at the time hung him out to dry, but the truth is the killer got away with it because DS Heaton took his eye off the ball."

The muscles in my jaw tensed and my right hand rose to grab the door handle. I dearly wanted to burst into the room to point out that he was still in school when Bruce Denton was murdered. Superintendent Charters had no idea what happened any more than anyone else. They knew the rumours. No one knew the truth, and no one ever would. That was a secret I would carry to my grave.

With a deep breath in and then out, I let my hand drop back to my side.

It was shaking.

Shadow of a Lie

Obsessive Compulsive Disorder, that was the name they gave to it. They also likened my condition to PTSD. When the whole case petered into nothing, every possible suspect finding a way to muddy the water enough to avoid being charged, I just couldn't let it be.

If there was a clue out there, I was going to find it. Someone had to have seen something. Someone had to know something that was yet to come to light. New cases came my way. Hundreds of them, in fact. But the Bruce Denton murder stuck with me, eating into my weekends and evenings as I went back to talk to his neighbours, his work colleagues and friends, the people living in the street behind him … Time and again, I begged them for any tiny detail they could scrape from the dark recesses of their minds.

After a time, some started to complain. Some even called it harassment. They felt they had answered the questions and had no more to give. Not all of them though. Bruce's parents were always pleased to see me; they wanted their son's killer brought to justice. However, like everyone else, they had no idea who might have perpetrated the deed.

Closing my eyes, I drew a deep breath though my nose. My boss was still bad mouthing me in the briefing room. I didn't want to let him say anything more, but slamming the door open and challenging him would bring me nothing but grief. Instead, I backtracked to the stairs and made sure to kick the bottom step so they would hear me coming.

I was almost at the briefing room when my boss stepped out of it and closed the door. I thought perhaps he might have a few words of encouragement to give despite his obvious feelings about me, but that was not the case.

Leering down at me with a smug grin, he said, "You're no good anymore, Heaton."

I blinked, caught off guard by the unexpected verbal attack. Trying to go around him, he moved to block my path.

"Sometimes I wonder if you ever were. Do you really think that idiot Dobbs is able to cover up your constant tardiness? The sooner you retire the better."

Sneering up into his face, I smiled when I said, "I've got twice your brain and I'm ten times the cop you'll ever be. Ask around, boss, you're a joke."

He snorted a laugh, trying to show I amused him, but the tic was back, a certain sign that my remarks had hit home and their accuracy was making him angry.

"Heaton, you contribute almost nothing. Maybe you were a hotshot thief-taker once, but you're over the hill now and about to be put out to pasture. This will be your last assignment and I'm making you someone else's headache. Try not to embarrass yourself too much, eh."

He turned around before I could respond and shoved his way into the briefing room, leaving the door ajar.

I fumed for a few seconds, my lips twitching as I fought against my desire to tell him exactly where he could stick his new assignment. It would feel good to speak my mind, but unleashing the words in my head would result in formal disciplinary action my superintendent would revel in dishing out. I couldn't give him the satisfaction. Also, he was right about most of it. I *had* stopped trying. It's what happens when people with less brain and less talent are constantly promoted past you because of a single event many years ago.

I drew another deep breath in through my nose and pushed my way through the door.

Sitting inside the briefing room, though he rose to his

Shadow of a Lie

feet at my arrival, was a young man of Caribbean descent who looked almost too young to be out of school. He wore a suit that had to be handmade and looked expensive. It told me everything I needed to know about the man inside it.

Walk into any police station in any part of the world and you will find a kid in their late twenties or early thirties, newly promoted, and wearing a suit they believe will impress their bosses. The older cops know better. They wear no-iron, stain-free suits they can buy off the peg and don't have to worry too much about when a late-night drunk vomits down it.

I wore a suit just like the kid's when I was his age.

Both men turned my way when I strode confidently into the room.

"Ah, Tony," the super chose to address me informally. A smile had replaced the scowl he offered me only moments earlier as though we were colleagues and friends. "This is your new partner, Detective Sergeant Long. He is, as I already explained, part of the task force assigned to tackle the backlog of unsolved murders."

We shook hands, his grip weak in mine. I didn't like him already. At least they only sent one man.

"Ashley," he gave me his first name.

"Ashley … Long?" I repeated his name and scrutinised his features. "You're one of the Longs."

The Long family had a big tradition of policing.

"That's right, Tony," agreed the superintendent. "Ashley's uncle is Commissioner Long. His father heads the Special Branch task force, and he has several other relatives in high-ranking positions across Kent and the Met."

I met my new partner's eyes, assessing him. Was it family pressure that drove him to join the police? Were they all looking down at him expecting great things?

STEVE HIGGS

The super had introduced me already, but I said, "Tony," for the sake of it.

"You have much in common with DS Long," remarked the superintendent with a smile.

"Oh?" I released the man's hand, noting that he continued to study me while his arm fell back to rest at his side.

"DS Long recently aced his sergeant's exam, Tony. Isn't that your big claim to fame?"

Despite the desire to spit venom in his direction, I smiled. "Yes. That's right, Sir. It made me think I was clever for a while," I replied pointedly, my gaze locked on DS Long's face.

He got what I was saying, but didn't respond.

Oblivious, the superintendent continued to talk.

"Now I want the two of you to work together, understood?"

He got a "Yes, Sir," from the pair of us though DS Long's was eager and mine came out barely awake.

"The Chief Constable for Kent wants as many of these old cases cleared up as possible and I expect the two of you to do better than the other teams across the county."

Of course, he wanted me to work hard and get results so he could look good. I felt like reminding him I had less than two months until my last day and nothing I did was going change my pension for the better. I could do the bare minimum quite happily. However, a glance at DS Long told me cruising through the next few weeks was going to be impossible, the man radiated barely restrained enthusiasm.

"DS Long has a list of cases. The two of you should pick those you believe stand the best chance of netting a result." He twisted his torso to look at me. "This is DS Long's assignment, Tony. You are to work alongside him as

Shadow of a Lie

local liaison – DS Long is new to the area – and to lend your many years of knowledge and experience."

The frown pulling my eyebrows down was epic enough to stop the superintendent speaking. It was only a few minutes since I last challenged him, but there was no chance I was letting this one go by without comment.

"You're putting the puppy in charge?" I demanded to know.

"The puppy?" DS Long faced me, an entertained chortle on his lips.

The superintendent was less amused.

"No, DS Heaton, I am not placing *DS Long* in charge." His voice carried the timbre of warning. "You have seniority, of course. However, as you were so swift to point out upstairs, you are weeks away from retirement and you are not, DS Heaton, the most proactive of police officers. DS Long will call the shots on which cases the two of you will investigate. It is his boss to whom the two of you are reporting. Is that understood?"

I'd asked for it, I had to admit. He was right about my lack of proactivity too. These days I did just enough to be certain that I wasn't creating or sideloading work to anyone else – that sort of thing can make a person unpopular very fast.

Off balance due to old memories resurfacing plus the unexpected and unwelcome emotions they brought making me act irrationally, I took a step closer to my boss. His eyes flared in surprise, but I wasn't about to back down. That's the joy of having nothing left to lose and only a limited amount of time left to suffer.

Raising my right hand, the index finger extended, I said, "We're not investigating the Bruce Denton case." It was a statement, but shooting for determined authority, my shaking hand betrayed my emotions to make me look weak

STEVE HIGGS

and afraid. Nevertheless, I had to stamp my foot. I could not ... would not put myself back in *that* situation.

My obsession with finding what was missed almost broke me. It damned near ended my marriage and drove a wedge between me and my daughter who rightfully accused me of giving all my time to it instead of her. To go back to that now ... if I so much as thought too hard about it ...

Superintendent Charters' lip twitched, a snarl trying to make its way to the surface only to be turned away by forced calm. "Watch your tone, Detective Sergeant."

To my right, DS Long watched the display without comment, his expression professionally unreadable.

"The cases to be investigated will be decided by DS Long as I have already stated, DS Heaton. It is not open to discussion or negotiation. If 'your' case is deemed to be one that can be solved with fresh eyes and fresh perspective, then it will be on the list."

"It is on the list," confirmed DS Long, his voice deliberately neutral.

I rounded on him, unable to stop myself. "You think you can solve a case I've been investigating since before you were born? Half the witnesses and persons connected to the case have died since. There are no leads, man! There never were."

DS Long said nothing, tempting me into filling the silence. Was he trying to get me to blow my top, was that it? I had insulted him, making a point about his age when I was probably younger the day they pinned three stripes on me. An outburst now would give him all the ammunition he would need to demand a new partner. One from a different station probably. I couldn't allow that. Not when there was a chance they would reopen the Bruce Denton murder case. I had to be involved.

Shadow of a Lie

DS Long would learn of my obsession and most likely see it firsthand. I didn't want that either, but I could not risk letting someone else find what I might have missed, so it had to be me. In fact, if I was with DS Long I could steer him away from the case. Shouting at him to leave it alone was likely to have the opposite effect.

Dropping my head and eyes to the ground, I knew the superintendent was about to lambast me for my behaviour. I needed to get in quick and repair the damage fast.

Snapping my head back up, I looked at my new partner, fixing it squarely in my head that I needed to think of him as precisely that now.

"DS Long I owe you an apology. I hope you can understand how I feel about the Bruce Denton case. I'd like to start over, if you'll allow me."

He shook my hand, his grip just as weak this time as the last.

The super watched over us both and I addressed him next.

"Sir, I owe you an apology too. The case has always brought deep emotions to the surface. I'll do my best to assist DS Long in his mission to resolve whatever cold cases he deems worthy."

I hated that the superintendent was so much taller than me. At six feet and five inches, he towered over my five feet eleven. I swear I used to measure over six feet in my twenties. Where did the inch go? Now *there* was a case that needed to be solved.

Looking down at me, the super acknowledged my apology with a nod, but wasn't about to extend to forgiveness.

Heading for the door, he said, "The chief constable expects results, gentlemen. *I* expect results."

He got a hearty 'Yes, Sir," from DS Long. I didn't

bother to reply, my head filled with images of Bruce Denton's mangled body.

The Superintendent's footsteps, loud and echoey in the hallway outside, faded into the distance leaving just me and Detective Sergeant Ashley Long, my new partner, shrouded in uncomfortable silence.

CHAPTER 3

DS Long folded his arms and tilted his head just a little to the left. I turned to face him.

"What?"

"You didn't mean any of that, did you? You apologised in front of your boss because you were being a dick, but you see this assignment as a punishment. Stuck with 'a puppy' for the next few weeks, right?"

I let a heavy breath deflate my lungs, exhaling through my nose in a kind of tired sigh. I had to tell him something, explain things in a way that would deflect him in the right direction, not the wrong one.

"The Bruce Denton case is …" I made a show of struggling to find the right word, "it's deeply personal. I tried to solve it for more than two decades before I was forced to give it up."

"Forced?"

The less I told him, the better, but I could sense he was going to keep digging unless I gave him a reason not to.

"I became … it made me sick, okay? It became all consuming. I … I couldn't not look at it. The more years I put into it, the deeper my obsession with solving it became." I took a moment, moving my head and eyes away to focus on the past.

DS Long waited, saying nothing.

"My wife almost left me. I was just never there. My days off, my weekends, I spent them trying to figure out if there was something I missed. There were suspects, and any one of them could yet be guilty, but there is no evidence." It wasn't hard to make my voice sound weary. Beaten. "No trace of a clue, no leads to follow. I cannot go back to *that* case. Other than that, whether I want to be stuck with you is irrelevant. We have our orders. I think we should just get on with it."

When DS Long didn't move, I grabbed a chair. The kid had a laptop with him, a police issue one with the encryption key. I figured he had data on there he would want to review with me before we did anything else.

"Shall we?" I asked, though implored might be a better term for the emotion I put into the question.

DS Long didn't move. He waited for me to look his way and only then did he break his silence.

"I read the case file in detail."

I closed my eyes and tried not to cringe. Had he not heard anything I said?

"Your investigation was solid. At least that's how it looked to me. In fact, it looked as though your superintendent, acting as the senior investigating officer, took a back seat and let you do most of the work."

"Well, things were different thirty years ago, kid."

"Ashley."

"Hmm?"

"My name is Ashley. I'm not kid or sport or junior. And don't ever call me a puppy again." He was trying to sound tough at the end, but couldn't quite pull it off. It might work on younger men, but I've faced too many criminals

Shadow of a Lie

who thought going down while fighting a cop would earn them kudos in jail to be impressed by a skinny kid in a good suit. "We're the same rank," he added.

"Okay, Ashley." I twisted through ninety degrees in my chair, so I faced him. "What's it to be? If you agree to leave the Bruce Denton case alone, I will do my utmost to assist you." My utmost wasn't going to match up to what he wanted, but that's what you get when you push a guy this close to retirement into doing things he would rather avoid. "Honestly, I'm doing you a favour by leading you away from it."

He eyed me sceptically, looking to me as though he was weighing up what he really believed. The Bruce Denton case was juicy. If our roles were reversed, would I let a reputedly lazy, over-the-hill, weeks-from-retirement has-been talk me out of pursuing it?

Surprising me, he settled into the chair next to mine.

"Okay. We'll put a pin in the Denton case. For now," he added. "It was going to be our first investigation. I was genuinely pleased when they said you were to be my partner."

I let a sad smile slip across my lips.

"Living up to the legend yet?"

"Hardly," he harrumphed. Resigning to his new situation, he said, "Look, all I'm saying is the Denton case needs some new eyes. You know as well as anyone that people miss things when they look at them over and over again. Fresh eyes might make a difference."

I chose not to argue. He'd already agreed to put it to one side which was all I wanted. I tapped his laptop with a finger to indicate I expected him to open it.

"Shall we review some of the other cases? I'm sure there must be several."

He didn't move for a second or so, continuing to watch

my face as though looking for something unspoken, hidden behind my eyes. It only lasted for a couple of seconds, but I could tell he wasn't going to let the Bruce Denton murder lie for long.

The kid - I was going to think of him in those terms even if I didn't employ them verbally - flipped open his laptop and brought it to life.

"There are six of us on the task force, headed up by a chief inspector who reports directly to the Chief Constable of Kent. The county has been likewise divided into six, though the northern half got the bulk of the personnel."

It was closer to London and more densely populated than the south. Significantly more densely populated, the press of people on top of one another creating friction as it always does in urban areas. That would be why they had more officers covering it.

Ashley hid his disappointment at being assigned one of the quieter regions, but I could see it bothered him. Just like me thirty years ago, he wanted to get recognised. The way to do that was to excel with big cases, to work with the right people in the right environments. He'd got lucky in being assigned to the task force only to find himself sent to the middle of nowhere and shackled to a deadbeat cop weeks from retirement. No wonder he wanted to go after the Denton case.

Well, tough luck, kid.

"The cases were assigned to each member of the task force based on area, age, and likelihood that new technology might allow us to produce evidence that never came to light during the initial investigation."

"How far back are we going?" I wanted to know, curious to hear if we might be going after some Jack the Ripper style figure from the nineteenth century.

"Thirty years. Here's the list." He twisted the laptop so

Shadow of a Lie

it faced me. "Further back than that and the algorithm determined the likelihood of finding a perpetrator alive reduced to less than thirty percent. My guess is they want to see arrests, not successfully closed cases with no one to pay the penalty."

We were sitting at the corner of the table that ran the length of the briefing room where the superintendent held his weekly meetings and got people together when he had a case worthy of team effort.

I used two fingers to turn the laptop just a little more, doing so to remove the glare from the overhead lamp. Now able to see the screen a little clearer, I had the kid explain the colour coding.

"Green is for the cases considered to hold the greatest likelihood of success. Orange is for those that might be worth investigation, and the red ones are those my boss and I believe were investigated thoroughly the first time around or have a lesser likelihood of being solved. Unless we solve a bunch of these really quick, I don't think it's worth looking at any of the ones in red."

I could hear something in his tone, a thing he was choosing not to say. Studying his face for a few seconds, I attempted to figure out what it might be. Was he hiding a lie? That was my initial assessment though I could not guess what it might be. I've been called many things in my life, but a natural detective is one that kept coming up. I have a knack for hearing lies and having recognised that ability, made sure to pursue it. People act differently when they lie, most of them, anyway. If one knows what to look for, there are facial cues, small gestures, even the way a person breathes can change.

Knowing what to look for and being able to sense when I was hearing the truth or otherwise has helped me to close more cases more quickly than my contemporaries could believe. Not that it ever did me any good. Not after Bruce Denton.

I scanned over the spreadsheet, noting unhappily that 'my' case was highlighted in green as one of those deemed worthy of attention.

DS Long pushed back his chair. "I'm going to the gents," he announced. "Where are they?"

I pointed along the hallway, my eyes never leaving the screen. "That way. On the left. Those ones are freezing though. Best to use the ones upstairs."

He murmured a thank you as he went out the door, closing it behind him.

There were thirty-seven cases, the bulk of them unsolved murders. Set out in a spreadsheet with a front page to show them all – which was where he'd applied the colour coding – and a separate tab for every case thereafter. That Bruce Denton's murder didn't fall into the red zone as a case where the original investigation was judged to be watertight felt like a slap to my face. Of course, I knew why they chose to question it. It was a horrible crime that shocked a town where murder was so rare it was people's grandparents who remembered the last one.

That wasn't totally accurate of course; there were cases every year, but nothing like the premeditated crime I failed to solve.

It hadn't helped that it was so public. In a slow news week, the national papers got hold of the story, someone leaking grisly details to make it all the juicier for the press. When I lost the best piece of evidence only minutes after obtaining it, it guaranteed my fall from grace. My superintendent at the time made sure everyone knew it wasn't his fault.

Moving on, certain I could steer my new partner away from investigating Bruce Denton's murder, a quick inspec-

Shadow of a Lie

tion revealed the tabs contained reams of information, most likely imported from the original case files. The senior investigating officer or SIO was named along with anyone else who worked on each case. Hyperlink brought up coroner's reports and there was more. Much more.

The more included a notes section where DS Long, I assumed, had already begun to compile thoughts and next steps for some of the cases. He was organised, I had to give him that.

There were names I knew, and a few cases I recognised. One was a French tourist, Michelle Canet, stabbed to death in Whitstable three years ago. I recalled a rumour of drugs, or a drug deal gone wrong and wondered if I had that right.

Another I picked out as familiar was Grace Snoke. It was the name I recognised. A forty-three-year-old woman who went missing from her Canterbury home. Her husband called the police when he woke in the morning to find her gone. They found what was left of her body three months later, but no arrest had ever been made.

Both those cases were in the green area and despite myself, I had to admit I was genuinely interested to see if there was anything there to find. Could I, in my last few weeks, solve a couple of old murder cases? It would be something to tell my wife.

I sniggered at myself. It sounded like a fun thing to do, but I knew the energy and interest required for such an undertaking had long since left me. At DS Long's age, I was like a terminator – utterly unstoppable. Even after Bruce Denton and the fall that followed, I believed I could recover my standing and status with hard work. If anything, in the years after I lost the evidence that might have caught his killer, I worked harder than I had before. Compensating, I guess.

However, over the course of the last decade, my energy levels have dropped and while the detective's mind remains keen, I have no desire to test it. I have become increasingly hostile to my superiors, highlighting their failures and arguing against petty policies that make no sense. So many of them arrived at where they are by saying yes and kissing butt, rather than by being true leaders. Superintendent Smart back in 1993 had been just like that.

My current boss wasn't much better.

The sound of feet coming down the stairs heralded DS Long's return. He had been absent for almost ten minutes.

"Number two?" I enquired, eliciting a frown from the younger man. Coming out of my chair I stood up and made it clear I was ready to go. "Just kidding," I teased. "Shall we?" I was indicating back along the hallway, the suggestion that we should leave the station obvious.

"You want to get started straight away?" he questioned. "You don't want to discuss the cases and which ones we should prioritise?"

I shrugged, stepping back out of his way so he could collect his laptop and a small Nike sports bag sitting on another of the chairs.

"I saw your spreadsheet. If not the Denton case, I'm sure you have another one to which you wish to defer."

"I do."

I shrugged again, not able to raise enough interest to ask which case he planned to tackle. "So let's go."

CHAPTER 4

DS Long drove a silver Ford Mondeo just like half the plain clothes officers in the country. I settled into the passenger's seat, silently fuming. Now that the terror of reopening the Bruce Denton files had eased, I was left feeling annoyed.

Anyone else in my position would be allowed to coast; it was an expected and unspoken reward for all the years of service. Instead, I was being made to babysit a junior detective with an inflated ego. I had seen the look in his eyes back in the briefing room; he genuinely believed he was going to solve some of these old cases. Cases that a fully staffed team of seasoned professional officers failed to crack when the evidence was fresh.

Unable to keep the words in my mouth, I said, "You know this is a crap assignment, right?"

DS Long twitched his eyes in my direction, but said nothing, waiting for me to expand on my statement.

"No one actually expects you or any of the other poor schmucks assigned to this task force to clear the unsolved cases."

DS Long smiled, but the emotion never made it to his eyes. "Isn't that all the more reason to do precisely that?"

"The optimism and indomitable spirit of youth." I sighed. "I remember when I was that dumb. The chief constable was embarrassed by the results of some audit. Right now, it's probably all the big wigs are talking about. It probably got discussed in parliament, but give it a week and the chief constable's attention will be elsewhere. A new problem will come along, and no one will care whether you close one of these cases or not."

DS Long flicked on his indicator, passing a slow-moving truck. "You may be right. However, I have been given an assignment. It was an order, not a request, and I intend to give it my best, just like I would any other assignment. And you are right, by the way, I am optimistic, and I refuse to be beaten. That includes when I get partnered with a pessimistic old fart who thinks leaving the office is a challenge."

I couldn't help the smile that clawed its way onto my face. It was a fair assessment if nothing else. I could have offered a retort, but I had no need to escalate things and in truth, I *was* enjoying being out of the office. Not that I was about to admit it.

We fell into an uneasy silence.

The earlier rain had given way to a cloudless sky. Dappled sunlight shone through the trees to our left until the woodland gave way to fields. They were devoid of life now, the summer crops already harvested to leave a patchwork of scruffy dark brown rectangles divided by thick green worms of hedgerow.

The North Downs, a series of rolling hills that dominate this part of the county ensured a continual rise and fall as we traversed the open plains between the towns and villages. Here and there we passed through a collection of

Shadow of a Lie

houses barely big enough to be called a hamlet though they each contained enough residents to support a public house and a church.

"Where are we going?" I enquired. We were heading out of Herne Bay, but that came as no surprise because the town is tiny. Two minutes in any direction and you are hitting the outskirts. Our nick covers the town and the surrounding villages where the population could be counted using fingers and toes in some cases.

To the west, the larger and busier seaside town of Whitstable had its own nick. Less popular during Victorian times when the concept of a holiday by the sea first became a thing, Whitstable came into its own when a famous artist remarked about the quality of light to be found there. It was utter guff, obviously, the light being the same everywhere, but a large natural oyster bed helped to boost the tourist interest through the 20th century while the development of Herne Bay dwindled.

It didn't help that people travelling down from London to escape the bustle of the nation's capital reached Whitstable first. Why stay on the train for an extra stop when the sea is right there beckoning you from the other side of your carriage's window?

To the east there was nothing worthy of mention until one reached Margate. We, however, were heading inland.

Ashley flicked his eyes to the rear-view mirror before answering my question, "Wingham."

I consulted my memory. Was there a case in Wingham on the list he showed me? I hadn't noticed it if there was, but my scrutiny of his cold case spreadsheet had been cursory at best. Straining my brain, because I knew the answer and it wouldn't surface, I caught a glimpse of the truth and found myself frowning.

"You're not talking about Craig Chowdry, are you?" I

both knew that he was and knew that he couldn't be. It made no sense.

DS Long nodded his head, his eyes never leaving the road.

"Yes. It's a prominent case ..."

I cut him off to point out what I knew to be a pertinent fact. "It's a missing person case."

"You're about to ask me why we are looking into a missing person case when there are murders to go around. The answer is quite simple: everyone knows he was murdered. They found more than a pint of his blood in a meadow half a mile from his house."

I cut him off again.

"I remember the case, thank you. I was a police officer at the time. You were still at school, right?"

DS Long snorted a breath through his nose. "University, actually. Were you involved in the case? I didn't see your name on the case notes anywhere."

It wasn't exactly my intention to wind the kid up. Not really. My dig about his age just slipped out, but he wasn't rising to the bait. Apart from the growl I got from him when he insisted I never call him puppy again, he came across as cool and unflappable, just like I used to be, and now that I was thinking about it, I could recall how annoying my colleagues used to find it.

Since I hadn't responded to his question, DS Long continued to talk.

"Sixteen-year-old Craig Chowdry went missing seven years ago. Just up and vanished one day. The SIO suspected a group of local boys. They were known to the victim, though he went to Hadlow College."

"Bright kid then," I remarked. Hadlow College wasn't just a private school where your parents needed to have some serious wonga to open the door, you also had to

Shadow of a Lie

qualify to attend. They boasted three prime ministers and a whole stack of industry leaders among their former pupils.

"Undoubtedly." DS Long brushed my comment aside so he could continue. "He was the only kid from the area who didn't go to the local school. I'm sure you know how that goes."

I did. Kids are pack animals, especially teenage boys. They want someone to pick on and the one who isn't part of the group will always be the target.

"Let me guess," I said, "He used to go to school with the other boys, but they went to the local comprehensive and their friendship ended when they left junior school."

"That would be correct, though you are assuming the friendship. They went to Goodnestone Church of England School until they were eleven. That much we know. Craig was also dating Sarah French, the sister of one of the boys suspected of being involved."

"But there's no body," I identified the key problem with his desire to investigate. No body means no one can be charged with murder unless there is solid evidence to prove a person did something to make the body disappear. If Craig Chowdry vanished seven years ago, then his former schoolfriends were all in their early twenties now. It was going to be a slog to prove it was murder which begged a question.

"Why do you want to pursue this one?"

DS Long nodded his head, sucking on his bottom lip as he thought about what he wanted to say.

"Had you read into the case as I have this past week, you would have spotted that the four boys suspected of involvement in Craig's disappearance all have very tightly constructed stories. They provide alibis for each other and their accounts of the day on which the victim went missing

35

STEVE HIGGS

support each other with no cracks or omissions. Under interview they were able to maintain their accounts without once slipping up."

"So they had a good solicitor who coached them and made sure their stories were straight," I concluded. I had seen it before.

DS Long took his eyes off the road for the first time since starting the engine. Looking directly at me, the expression conveyed the deep meaning behind his words.

"They didn't have a solicitor."

A frown arrived unbidden on my forehead. No solicitor? Most people end up with the duty solicitor when what they really need is a committed and motivated professional assigned specifically to their case. Such a person might have been able to make sure the boys' stories didn't contradict each other and that they remembered the same things happening at the same time. The likelihood of that occurring otherwise ... well, it wouldn't happen. It didn't happen. It would have been highlighted instantly by the prosecution counsel, but the case never came to court because Craig's body was never found.

His eyes back on the road, DS Long sounded satisfied when he remarked, "I thought that might get your interest."

It had. The lack of a solicitor wasn't all that unusual. The boys would have been questioned with a parent or guardian present who may have felt there was no requirement for legal assistance. Sometimes they mistakenly assume it will make their child look more guilty. Other times, they believe their child to be innocent and knowing they will have to wait for a solicitor to show up, decide they have better things to do.

However, if I took Ashley's claims at face value, then

Shadow of a Lie

there was something fishy going on and the senior investigating officer would have identified it instantly.

"There's nothing on record to show he was even aware," Ashley replied when I raised the question. "I mean, he must have been, but it's not shown in the case notes. The whole thing fizzled out and the four boys were released without charge."

I could have quizzed him on why he felt the four boys, now men, were guilty, but the more pertinent questions were all to do with why he thought he would be able to prove it seven years on. The mild interest he managed to pique was already waning, so all I said was, "This is it then? Figure out what happened to Craig Chowdry and get your name in the papers." It was another dig at him, but if he said he wasn't going after it for the attention it would get, I was going to call him a liar.

"First." He had a big grin on his face when I looked his way.

"I'm sorry?"

"First. We are pursuing this one *first*. I can't focus on just one of these cases and hope I can bring it home. That won't be good enough even if we do identify and catch Craig's killer. And what if we focus on one case and fail? I'm afraid, Tony, you and I are going to look into every last one of these cases. It's going to be a busy few weeks."

I said nothing and could feel Ashley glancing at me.

After thirty seconds of silence, he said, "Not going to remind me we agreed to leave Bruce Denton alone?"

I huffed out a breath and tried to ignore the mounting stress making my stomach twist. He was going to keep prodding and poking, that much was obvious. And his ego was even worse than I first thought; he believed he was going to solve not one case, but several of them. Cases that were investigated into the ground years ago by teams of competent officers.

Refusing to meet his gaze, I reaffirmed my earlier position.

"I – I can't," I stuttered. I clenched my hands, wiping sweaty palms against my thighs. I sucked in a deep breath and tried to control it.

Ashley side-eyed me, a slight frown creasing his forehead when he took in my agitated state.

"I hope you're ok just talking about it," Ashley remarked casually like my confessed obsession over Bruce Denton was no big deal. "I know we agreed not to pursue it, so let's call it ... professional interest. One cop talking to another about a case. I'm sure you're ok with that." He wasn't asking my opinion.

He was being persistent.

Problematically so.

I sucked in a deep breath and closed my eyes, rubbing my palms against my trousers again as I fought to shut out the ghost in my head.

Ashley took his eyes off the road. "Hey, are you okay?"

"Pull over," I blurted the words, getting them out quickly as though fearing my lips might be about to stop working.

"You going to throw up?"

I felt the car slow, Ashley taking his foot off the accelerator and checking his rear-view mirror. There was nowhere to pull over, no layby in which to take a pause, but he was going to have to stop anyway.

"Pull over!" I repeated adding volume and urgency. It was enough to jolt my new partner into action. I had my eyes closed so didn't see it, but felt when the wheels on my side left the road. Crunching gravel and the whack of

Shadow of a Lie

stringy weeds against the paintwork ended when the car slewed to a sudden stop.

"Don't throw up in the car, man!" Ashley slipped his seatbelt and invaded my personal space to get to the door handle on my side. Fresh air flooded in, carrying with it the heady scent of recently disturbed dirt.

I fumbled for my own belt, pressing the button and twisting to face the open door when it whipped past my face.

Ashley hovered, unsure what he was supposed to do while I tried not to hyperventilate. I had my arms wrapped around my body, hugging myself, and I rocked gently, reminding myself of all the things the appointed psychiatrist had said – the coping mechanisms.

Ashley enquired if I was okay and if there was anything he could do, but when I failed to respond the first two times, he gave up. A short while later, I could hear him tapping away on his phone.

I had no sense of time, but five minutes must have passed before I felt able to speak. Unlocking my jaw, I managed to utter, "Whoever killed Bruce Denton got away with murder. Plain and simple."

Ashley was behind me still, sitting in the driver's seat, so I couldn't see his expression, but there was defiance in his voice when he said, "I don't believe in that scenario. No one is clever enough to leave no evidence at all. Someone will always see something."

I opened my eyes and lifted my head. The glorious Kent countryside was there for me to marvel at. Birds were tweeting in the trees, plump blackberries sprouted from their thorny brambles all along the hedgerow and to the west beyond the trees the fields rose and fell in elegant, rhythmic humps. It was far from its best on this dreary October day, yet glorious, nonetheless.

I wanted to appreciate it, but my gut felt like I had eaten a bowling ball and I wanted nothing more than a safe, dark space in which I could hide.

My episode had come as a shock to my new partner, that much was obvious and predictable, yet his persistence remained. I could not argue with his statement, yet at the same time, I could not allow him to reopen the Bruce Denton case. I couldn't.

Not ever.

CHAPTER 5

SLOWLY, I ROTATED BACK INTO MY SEAT SO I FACED THE windscreen once more. I could feel his eyes on me and kept mine aimed firmly down the road to our front. Surely, he could see my distress. Using it to push him away from 'my' case might not be an honourable tactic, but I was willing to employ any strategy that worked. I would not allow it to be reopened.

"Are you okay now?"

I nodded but didn't give a verbal answer. Instead, I nodded my head at the road. "You can get going again."

Ashley watched me for a few seconds, leaving me with the impression he was waiting for me to turn my head and make eye contact. When I kept my face firmly forward, he took hold of the steering wheel, checked his mirrors, and eased us back onto the road.

Trying not to mumble, I did my best to put an end to the subject.

"I want you to try to see this from my perspective. That case killed my career. Think about your aspirations, where you want to get to, what you hope to achieve with your

STEVE HIGGS

career. You don't have to say what's in your head, but I was going to be the chief constable for Kent."

He took his eyes off the road, twisting his head around to look at me. He wanted to check if I was being serious.

I was.

"I was twenty-four when they promoted me to sergeant." His eyes were pointing ahead again, but I got to see when they widened. No one makes sergeant at twenty-four. "When I sat the NPPF, I came top in the country. Not the area or the county, but the entire country."

He glanced at me again.

"I studied a degree in criminology before joining as a detective, and everything I did, every choice I made was about getting to the very top. For nearly four years, I was the golden boy. Right up until Bruce Denton got himself bludgeoned to death in his home. Everything stopped for me at that point. The case attracted the national press, and my superintendent went on the national news making a statement about our confidence in catching the killer. The fool made it sound like we were on the verge of making an arrest."

"But you did make an arrest."

The angry face of Trevor Smith swam back into my brain. He was always angry when I thought of him.

When I said nothing, Ashley continued.

"He was the father of a girl you thought Bruce might be sleeping with even though she was a student at his school and only fifteen years old."

"You've read the file," I accused, unhappy to be talking about it again. "So you know he fit the profile. The man had a short fuse and a prior for bottling a guy in a bar when he was younger. His wife provided an alibi which I never believed, but if it *was* him, there was no evidence beyond the circumstantial. The girl denied the relationship

Shadow of a Lie

and there was no trace of her or her father inside Denton's house."

"What about his former lodger or the ex-fiancée?"

I felt a muscle in my jaw begin to spasm, right at the back behind my right ear. If Ashley noticed it, he chose not to comment. How had he done this? My sole aim was to avoid the subject of Bruce Denton's murder and here we were talking about nothing but.

I was going to force a subject change, but the powers that be intervened, my saviour arriving in the form of the disembodied satnav voice. We were less than a minute from our destination, the station in Wingham.

I was familiar with the name of the man who investigated the Craig Chowdry case seven years ago: Chief Inspector Hector Pascoe, but I was sure we'd never met.

I simply ignored Ashley's last comment, riding the final half a mile to Wingham nick in silence. There were other cases to investigate, and I would make sure they proved distraction enough to keep him away from Bruce Denton.

CHAPTER 6

THE LOCAL NICK IN THE COUNTRYSIDE TOWN OF WINGHAM is a converted house on the corner of a street one road back from the main thoroughfare. Painted white with stone chip rendering over the original brickwork, which would have looked much nicer in my opinion, it was in need of a refresh. Otherwise, the exterior was in good condition, what one would expect: no station chief would allow the gutters to clog or for weeds to grow, not when their boss might pop in unannounced at any point.

Probably Victorian, though I'm no expert on architecture, I knew the rooms inside were big, and the boss's office, which dominated the front of the building upstairs, was bigger and better than the superintendent's in Herne Bay. Out the back, an extension provided a custody centre as well as additional space for equipment.

This had to be my umpteenth visit over the course of my career so I knew to go around the back and not to bother going in through the open front door where civilians would find a sergeant in uniform working the reception desk.

Shadow of a Lie

I tried to do the maths to figure out how long it had been since my last visit, but settled for 'more than five years'. Little had changed in the interim. The posters looked the same and I found myself wondering if some of the cobwebs in the corner might have been there as long.

The chap on the custody desk looked up from a magazine when we walked in, a frown creasing his brow.

"Tony? What brings you to this neck of the woods?"

I knew Vince Appleton purely from being around long enough that I'd met people. He was roughly the same age as me and our paths had crossed a bunch of times.

"Hi, Vince." I shook his hand. "Need to see your boss. I got assigned to a new task force looking into unsolved murders."

"Oh, yeah. I heard about that. Didn't realise they were recruiting fossils for it though."

I took the banter without comment. "Is the DCI in?"

Vince said, "Yeah. Upstairs, turn right. It's the big office at the front." Nodding his head at DS Long, he added, "Good luck working with this one."

I thought Ashley might ask what he meant by his comment, but he chose to let it go.

Walking up the stairs, I saw another man I knew. Unlike Vince, he was not a person I could claim to get on with. Not due to an incident in the past, but because he is an utter dick.

Detective Sergeant Glenn Beckett stopped at the top, looking down at me when he asked, "How on earth are you still serving? Isn't there a mandatory retirement age or something?"

I gave him a two-word reply, unable to find enough interest to do more. He laughed at our backs when we passed him and descended the stairs in our wake.

45

STEVE HIGGS

At the top of the stairs, we found the DCI's door open. He looked up as we approached.

With eyebrows raised, he asked, "You gentlemen need to see me?" He was asking if he could palm us off onto someone else; his time too precious to waste if he could avoid it.

Detective Chief Inspector Hector Pascoe is a tall man of mixed racial heritage. As head of the station he knew all about the task force assigned to reopen old cases, but was surprised to find the Craig Chowdry missing person case included.

"What is it that you propose to investigate?" he questioned, clearly believing there was no case to pursue. "I mean, it's not for me to create any barriers, not if this is what the chief constable wants, but there really is no case. We never found a body, and apart from a couple of conflicting witness statements, all we ever had was four boys seen getting a little physical with Craig earlier the same day he disappeared. They were questioned at length, but couldn't have done it."

DS Long jumped in, something I was beginning to see as a habit.

"Sir, Craig Chowdry's blood was found half a mile from his house in a meadow. It was estimated to be more than a pint, a considerable amount of blood for someone to lose."

"Your point is?" DCI Pascoe wasn't fighting our investigation, but he wasn't happy about it and why should he be? We were going to trawl through his work, questioning what he and his officers did and why they were unable to bring the case to a conclusion. I felt much the same about the Bruce Denton case.

"My point, Sir," DS Long replied, "is that no blood

Shadow of a Lie

trail was recorded leading to the site of the blood they found. Craig lost a lot of blood in one spot and then managed to leave the area without spilling any more. That, Sir, is something I find highly suspicious."

I remembered the television coverage the case received at the time, but had forgotten that element.

"As did I," replied the DCI cooly. "You are going to suggest he was murdered, and his body wrapped somehow before being moved. It is an obvious conclusion to draw, and we explored that theory at length."

I stayed quiet while my partner dug himself a hole. DCI Pascoe was choosing to remain polite, but I could see DS Long was beginning to get under his skin. He knew there were other cases we could be pursuing, and would rather we did just that. He wasn't going to say it outright, but he was trying, quite carefully, to sow doubt into DS Long's mind and steer him, ever so gently, away from the case.

I wondered if he might have had more luck had I not already convinced him to leave *my* case alone.

"Yes, Sir," acknowledged my partner dutifully, "Yet no body was ever found to corroborate or confirm what might have happened, leaving you to prove his murder by means of a confession. Your investigation focused on four boys who knew Craig Chowdry. The witness statements recorded at the time state that he was seen talking to them outside the Shop Ryte store on Canterbury Road. One witness, a Mrs Rose Winslow, claimed their discussion was heated and she saw one of the boys push Craig."

DCI Pascoe waved for Ashley to stop talking.

"Yes, yes, I know all that. I brought them in for questioning two days after Craig was reported as missing. They didn't like Craig because he thought he was better than them. Whether he did or not I never found out, but that was their opinion. They might have left him alone if he hadn't been dating Daniel French's little sister. Daniel was the ringleader, dragging his pals into his plan to scare Craig away."

"So you think they did it?" there was no mistaking the animation in Ashley's voice.

DCI Pascoe aimed a look of disdain at my new partner.

"Did what, kid? We found some blood, but it was a survivable quantity and could have been collected over the course of several days."

DS Long interrupted the DCI. "You're saying he could have faked his own death? A sixteen-year-old?"

Forcing himself to be patient, DCI Pascoe said, "No one knows what happened to Craig Chowdry, Detective Sergeant Long, that's the point. There was nothing to suggest Craig Chowdry did anything other than run away. And if you're about to question that, I'll tell you why I think he did."

I was all ears.

"Sarah French was fourteen. Craig Chowdry was sixteen. She refused to divulge whether they were having sex or not, but her brother claimed they were, that was his big beef. Maybe the kids roughed him up a bit as a warning; they never admitted as much, but he had far more reason to fear prosecution for sex with a minor. Good luck if you think you can prove otherwise."

There was something about the way he chose his words that made my brain itch. I had been watching him ever since he first looked up from his desk, observing his mannerisms and movements. He poked the air with his right index finger when he had a point to make. He tilted his head to the right whenever he was being asked a ques-

Shadow of a Lie

tion. There was a visible pulse in his neck, his carotid artery sending blood to his brain. It ticked away at a steady pace.

When he delivered solid facts about the case such as ages, places, names, he looked directly at the person he was addressing. However, when he had to speculate, as he just had regarding whether the four suspects might have attacked Craig physically, his eyes cast down to the floor. It was only brief, and happened right before he delivered his response, but it was unmistakable.

Ashley ought to have known to back off at this point. We were at the nick in Wingham only as a courtesy to DCI Pascoe and needed no permission to investigate a case he once headed. DS Long's orders – mine too now, I suppose – came from the Chief Constable of Kent. My partner hoped the DCI might be able to provide some insight into the case, suggest something he'd suspected but was unable to investigate at the time. However, that wasn't the case and the approach he chose had succeeded only in putting the local chief's back up. The pulse in his neck was going twice as fast now, a sure sign he was getting ready to blow his stack at the two interlopers getting into his business.

Nevertheless, whether he couldn't read the signs or just didn't care, my new partner ploughed onwards.

"Sir," he said with a smile that suggested the DCI was being foolish, "surely you can see that Craig Chowdry had no good reason to run away? His family had money enough to send him to one of the best schools in the county. Even if he was involved with the underage Miss French, such cases are nigh impossible to prove unless the minor makes an accusation. Even then, he could deny the act and claim she must have lost her virginity to someone else."

I felt it acted as a demonstration of his youthful inexpe-

STEVE HIGGS

rience that he would waste his breath explaining what the DCI already knew. There was a part of me that wanted to back away and let him continue to dig the hole he now stood in even though the kid seemed utterly oblivious. It was tempting, but for my own benefit, I chose to save Ashley from himself.

DCI Pascoe looked like Mount Vesuvius about to consume Pompei when I chose to speak.

Clearing my throat to draw attention my way, I said, "Please excuse my partner, Sir. He's not suggesting there was anything wrong with your investigation. We are, however, as you know, tasked with reopening some of these old cases and this one is on the list. We'll do our best not to get in anyone's way. Our visit today is a courtesy to let you know we will be digging into one of *your* old cases and that we will be operating in your area. Of course, I think it's just a formality to confirm there really is nothing to investigate."

DCI Pascoe didn't say anything for several seconds, the time stretching out while he scrutinised the pair of us.

"Just a formality?" His thunderous face calmed a little.

"Indeed," I replied. "Was there anything left out of the case, Sir? Anything you believe was missed during the initial investigation that might come to light now?"

The skin around his eyes tightened, making me think he might start shouting. However, he was getting pure innocence from me, nothing in my expression to suggest I thought there might be any merit to our efforts.

"No, there was nothing left out," he stated firmly. "Craig Chowdry vanished, DS Heaton, and with the exception of the blood, there was no reason to suspect foul play."

I offered him a pleasant smile.

Shadow of a Lie

"Thank you, Sir. That's really helpful."

"But you intend to reopen the case?" DCI Pascoe pushed me to confirm.

I wasn't going to reopen a thing and might have expressed precisely that had my partner not opened his mouth again.

"Yes, Sir. We'll need an incident room we can work out of, please. I requested all the evidence from general storage yesterday. It should be arriving later today."

Oh, yes, Ashley said we would be working multiple cases simultaneously. I guess this was always going to be one of them.

The vein in DCI Pascoe's neck sped up again.

"I suppose you would like a couple of my officers to make sure it is all accounted for to maintain the chain of evidence?" His voice was like a shark fin breaking the surface as it sped toward the unwitting swimmers.

DS Long could have appeased him by offering to handle it himself, but he didn't. Instead he chummed some more blood into the water.

"The chief constable has asked for full cooperation." He was throwing the memo the DCI must have received in his face.

"And you'll get it!" DCI Pascoe raised his voice.

It hadn't taken all that much provocation to make the DCI lose his cool. Some people are just like that, of course – never too far from displaying their stronger emotions. I didn't think that was the case with DCI Pascoe though. I was witnessing something else, and I thought I knew what it was: Nerves.

Seizing the moment, I delivered a question. It was an easy one, but I wasn't interested in the answer, so much as I wanted to see how he answered it.

STEVE HIGGS

"Sir, do you think Craig Chowdry ran away?"

"Yes."

The DCI didn't hesitate to give his response. He required no thinking time and delivered it in a confident tone. He was also lying. It made me rather curious. So curious, in fact, that I asked another.

"Sir, do you believe the four boys are innocent?" I didn't need to clarify which four boys I was talking about and gave him a simple yes/no question rather than ask his opinion about the validity of reinterviewing them.

"Yes. If I thought anything else, we would not be having this conversation."

I nodded my head, more curious than before. While my 'ability' to read people's facial cues is hardly proof, it has rarely been wrong. DCI Pascoe, the senior investigating officer in the original case was lying about the key conclusions drawn. Lying to the two men about to reopen the case.

I thanked him, apologised for taking up his time, and promised to cause as little disruption as possible.

The moment we got outside, Ashley started on me.

"What was that? Why did you cut me off in there?"

I continued walking, heading to the car, while over my shoulder I said, "Because you were making a fool of yourself. And by extension, me. Explaining things to a seasoned DCI like he doesn't know which way is up? Why were you pushing him so hard?"

"Because there are obvious flaws in the investigation. I wanted to push his buttons to see how he would react. He got defensive."

"Mother Teresa would have been defensive," I countered. "In fact, find me a cop in the world who doesn't get their back up when you attack their work." I spat the words, but Ashley was right. Not about DCI Pascoe being

Shadow of a Lie

defensive, that was a natural reaction to Ashley's persistent annoyance. He was right about the flaws. DCI Pascoe was hiding something and was content to lie to my face. I took his statements and turned them around: The boys were not innocent, and Craig Chowdry didn't run away. However the case didn't get solved because there was no evidence to work with. It wasn't the first time, and it wouldn't be the last, but DCI Pascoe's willingness to conceal what he really believed demanded some exploration before I shared my thoughts with my young partner.

We had reached the car, but when I went around to the passenger side, expecting Ashley to unlock the doors, he followed me and got into my personal space.

"I am in charge of this investigation." His voice was still calm and measured, but his body language gave him away; he was getting angry with me.

I didn't let that bother me too much. "And I am here because your boss recognises that you are too new and inexperienced to go at this alone. Your youth makes you impetuous."

"And your age makes you slow and cautious. Your boss called you lazy and he was right. Is that why Bruce Denton's killer is still out there?"

I felt my fists clench and saw that he noticed. I wasn't going to hit him. In all my years of service I'd never struck another officer, but I will admit the desire to knock the smug confidence off DS Long's face.

He looked up from where my balled fists hung poised by my sides, meeting my eyes with an expression of calm, almost detached, nonchalance.

"You know I'm a black belt in three different disciplines, right?" He followed the question by calmly pivoting onto his left foot and raising his right leg high in the air so he was more or less doing the splits while standing on one

53

foot. His pose could have come straight from a Jackie Chan movie poster.

Feeling foolish, I relaxed my hands.

Setting his right foot back down next to the left, he said, "I have no desire to fight with you, Tony. Not about which cases we pursue or how we pursue them. In fact, I will happily discuss the topic with you at length. However, I believe there is merit to investigating Craig Chowdry's disappearance. You want me to ignore the Bruce Denton case, so how about this? I'll shuffle it to the bottom of the pile if you stop battling me and throw your undoubted talent into helping me solve some of the other cases. Is that a deal you wish to strike?"

How did this kid keep getting the upper hand? How was it that he was talking to me like he was the master and I was the petulant child to be tamed and teased along the right path?

I was angry again, but not so consumed by my rage that I couldn't see I was being offered the very thing I wanted. The thing I *needed*.

"Stopping you from investigating Bruce Denton's murder is a mercy," I assured him, "and yes, I will throw myself into the other cases, including this one, *and* I'll make sure you get all the credit." What I chose not to say was how invigorated I felt to be looking into what might have happened to Craig Chowdry. I hadn't felt like this in years. From the wobbling low point of haunted stress I felt when I thought I might be forced to look at Bruce Denton again, to a strange high now that I had a sniff of a real test for the first time in years.

DS Long said nothing. Not straight away. His lips were pursed in thought, the questions rattling around inside his head known only to him.

When he thrust out his right hand for me to shake, I

Shadow of a Lie

wasn't expecting it and flinched slightly, thinking he was launching an attack.

"Truce?" he offered.

"Truce." I repeated the word, but already believed it would be one based on mutual distrust.

CHAPTER 7

"THIS IS THE WORK ADDRESS WE HAVE FOR ANDREW Curzon," DS Long announced, his voice like a pin to the bubble of my memory. Drifting along on a daydream in the passenger seat, images of Bruce Denton's broken body had chosen to return, uninvited as they always were.

He was turning off the road, angling the car's front end down a short driveway.

"Andrew Curzon," I repeated, committing the name to memory. "It would help if I knew a little more about this case."

DS Long made a face, one that might have been intended to convey apology, but could equally have meant 'tough luck'.

"Yeah, I get that," he said, placating me somewhat. "We can go through them together later if you like. And I can send you a complete copy of my files; you'll need that anyway."

Obviously.

The more I thought about it, the more I could see that I'd been ambushed. My superintendent hadn't suddenly discovered he was to assign one of his detectives to accom-

Shadow of a Lie

pany DS Long. In all probability he'd known for weeks yet he chose to keep it secret.

Had he not done so I might have been able to bring myself up to speed with the cases to be investigated. Equally, I suppose, I might have come up with a better reason why I couldn't be a part of the task force. Acknowledging the soundness of my boss's strategy, I glared gloomily out of the window.

We were approaching a farm; trust me when I say there are a lot of them around this area. Kent is known as the garden of England for all the arable land and food it produces. The trees were losing their leaves fast now, but in so doing the lush green of summer growth had given way to hues of autumn gold. Falling by their thousands, the leaves littered the roads where they created a carpet of yellows, oranges, and browns. In a week the branches would be bare and the leaves would be a churned, rotting mess good for nothing more than clogging the drains. Today, though, the countryside was glorious.

The car's built-in satnav announced our arrival a hundred yards before we reached the farmhouse. It was surrounded by barns, most of which were open along one side. From my angle, I couldn't tell if they were empty or full. For that matter, I didn't know what sort of farm it was. There were tractors and trucks parked to our left, and to our front a plethora of dangerous looking farm machines. Clearly designed to work, not look nice, they stretched into the distance in a field beyond an open gate.

Shutting off his engine, DS Long reached around to behind his seat where he found his backpack. From it he took his laptop which he flipped open and placed on his lap.

"Okay, here are the cliff notes: Andrew Curzon is the one who was seen giving Craig a shove. That evidence came from Rose Winslow, but she died last year aged eighty-seven, so there's no chance to interview her again. The altercation occurred at approximately 1445hrs on Monday, August 12th, 2016, outside the Shop Ryte supermarket in Goodnestone."

We had passed through Goodnestone on the way from Wingham. It was a real 'blink and you miss it' place with a pub, a church, and a convenience store. They could call it a supermarket if they liked, but the term was misleading since you'd be lucky to fit more than about four customers in there at one time. I'd never been in it, but could tell from the size of the old, Victorian terraced house in which it was built that it would be stacked to the ceiling with shelves of everything they could possibly sell.

"Curzon was arrested?" I asked, forcing myself to attune my thoughts to the case.

Long shook his head. "No. He was brought in for questioning as were three other boys, Daniel French, Shane Travers, and Timothy Botterill. They were all released without charge."

The case excited me, largely because I believed DCI Pascoe was hiding something, so it was with interest that I challenged my new partner.

"Released without charge means there was no evidence to warrant keeping them."

Ashley turned in his seat, facing me and looking right into my eyes when he asked, "So why were they held for more than forty-eight hours?"

I blinked. Holding a suspect without charge for more than twenty-four hours rarely occurs unless they are suspected of a serious crime such as murder.

"All four were held that long?"

Ashley nodded in reply.

A frown crept over my face. "Why didn't you ask DCI

Shadow of a Lie

Pascoe why he held them that long? He must have had a reason."

Gripping his door handle to get out, Ashley paused. "I'm sure he did. I would like to find out what it was though, not have him tell me. You asked me why this case when it appears to be a missing person and not a murder. Because it stinks, Tony. Because it stinks. They didn't find the body and that would have made things difficult, but there is something very wrong with the investigation and I should like to find out what it is."

CHAPTER 8

"Can I help you?"

The question came from a man exiting the farmhouse. He was in his late fifties with brown hair going to grey along the sides. A shade over six feet tall, he had a steaming mug of tea in one hand and what looked to be a ham and cheese sandwich in the other. I'd seen movement inside the house when we pulled up and guessed this was the farmer coming to see who we were.

That we were police officers ought to have been obvious – I am used to people identifying what I am before the need to introduce myself, but the man now leaning on the gate post leading from his flower garden had a questioning look on his face.

DS Long held out his warrant card for the farmer to see and introduced himself and then me.

"Good morning. Are you the owner?" Ashley enquired.

The man was chewing a large mouthful of bread, meat, and cheese and we had to wait for him to swallow and slurp his tea before he could respond.

"I'm Brian Curzon, yes. Is this about my Andy? What's he done this time?"

60

Shadow of a Lie

The question made it clear the former suspect in Craig Chowdry's disappearance had a history of misbehaving.

I watched from two feet behind my new colleague, content to let him lead so I could observe. Andrew Curzon's father was relaxed, unconcerned to have two police detectives at his door. His facial cues and mannerisms were not that of a man with a dark secret he wished to remain hidden, so if his son were guilty of murder, he knew nothing about it.

Ignoring Mr Curzon's question, DS Long pressed on.

"Mr Curzon, our visit today is to do with Craig Chowdry." He left it at that, falling silent to gauge Mr Curzon's reaction.

Mentally I noted that Ashley had a natural inclination for the job. He hadn't asked a question, which at first I thought to be an error. However, I realised it was a deliberate tactic and I waited to see if Mr Curzon was savvy enough to choose to not respond.

He wasn't.

"Craig Chow ... You're digging that old case up again?" Andrew's father was unhappy, his face pinched with disbelief. He gesticulated with his left hand, a chunk of cheese slipping from between the slices of bread as he jabbed the air with it. "The kid ran away! Everyone knows that. My boy had nothing to do with his decision to leave!"

Once again, Ashley stayed silent, tilting his head slightly to one side as he examined Brian Curzon's reaction. It had the desired effect, tempting the man into saying more to fill the silence.

"That Craig, he was the troublemaker. Ask anyone. Messing around with an underage girl. It ought not to have been allowed."

This was good. Mr Curzon was babbling excitedly,

STEVE HIGGS

providing nothing substantial yet, but when a person being interviewed wants to talk, you let them. Every time.

"Dad!" snapped a voice from our right.

I twitched my head around to find a tall man in his early twenties heading our way. Obviously, the son of the man we were talking to, not just because he called him dad, but because I would be willing to bet photographs of the senior man from thirty years ago would be hard to differentiate from ones of his son now. Andrew stood an inch taller than his father and had a flatter core, his father's settling into doughiness like so many men once they hit middle age. I know mine had. Otherwise, only their age difference set them apart.

"Don't talk to them, Dad," growled the younger man. His phone was ringing, the device out of sight in a pocket somewhere.

"Andrew Curzon?" Ashley sought to confirm, though we had both seen the picture of the sixteen-year-old version.

"Yes, that's right," Andrew said with a snarl, his face set to an unpleasant grimace. "Now hop it, the pair of you. I've done nothing wrong."

Once again, I opted to stay quiet and observe. Andrew was irritated, that was clear, but I was more interested to find out why. It could be as simple as a history with local cops. If he was in semi-regular bother with the law, and wasn't currently aware that he'd committed an infraction, he might feel that he was being unfairly targeted. I doubted that was it though.

Glancing down at his hands, I wondered if they might be shaking from a burst of adrenalin. They were not, but they were balled into fists, his knuckles showing white, so there was no way to tell. His phone had stopped ringing,

62

Shadow of a Lie

but less than ten seconds after the caller gave up, it started again.

Undeterred by Andrew's attitude, Ashley said, "Andrew Curzon, my name is Detective Sergeant Long. This is Detective Sergeant Heaton. We have some questions for you about Craig Chowdry."

"Craig Chowdry? Really?" His surprise ought to have looked genuine, but his expression failed to convince me. What's more, now that the subject of our visit was aired, his face reflected amusement. "Ask away," he invited with a confident smile. It was as though he welcomed our enquiries.

Ashley flicked a glance in my direction to check I was seeing it too. When approached and questioned by the police even innocent people trip over their own words and struggle with what to say and what to leave out. The calm assuredness currently on display was alien to me. I had never seen anyone so unbothered in all my years.

Ashley refocused on Andrew when he asked, "What happened to Craig Chowdry seven years ago?" It was a good question because it invited opinion or conjecture. What story would Andrew deliver?

Sneering triumphantly, Andrew said, "He ran away. Everyone knows that." It was the same thing his father said. The same story intimated by DCI Pascoe.

There was nothing to prove it held the slightest shred of truth and that was what made it such a magical answer.

"I'm not so sure he did," remarked my partner. It was six words, but they contained a lot of subtext. In many ways it was a challenge, my colleague subtly saying, *'I know you boys killed him and I'm going to prove it'*. Again, I was impressed by Ashley's cool demeanour and the way he manoeuvred his suspect. "More than a pint of his blood was found, Andrew. A person doesn't lose that much without needing medical assistance." There was no question, just a subtle hint.

I thought Andrew was going to shout and swear and reaffirm his position on the subject of Craig Chowdry's whereabouts. His posture, the set of his jaw, the way his fists were clenched all told me he was angry. More than angry. Yet he was doing a masterful job of keeping it in check and his words and the way he delivered them contrasted vividly with his body language.

With a shrug that bordered on nonchalance, a half-smile found its way to Andrew's face.

"I wish I could help you, I really do. Craig and me were buddies back in the day. You're going to ask me why I shoved him, that's what is in the report, right? That's why they picked me and the others up the first time, and I'll tell you the truth: I was trying to get him to fight me."

Andrew was talking, so much like we had with his father, Ashley and I stayed quiet so he could tell his tale.

"He was banging Danny's little sister, Sarah. She was only fourteen and before you ask how we knew for sure, Danny found the used condom wrappers in his sister's bedroom. Craig had the gall to do it in Danny's house. We were going to put a stop to it, that's all. But the coward wouldn't fight me. That old lady shouted at me and when I was distracted looking at her, Craig ran off. Fast as his little legs could go." Andrew mimed running legs with two of his fingers. "Danny yelled after him, promising we would catch him sooner or later and that he would get what was coming to him, but Craig ran away the same day. He knew what he'd done, and we never saw him again. Was I going to slap him around? Sure, I'll not deny it. Did I? No, I never had the chance. One shove, that was all I got."

Shadow of a Lie

He stopped talking, folding his arms across his chest in a pose that was meant to show how relaxed he felt. Others might have fallen for it, but I didn't. There was perspiration above his brow and I believed the folded arms were to hide his shaking hands. He was nervous, anxious, and I believed he had every reason to be.

His phone rang for what had to be the sixth time in the last two minutes, and I chose to break my silence.

"Do you want to get that?"

Andrew's eyes twitched across to meet mine and he forced a smug smile.

"Nah. If it's important, they'll call back."

"They have called back," I pointed out. "Many times. Who could need to speak to you so urgently, Andrew? Why now?" The timing of the calls was suspicious. Why such urgency? It could be nothing, but a little itch told me the call was about the two detectives unexpectedly in the area asking questions about Craig Chowdry. "Why don't you go ahead and answer it, Andrew?" I pressed, my eyes never wavering from his.

His eyes narrowed. "I'll call whoever it is back later, thank you."

"Why? What are you hiding?" Now I was pushing him.

He opened his mouth to spit an answer, his anger rising to the surface, but his father stepped in.

"Go in the house, Andy. These gentlemen are trespassing."

"No, actually, we are not," argued Ashley.

I touched his arm lightly. "It's fine. We can leave now. We have what we came for."

DS Long shot me a questioning look, but I was already turning away, heading back to the car.

The Curzons were disappearing through their front

door by the time I slid into my seat. Ashley clambered in through the driver's side, his forehead rippled with a deep frown.

"What was that?" he demanded, snapping out the question before his butt could meet the material of his seat. "We are not trespassing, and Andrew Curzon was talking. You let him off easy."

Choosing to look at the farmhouse rather than my irritated partner, I said, "It doesn't matter if we are trespassing or not. They have every right to go inside their house and refuse us entry. They could have done that straight away, but they didn't and for that we should be thankful because you were right, there is something to this case. We should move swiftly to visit the other three boys ... men now, I suppose, who were with Andrew. We should talk to Sarah French too. I want to hear her perspective."

Ashley raised one eyebrow. "Seriously?" His tone was derisory. "Suddenly you are all interested. What changed?"

"They did it." I'm not claiming to possess a supernatural ability to determine guilt, but Ashley was right about the case. It stank. Andrew Curzon's brash confidence, his almost mocking tone made me believe he had reason to believe he was untouchable. His answers came too easily, and I had a nagging, unpleasant theory for why that might be.

Ashley said, "I think so too. That's why I wanted to reopen the case." He fell silent for a moment before asking, "What did you mean by 'We've got what we came for'? What is it that you think we got?" He was challenging me again.

"We didn't get anything," I replied, my eyes still fixed firmly on the farmhouse. "Andrew Curzon doesn't know that though. Right now he's rattled. The calls were from

Shadow of a Lie

one of his mates, the ones involved in the altercation with Craig outside the Shop Ryte."

"How do you know that?"

Now I turned my head to look straight at him. "That's the wrong question, Padawan. What you need to ask is how they knew to call."

CHAPTER 9

WE WERE DRIVING ALONG YET ANOTHER COUNTRY LANE, sunlight creating a strobe-like effect on the windscreen where it broke through the canopy of branches overhead. Ashley wore sunglasses, the constant flickering bothering him not one jot. I was forced to close my eyes or look at the carpet which I refrained from doing because it would make me nauseous. Reaching up, I pulled down the sun visor on my side.

Ashley wanted to visit Daniel French next. The older brother of Craig's girlfriend was at the centre of the mystery. If Craig was targeted and murdered by the boys, Danny was the one behind it – Andrew Curzon had said as much.

Danny worked at an insurance company in Wingham, in an office that sat above a bakery on the main street running through the town. There was parking around the back with signs advising the spaces were reserved for staff displaying permits.

Ashley angled the nose of the car into the only available space and parked it anyway – perks of the job. A

Shadow of a Lie

window opened above our heads as we were exiting the vehicle.

A terse voice from above our heads said, "You can't park there. The signs clearly say it's for staff only. I can have you clamped in five minutes." Her tone suggested she took great joy in bossing people around whenever she could and that she was used to being obeyed.

I knew without needing to look that her desk was set next to the window so she would see anyone who chose to disobey the signs and would gleefully call the local clamping firm to deal with any offenders. The number was probably locked into her phone for ease of access.

Ashley held up his warrant card. "Police," he replied, the single word all he felt the situation needed.

Aiming a smile at the officious woman glaring down at us with disappointment and indecision etched onto her face – she was trying to decide if she could just have the car clamped anyway – I said, "Me too," and left it at that.

A door set into the rear of the building declared *Hanson Insurers*. It was an old, detached cottage that stank of freshly baked bread and would have driven me nuts and made me fat if I had to work anywhere near it.

We were in the right place at least.

A buzzer set into the door connected us to what sounded like the same officious woman we had just upset, but she let us up when Ashley announced who we were.

At the top of a set of narrow stairs, another door blocked our path, but this one wasn't locked. It opened into an open-plan office where a dozen or so people in office-wear sat behind desks staring at computers. Everyone looked up or glanced our way with one exception.

Daniel French kept his eyes studiously locked on his computer screen. The picture in the case file was of a

69

STEVE HIGGS

sixteen-year-old boy, but while he now wore a trimmed beard and had put on some muscle, he didn't look a whole lot different.

"Daniel French," Ashley spoke clearly and at a volume above normal conversation.

Inevitably, Daniel looked our way. How could he do anything else?

"Yes?" he enquired, acting innocent when I believed wholeheartedly that he knew who we were and why we were in his place of work.

Ashley held up his warrant card again. "Can we have a word, please?"

"I'm working."

"This won't take long. I'm quite sure your boss will permit you to take a break."

A woman with flaming red hair above a green satin blouse and a black pencil skirt appeared from a private office set against one wall. I will admit I noted her figure, since it was the sort of figure a man unconsciously notes, and guessed she was the boss.

"It's fine, Danny," she spoke to him while glancing at us. "Take as long as you need."

Danny didn't want to take any time at all. He was quite happy not talking to us, but that option was gone now, so after deliberately taking his time to finish up whatever he was working on, he slowly got to his feet, drained the contents of his coffee cup, and reluctantly walked toward us. He was tall – six feet four inches or thereabouts, and lanky with it. Unlike Andrew Curzon, who was tall but had muscle, Daniel was skinny, but they both bore the same distrusting, hard eyes.

I watched closely, my eyes scanning his pockets. He wore a plain, light blue oxford shirt with the top button undone and charcoal grey trousers. There was no sign of a

Shadow of a Lie

phone in his front pockets and when he passed me I could see it wasn't tucked into the back pockets either.

Looking back across the office, two of the workers were whispering to each other, their furtive eyes glancing at me. They had spotted me staring at Daniel French's bottom.

Letting that go, I excused myself to use the restroom just outside the door and promised to meet my partner in the carpark. I didn't need to relieve myself, or so I thought until I got in there, but coming out a minute and a half later, I bypassed the stairs to go back into the office.

There, acting as if I had every right to wander around their workspace, I went to Danny's desk and picked up his phone.

"Are you allowed to touch that?" asked a voice. I turned to find the officious woman's thin lips and beady eyes aimed in my direction. She was sitting next to the window that looked down over the carpark.

Shooting her the same smile as before, I said, "Good question." I only needed a few seconds to check the call log on the phone. I was playing a hunch that he would have received a phone call warning him of the two detectives in town asking questions and wanted to confirm that was the case.

If he'd been warned, I wanted to know who made the call.

Unfortunately, holding up the phone, I couldn't get past the facial recognition software to open it. The officious woman was rising from her seat, a deep-set frown contorting her features. I placed the phone back where I found it and started toward the door.

She stopped walking having only moved a few feet from her desk. Her fists were balled and placed on her hips, a stern expression following me all the way out.

Back in the carpark, I found my partner grilling Daniel French.

CHAPTER 10

"HE'D BEEN COACHED," ASHLEY STATED.

I agreed. "That was my impression too." Daniel's answers, much like his more excitable friend, Andrew, were well thought out and he took his time to deliver them. I've interviewed thousands of suspects in my career and none of them ever came across as well as Daniel French. It was another indicator that things were not as they should be.

We got back into the car and Ashley started the engine.

"I think we should head back to the station."

Ashley checked left and right before pulling out and asking, "Wingham? You want to speak with the DCI again?"

"No, we don't have anything yet. I want to do some research."

"Into what?"

I thought about my answer for long enough that Ashley repeated himself.

"Into what, Heaton?

"You can call me Tony."

"And you can call me Ashley, but so far you haven't. You've called me kid, and puppy."

STEVE HIGGS

He wasn't wrong. Thrown for a loop by the sudden and unexpected assignment, and the possibility that new eyes might scrutinise the Bruce Denton case, I had been acting only a few degrees south of hostile since we met.

Huffing out a hard breath, I did what I knew I ought and played the part of the bigger man.

"Sorry," I offered, hating that I needed to apologise. "I wasn't expecting ... this." I gesticulated to indicate I meant the whole situation. "Can we start over?" It was the second time today I had felt the need to apologise and ask for a do-over.

Ashley was gracious enough to let it go. "What is it that you want to research? My plan was to speak with all those involved today."

"We already interviewed Andrew and Daniel and agree they had been coached on what to say. I think it safe to assume Shane Travers and Tim Botterill will give us the exact same story only told from their perspective. That being the case, for now at least, I see nothing to be gained by speaking with them. What we need to do is find something that will allow us to undermine their version of events. That way we can disrupt their practiced answers."

"Find something?" Ashley picked out my ambiguous phrasing.

"Also," I pressed on regardless, "I want to look at burials in the area at that time."

His eyebrows shot up, instantly understanding the reason why.

"You think the body could be in someone else's coffin?"

"Maybe, but that's not exactly what I had in mind. The whole area was searched by teams of police and volunteers and no body was found. I remember it well. Police divers dredged the rivers and lakes, so there's no reason to think Craig Chowdry ended up in a shallow grave, or ditched in

Shadow of a Lie

a water course. That leaves a lot of options, but to make his body disappear so completely, they had to come up with something clever and I remind you we are talking about four sixteen-year-old boys and none of them are rocket scientists."

"But it could be in a grave?" he questioned.

"They had help." It was the first time I had voiced that particular opinion out loud. It steered away from his question, but prompted a series of more interesting ones. "Andrew and Daniel were lying today. I think they know exactly what happened to Craig Chowdry, but teenagers don't possess the wherewithal to dispose of a body so completely, and they didn't coach themselves."

Ashley narrowed his eyes. "What are you saying?"

He knew precisely what I was suggesting, but didn't want to say it first. The chilling and very easy conclusion to draw was that someone at Wingham nick called one of the four boys the moment we left there. It would have to be someone involved with the original investigation, which narrowed things down fast.

"This goes back to the point you raised about their interviews in 2016. You identified how neatly sewn together the boys' stories were. How none of them overlapped or contradicted the others."

"That's right."

I gently nudged him to make the jump. "They moved the body from a field without getting any blood on their clothes – had they done so the forensic team would have found it when they looked for evidence. We know they didn't have a solicitor, so who could have coached them and helped them hide a body? Who would have enough knowledge to be able to bamboozle the investigation?"

Ashley's mouth was open, unspoken words waiting in his mouth. His eyes were wide and questioning.

"You think a cop helped them?"

"I think Andrew Curzon was being called by one of his friends, or perhaps by the mystery person who helped them to cover up the murder seven years ago, but he'd already gotten the message from someone else, that's why he wasn't interested in answering the persistent caller. Did he seem shocked to have two detectives at his place of work?"

"He did not," Ashley acknowledged. "And he tried to look surprised when I mentioned Craig Chowdry, but I think he was acting."

"Daniel and Andrew were ready for us, so you tell me: how did they know we were coming? Who knew we were here and what we were going to do?"

"DCI Pascoe." Ashley breathed the name, horrified to be able to draw such a conclusion. It sat with him for a moment that ended when he shook his head like a person trying to clear an Etch-a-Sketch. "Give me one reason why he would," Ashley dared me. "Why risk his career and everything else for four kids? What could possibly motivate him?"

"Well, among other things, Ashley, that is what we have to figure out."

CHAPTER 11

LOOKING PENSIVE, SHANE TRAVERS ASKED, "HOW MUCH do you think they know?"

Tutting, Daniel replied, "They don't know anything."

"But Andy said ..."

Danny cut him off. "What? Andy said what, Shane? That they looked confident and acted as though they knew something we don't? If they knew something, they would be making arrests, not asking questions."

"All I did was repeat what the old one said when he left," Andy felt it necessary to defend himself. "He said, 'We've got what we came for'. He sounded pleased with himself."

Tim butted in. "We were told what to say and how to act. If you can do that, Shane, you have nothing to worry about. They will never find the body, so provided you don't do something stupid like confess, they can't touch us."

"Confess?" Shane repeated the word. "How could I confess? I didn't kill him."

"No," agreed Danny, "But you know who did and you swore to keep the secret. Telling the truth now would ..."

"It would get you killed," growled Andrew, the biggest

77

of the four by a significant margin. Nature had chosen to make him tall and broad and life working on his dad's farm ensured he grew muscle. By contrast, Shane was a foot shorter at barely five and a half feet. He was also scrawny and skinny with spots, glasses, and a lack of confidence to match.

Twitching when Andy came towards him, Shane backed away. "I ain't gonna say nothing, am I? I was just asking why the cops made it sound like they were onto us."

Andy kept walking, crossing the room to get to Shane where he leaned in close to get his face within an inch of his friend's.

"Just remember the promise you made, Shaney boy, and everything will be all right. You carry on like nothing has changed because nothing has. It's just two cops digging around. They don't know anything because there is nothing to know. Like Danny said, the body won't be found. In a week they'll be gone, and you'll wonder what you were worried about. So just hold your nerve." He patted the right side of Shane's face with a rough, calloused hand. Once. Twice. Both times a little harder than could be considered friendly. "Agreed?"

"Yes. Sure," stammered Shane, moving to the side and sliding along the wall to get away from the larger man. "I know what to do. I never said I didn't."

"Why now?" asked Tim, the quietest member of the group. When the other three looked his way, he expanded, "I mean, what changed to make Craig Chowdry interesting again? There's been nothing in the press since the initial investigation."

"It's because of some new task force," Danny explained what little he knew. "That's all I was told. Something about a backlog of unsolved murders. He said not to worry, and to make sure we stuck to the same story and stay calm."

Shadow of a Lie

"So stay calm," echoed Andy, looming over Shane once more.

Danny moved toward the door. "Above all else, we need to act normal. That means we should carry on our normal lives and do nothing unusual."

"Like having a clandestine meeting in a barn on Andy's dad's farm," sniggered Tim, his humour not appreciated one bit.

Danny nodded. "Yes, exactly like that, Tim. I'm going for a pint just like I always do on a Thursday. You should all do what you usually do."

"In that case," Andy smirked. "I think I'll shag your sister."

CHAPTER 12

OUR APPOINTED INCIDENT ROOM ON THE GROUND FLOOR OF Wingham nick was twenty feet by about ten with a cheap linoleum floor, pin boards down one wall, white boards down another, and three desks plus a long table down the middle where we could lay out evidence.

Ashley expressed concern that the evidence from 2016 might not have arrived. The call he expected to confirm its receipt never came, but we found it all loaded neatly in boxes stacked against the wall to the left.

We would be working out of the incident room for the duration of the case, so getting organised was imperative. Under any other circumstances, we would have a couple of constables to help, but this wasn't our nick, and given the extreme nature of our suspicions regarding personnel working here, it was very much for the better that we included no one.

"Are you going to help?" asked Ashley, pinning photographs to a board on the wall to my right. This came after almost an hour of silent work, Ashley opening boxes to examine the contents while I focused solely on digging around on the internet.

Shadow of a Lie

Without looking up from my laptop, I said, "I am helping. I'm researching."

"You're just going to leave me to unbox all this stuff myself."

"Most of it can be left in the boxes. It got them nowhere last time and we have their notes pertaining to any pertinent items."

It was nearing five o'clock and I hadn't worked as late in a long time. Years for sure. I had put those days firmly behind me, but I was still at it after hours today and genuinely exhilarated to find myself immersed in a case that felt like a challenge.

To ward off further complaints, I rose to my feet. "You want a coffee?"

Ashley thought about it, but nodded, deciding it just wasn't worth the effort of battling me over every point. Every nick has a brew room somewhere and I knew from old where to find the one in Wingham. Spooning coffee granules into two mugs, I mentally noted the need to donate some money or a jar of coffee. Such things are not covered by the budget and exist only because the cops pay into a central fund. Back at Herne Bay the brew fund is managed and collected by Doris. The arrangement would be similar here and I knew helping ourselves would be seen as taking liberties if we failed to contribute.

To accentuate the point, a deep voice from behind me rumbled, "That's for the cops that work here." I turned to reply and found a hulking giant of a man hanging through the doorway, using one hand to grip the top of the doorframe. His surly attitude was nothing new.

DS Beckett had to be close to six and a half feet tall, so the hand on the doorframe might have been to stop his head hitting it. He wasn't just tall though. Even in a shirt and tie, the muscle beneath was obvious. Certain he'd been

STEVE HIGGS

mainlining rhinoceros' steroids from an early age, I believed he could turn up to fight at an American wrestling event without anyone questioning his right to be there.

Smiling, I said, "But we are working here. Besides, I'm sure no one would deny a single cup to a visitor. I promise we will bring supplies tomorrow to more than cover what we use."

"Make sure you do," Beckett rumbled, pushing back out through the door to continue on his way.

Choosing to ignore Beckett's interruption I asked Ashley, "How do you want it?"

"Black and strong," he grinned. "Just like me." With a nod toward the door, he asked, "Who was that?"

Dropping a heaping spoon of the granules into a mostly-clean mug, I said, "Detective Sergeant Mavis Beckett."

"Mavis? Really?"

I sniggered at my own comedic brilliance. "No, not really. I just wanted to see what would happen if you called him Mavis."

Ashley shook his head, but smiled, enjoying the first hint of banter between us.

Waiting for the kettle, I elected to break the ice a little further. We were no longer glaring at each other as we had been for most of the day, but the air was far from friendly.

"You have a partner at home?" I enquired, making small talk because it was the right thing to do, not because I was in any way interested. "A significant other?"

"A fiancée," he replied.

I suspected as much. Sitting next to him in the car, there was a trace of a feminine smell about his clothing, the kind of scent that gets transferred when two people embrace. Also, I observed him pay little attention to the women we met during the day. No surreptitious glances at

82

Shadow of a Lie

a firm bottom or voluminous chest. That could have resulted in me questioning his sexuality, but he paid even less attention to the men. He was content with his partner, a condition that rarely lasts in my experience.

Imparting a few words of wisdom, I said, "be sure to keep a photograph of your good lady in your wallet when you get married."

Ashley jinked an eyebrow in question. "What for?"

Fighting to keep the mirth from my face, I replied, "To remind you why there is no money in it."

He shook his head in an amused manner.

"You're married?" he pointed to my ring, but asked the question cautiously like he was worried I might be a widower or recently divorced and unable to let go.

"Thirty-one years this December."

He pushed out his lips and raised his eyebrows slightly. "Congratulations."

"Thank you." I'd always found it odd that others would congratulate a couple on staying married when that was what they were supposed to do.

He followed up with a natural next question.

"Kids?"

"Just the one. She is about to turn thirty."

The conversation stilted, neither of us able to think of anything else to say. The kettle clicked off, giving me some-thing to do and a few seconds later we were returning to the incident room where I got straight back to research.

For the most part I was reviewing the Craig Chowdry case, bringing myself up to speed since I knew very little about it other than what Ashley had been able to tell me in the car and the little I could remember from the news seven years ago.

I knew DCI Pascoe led the investigation in 2016. The other officers involved with the case were listed and I

STEVE HIGGS

realised I recognised one of the names: Detective Sergeant G Hunt.

Gary Hunt was retired. A few years my senior, we met somewhere around 2004 when a case he was working ran into one of mine. I made a note to look him up. He would remember the Chowdry investigation and that would be of use.

My brow wrinkling, I picked up my phone and scrolled through the list of contacts. I hadn't spoken to Gary in years, but we got on well enough back in the day.

Hesitating for a moment, my finger over the call button, I decided it couldn't hurt to ring an old friend.

"Hello," a familiar voice echoed in my ear.

"Gary. It's Tony Heaton."

"Tony?" He said my name like he was trying it out. He knew it, but needed a few seconds to align his memory. "Tony! Hey, how's it going? To what do I owe the pleasure of this call?"

"I just found your name on an old case I'm looking into."

"Oh?"

"Craig Chowdry." I said the name and left it at that.

He repeated it, "Craig Chowdry. Now that's a case I haven't thought about in a while. You say you're working on it? Did they find him? I haven't seen anything on the news."

"No, nothing like that. Listen, I just got handed the case today. I might have some questions and wanted to check you would be around to answer them."

"Sure. Anytime."

I thanked him, chatted for a couple of minutes just to be polite, and left him to his evening.

I also poked around burial records which are available online for a small fee. They were listed by parish as there is

Shadow of a Lie

no central registry, so a person must go almost church by church to determine if there is anything at all to discover.

I didn't have to do that though; I could focus on the church in Goodnestone – St Batholomew's. From the map Ashley showed me and which was now pinned to one of the cork boards, the blood they found was on a straight line from Craig's house to the village centre.

Craig's family had lived on the outskirts of the community, in a row of plush, detached houses built in the eighties. Craig's father worked in London as an IT guru and his mother was a dentist. It was a wonder they sent him to the local school before packing him off to Hadlow College. With their money they could have sent him to a private place the moment he could walk.

If I drew a line from his house through the meadow where they found his blood and kept going, it crossed a road – the B2046. Andrew, Daniel, Shane, and Tim were spotted by Miss Jane Wallace trying to cross the road at approximately 1712hrs on August 8th, 2016.

In her statement, she claimed to have almost run Tim over when he stepped into the road. They claimed to have been looking for Craig following the altercation outside the Shop Ryte and unable to find him, but it placed them in the vicinity of the blood. Directly across the road, if one continues the straight line, is the church and the churchyard.

Hence my interest in burials at the time.

There were none listed, but that didn't mean I could rule it out. Two people were buried the previous week: John Halshaw, eighty-four, and Matilda Wren, ninety-six. The soil above their coffins would be soft and easy to remove and they wouldn't need to take it all out, just enough to make sure Craig's body was far enough below the surface that it would not be dug up by wild animals.

STEVE HIGGS

Still, I had no evidence to suggest that could be the case, just a hunch. It wasn't something I could use to get the graves dug out again.

My phone rang just as I was opening a new tab. A glance at the screen confirmed who was calling and I reached to pick it up, knocking my cold coffee over in the process.

I swore and leapt from my chair to evade the spreading puddle of dark brown doom. Ashley looked up from his screen, pushing his chair back a little with an amused expression on his face.

Whipping papers out of the way and looking around for something I could use to mop up the swamp of liquid now coating a third of my desk, I removed anything absorbent from its path.

"Here," said Ashley, helpfully passing me a small towel.

I mumbled a thank you, laying it over the spill where it instantly soaked up much of what was there.

"Where did that come from?" I asked, glad for the towel but curious about whether he had in fact used magic to produce it.

"My bag," he replied, his attention back on his laptop. "It's got my gym gear in it."

My phone had long since rung off, leaving me to return the call. But first I needed to visit the gents because the coffee I didn't catch dripped onto the floor with a running-water sound that had instantly triggered my bladder.

The call had been from Mary, my wife, to check what time I thought I would be home and whether she could prepare me anything for dinner. I'd sent a text earlier that afternoon to let her know I would be late.

My reply told her I would throw something in the oven when I got home and not to wait up for me. I had intended to go home sooner, but enthralled by Craig Chowdry's

86

Shadow of a Lie

disappearance the time had passed almost without me noticing. Seven years ago ... well, I couldn't now tell you what I was working on at the time, but it had been enough to distract me. The missing teenager from a village a few miles away had caught my attention, but it was being investigated by other officers, so like the rest of the country, I got my updates from the TV. However, I could recall remarking to my wife that the missing teenager was almost certainly dead.

I was getting hungry and needed to leave, but it wasn't until Ashley rose from his chair, announcing his intention to call it a night, that I realised how late it had become.

"Have you found much?" he asked, folding down his laptop and swivelling his chair around to wrestle it into his bag. We had barely spoken in the last two hours. "I'm heading home, but I assume you would like a lift back to Herne Bay."

I blinked, confused for half a heartbeat until my brain caught up. Caught up in the case, it had not occurred to me that my car was miles away, back in Herne Bay where I parked it this morning.

Quickly gathering my things and patting my pockets to be sure I had it all, I followed him to the door.

"Yes, thank you. I need a ride home."

"Home? Or back to the nick?"

I almost said 'home' but stopped myself. If he dropped me at my house, he would then have to come back for me in the morning and I had a sneaking suspicion he would want to start earlier than I was used to waking.

"The nick, please."

We left Wingham nick via the detention centre at the back, giving a cursory nod to the duty officers on our way out.

STEVE HIGGS

In the car, silence ruled until Ashley reminded me of his earlier question. "So did you find much?"

I shook my head. "No. I looked at deaths and burials in the area around the time Craig went missing, but if that's what they did with his body, I doubt we would ever be able to get an exhumation order unless someone confesses."

"Anything else?" He didn't say it, but he was challenging me to confess that was all I'd done with the last four hours.

"I went through the case file," I pointed out, a frown compressing my eyebrows. "Because, you know, I'm investigating a case I know next to nothing about. The investigation appears tight. Pascoe followed all the steps, asked all the right questions. I still think the boys were coached; their answers are too perfect." I was doing nothing but reiterating a point we had already discussed. However, the possibility that someone inside the investigation helped to cover up the murder and make sure the four boys got away with it was a dodgy subject to discuss.

If we were to prove that was the case, we would need to collate watertight evidence, not just of witness tampering, but of a deliberate attempt to pervert the course of justice. It meant we were operating inside enemy territory and would need to tread carefully. It made my heart race just to think about it.

"We need to proceed with extreme caution," Ashley coached unnecessarily. "If you are right, the four boys won't give us any answers, might refuse to be interviewed at all, and DCI Pascoe will be watching us like a hawk."

I said, "There was one witness report that places them near to the site where Craig's blood was found."

"Jane Wallace," Ashley gave her name to show he knew who I was talking about. "She claimed to have seen three

Shadow of a Lie

of the boys coming through Catshole Copse where it ends at the B2046."

"Yes. They explained their reason for being there, and in many ways it helps them because she would have mentioned it had they been carrying a dead body."

"I'm going to interview her in the morning, see if there is anything new she might recall."

We continued to discuss the case and our next steps all the way back to Herne Bay. Outside the nick, he cruised to a stop at the kerb. I patted my pockets once again, mostly to confirm I had my car keys, then levered myself out of his car.

I bade him goodnight and let the door shut only to hear the window powering down as I turned away.

"I'll meet you outside Herne Bay nick at eight," he called and was already pulling away when I twisted to show the disdain on my face. His confidence that I would show up at a time he dictated undid some of the collaborative camaraderie beginning to develop. It felt a bit like my olive branch had been slapped away.

Eight might not be early for most people, but I was usually just sitting down to breakfast at that time, and I liked my routine. Let the young run around being keen. Mature folks would achieve more by pacing themselves.

CHAPTER 13

MARY WAITED UP FOR ME EVEN THOUGH I TOLD HER NOT to. She was like that though and it wasn't so late that she would have been in bed asleep. More usually, she retires to read before ten each night, but had chosen to curl into her chair with her current book so she could quiz me about my day.

"I have a new partner," I revealed while taking off my jacket.

"New partner? Is there something you're not telling me?" she teased. "I thought you were retiring in a few weeks."

"I am." My stomach rumbled, reminding me that lunch was a very long time ago now, but my feet led me to the drinks' cabinet not the kitchen. There I found a bottle of Scotch in desperate need of emptying.

Mary expressed her disapproval silently, her face saying everything.

I explained myself with two words, "Bruce Denton."

Her eyebrows shot for the ceiling and her right hand went to her heart.

90

Shadow of a Lie

"What about him? Have they ... have they found something?"

I grimaced as the neat whiskey burned a path through my body, warming me and taking away the stress of the day all in one go like a magical elixir. With a shudder, I faced my wife to address her questions.

"No, nothing like that." Resting against the arm of the chair adjacent to hers, I regaled her with the events of my day. I left out how rattled I felt when I thought I would be forced to reopen the case that became such an obsession. Mary knew only too well how many hours of our marriage were spent apart because I refused to leave it alone.

A couple of minutes in she interrupted me to confirm whether I had eaten anything or not and rolled her eyes at the truth. I was drinking neat whiskey on an empty stomach, and she wasn't going to let that pass.

Leading me to the kitchen, she swiftly produced a toasted cheese and ham sandwich. Between bites, she listened to me jabber about the Craig Chowdry case – which she didn't remember at all – and my new partner who she said sounded just like me when I was his age.

I didn't like the comparison, though I worried it might be accurate.

With my supper finished, and though I had no intention of getting to the nick in time to meet Ashley's eight o'clock start, I wasted no time in getting to bed. The whiskey would dull my raging memories and help me sleep.

Mary kissed me goodnight, but kept her light on, continuing to read and waking me gently at what felt like only a few moments later to tell me I was snoring like an asthmatic warthog. I turned over and that was that.

CHAPTER 14

ASHLEY CHOSE TO DEFY PROTOCOL AND WAS GONE BY THE time I arrived the next morning. According to Gavin Dobbs, he waited until eight fifteen, sent me a terse message, which I had received, and left by himself.

The message had popped up on my phone while I was eating breakfast, a delightful plate of smoked salmon and scrambled eggs with freshly toasted sourdough bread dripping with butter and a scattering of chives. Mary didn't want me to eat the bread or the butter, scolding me for ignoring my dietary needs in favour of flavour. Thankfully, she held back from reminding me my trousers were already tight and kissed me goodbye as was our custom.

Dropping into the chair at my desk, I called Ashley to ascertain his whereabouts. He didn't answer. Automatically, I assumed he was choosing to ignore me, but my phone rang while that thought was still forming.

"Where are you?" Ashley demanded.

"At Herne Bay nick. It is ..." I checked the clock on the wall, "eight forty-seven. This is the earliest I have arrived at work in a year, Ashley. That's all for you. Could you really not wait for me?" I was teasing him, being delib-

Shadow of a Lie

erately annoying in the face of his powerplay. He wanted to dictate timing and directions, and I am just too old to let it work that way. "Tell you what. Come back for me in a bit and I'll buy some sticky buns and coffees."

I got an expletive in reply followed by, "Get yourself to Goodnestone. Call me when you arrive. I'll interview Jane Wallace without you."

I would have challenged his decision, but he had already hung up.

"No sticky bun for you then," I remarked to myself. I had an address for Jane Wallace, but just as I thought about heading there to find my partner, a different course of action floated into my head. It sounded much more promising and interesting, so that was what I chose to do.

Goodnestone is about a thirty-minute drive from Herne Bay, but hampered by roadworks on the A257. Temporary traffic lights had created a tail back that added ten minutes to my trip, so I arrived in Goodnestone a little after nine thirty.

My car is an old, battered Vauxhall Astra estate with a two-litre diesel engine that rattles and smokes. It is old enough to have been to university, graduated, found a job, got married, and had kids. It was blue once, and still is, I suppose, but what started as small patches of rust are threatening to join forces, and the paint that remains is weather worn and faded. The radio antenna got ripped off years ago, there's a crack in one corner of the windscreen, and the seats are lumpy.

I love it.

I've never been a car person as my choice of automobile indicates. However, it worked, I took it to be serviced every year, and I took great joy in how little I needed to care if it got scratched.

Ashley expected me to link up with him, but if he was

prepared to leave me behind and set off on his own, he could hardly complain when I did the same. Besides, I'd worked by myself for most of my career, teaming up with others only when and if I had to. Without a partner I was unencumbered, undistracted by their ideas and opinions, and able to focus my skills on the task at hand: finding what the killer forgot to cover up.

I parked on the grass verge on the B2046 right about where Jane Wallace should have seen the four boys exiting the woods. I wanted to see it for myself, immersing my mind in the crime and how things might have played out on that fateful day.

Though it would be inaccurate to describe the temperature as cold, it was cool enough to make me thankful for my coat. The sky above was grey, but not with the kind of clouds that bring rain. They gave the air a damp feeling, one that reminded me of my youth spent playing in the woodland near my home.

There was a path through the copse of trees on the western side of the road. It was old and a little overgrown, though the brambles, nettles, and everything else were dying back this far into autumn. Assuming my map skills were up to scratch, and I wasn't in the wrong place, I could see the way the boys must have come. For those not driving a car, the route provided a shortcut from the estate where Craig's parents once lived to the village where I guess kids might congregate.

The road formed a tight bend which provided a possible explanation for why Jane Wallace found Tim in the road. Standing on the western edge, it was impossible to see traffic coming from either direction. Only when I crossed to the far side, closest the village, could I see a worthwhile distance.

Murmuring to myself, I said, "He was checking to see

Shadow of a Lie

if the coast was clear." If they killed Craig in the meadow where the police found his blood, they would have been out of sight from the houses. However, they couldn't go back that way, so their only choice was to head for the village.

Reaching the road, they placed Craig's body down, and sent Tim forward to scan for cars. Jane Wallace skidded to a stop to avoid hitting Tim. She was undoubtedly going too fast, but must have scared the living daylights out of the four boys who would have feared discovery. The undergrowth in August would be tall though. I could see now that it had grown to a height of several feet before the changing seasons made it wither.

My thoughts were nothing but educated guesses, but starting from a point of assumed guilt, the theory worked.

Pushing on, I crossed to the village side of the road, moving east. I had to fight my way through some of the undergrowth. While the summer growth was dying back, the hardier brambles were only just bearing their fruit. Unrestricted by man, they grew rampant, great snaking tendrils looping in and around as they sought the light and competed for the best spots.

Mercifully, they thinned only a couple of feet in, though I appeared to have an arterial bleed from a thorn wound to my left ankle and a nettle had deliberately, and with great malice, chosen to sting the underside of my scrotum. What I needed, I remarked to myself on reflection, was a Robocop suit. I felt fairly certain Robocop never felt the need to massage irritated testicles in the line of his duties.

Beyond the initial overgrowth, it was possible to see the edge of the village. The tower of St Batholomew's Church was the first thing anyone would spot, and I used it as a guide to find my way through the trees. Reaching the edge of the woodland, I turned around to look back. Had the four boys come this way?

It would have been a tough slog, but the case notes made no reference to any scratches or wounds they might have suffered. Was I just wrong?

I pushed on into the churchyard, scanning the morbid scene as though I might somehow be able to guess where Craig's body might lie. It would have been so easy to slip into the churchyard at night to dig just a few feet down into one of the fresher graves. Is that what they did? I could picture their haste to move the body, to get it tucked out of sight. But if they returned when it was dark in August, would their parents not have noticed their teenage boys leaving the house? Were they recorded as arriving home late that night? Had the questions even been asked? I ran through the interview notes in my head, unable to recall the subject being broached.

I pushed the thought to one side. Skirting the church, I arrived on Lunsford Lane. Shane Travers lived close by, but then all four boys lived within a half mile of each other. They had to; it is a small village.

I had seen enough for now, so I retraced my steps, hopping back over the church wall and fighting through the undergrowth once again though it was easier on the way back, my passage the first time having left a path to follow.

I paused when a little gong chimed in my head. Four boys passing through the thick undergrowth would have created a distinct furrow. Surely DCI Pascoe would have come to look for himself, so was there an obvious passage through the woods?

For a moment, I was almost excited, but with a tut, remembered this was an established shortcut to the village.

Back at the road, I made my way to the white line

Shadow of a Lie

running down the middle and looked around until I spotted the telltale gap in the foliage. To my left as I looked to the east, a path meandered through the trees on its way to the houses beyond. Had I spotted it before, I could have avoided the slog through the undergrowth and accompanying injuries thus sustained.

Regardless, the four boys came this way from the direction of Craig's house and must have ended up in the village. Staring through the trees, I knew the missing teenager's body was almost certainly somewhere in Goodnestone.

It sent a chill down my back.

At my car I swiped at my clothing to remove pieces of plant and some spiderwebs before getting in. Next on my list was Sarah French. A woman now, not a teenage girl, she had moved out of her parent's house and in with her boyfriend: Andrew Curzon.

CHAPTER 15

I PULLED UP OUTSIDE THE ADDRESS FOR SARAH FRENCH and saw too late that Ashley was pulling in behind me. Given the option, I would have continued to avoid him today. Well, for a while at least. Truthfully, the last hour of poking around on my own had been quite enjoyable. The thrill of the chase and all that.

I was slower to exit my car than my partner and found him lounging against his car looking like he was debating the merits of strangling me.

"Finally decided to show up then?"

"I've been exploring the woods, thank you," I replied, matter-of-factly, but also with a tad more cheer than the situation called for. "How was Jane Wallace?"

"Cooperative, but ultimately of no help. She remembers the incident only because she reacted to a request for information on the local news channel. They were asking about the missing teenager and showing the faces of the four boys she saw on the afternoon of August 8th. She recognised them as the same kids. Beyond that, I don't think she knows anything."

Ashley was annoyed with me, but he was more inclined

Shadow of a Lie

to focus on the case and the worrying trend we had unhappily identified.

"I think we need to watch DCI Pascoe." It was a bold statement and not what I expected my young colleague to suggest.

"You know you can't accuse him until you have absolute proof, right? If you even attempt to do so, I will distance myself from this case and watch you burn."

Ashley shot me a look. "You're the one who said it first. In fact, you were suspicious when we left the station ten minutes after meeting him for the first time."

"Suspicious is a long way from accusing a senior detective of a serious crime! Your career will stop dead, and it will cause me all manner of headaches even after I retire. You'll forever be known as the cop who went after one of his own."

"So you have no intention of going after him even if he's behind it?"

"That's not what I said." I lowered my voice, conscious we were having this discussion in broad daylight. "If DCI Pascoe deliberately altered the course of justice in the original case and helped the boys to make Craig Chowdry's body vanish, then I am all for seeing him go down. What I am pointing out to you, which, by the way, should be patently obvious to anyone with eyes, is that you cannot even say the words 'dirty cop' unless you have all the evidence in your hands. Anything else is career suicide."

Ashley drew in a slow breath through his nose, holding it for a two count before slowly exhaling. He was calming himself and taking a second to process his thoughts.

"Okay, you're right. Even if there was a cover up, it doesn't have to have been Pascoe. There were other detectives involved in the case."

"Yes," I nodded. "A host of other officers in relatively

key positions. I know one of them, a DS called Gary Hunt. He's retired now, but I was planning to fire a few questions his way when we know a little more. Shall we have a chat with Miss French?"

CHAPTER 16

MOVEMENT BEYOND THE FRONT DOOR'S PANE OF FROSTED glass revealed someone coming toward us. Sarah was in at least. Employed as a shop assistant at Grogan's Farm Shop just outside the village, Miss French had been living with Andrew Curzon for two years.

The house was a small, terraced place, the like of which one can find all over the county. I knew without needing to see that the front door would open into a hallway containing a set of stairs leading to the bedrooms. The room at the front of the house would be the living room, but defying the term would be so small it had barely enough room for a sofa and a television.

Moving further in one would find a dining room and beyond that a galley kitchen. Strangely, that wasn't it and beyond the kitchen lay the bathroom and toilet, a throwback from the old Victorian design that placed the toilet outside.

Millions of houses were made just the same and had been converted by generations of homeowners to make them more liveable. In many cases this meant removing the chimney breasts to provide a little extra space in the affected rooms once central heating had been installed, but others I had seen included a full reimagining of the layout to make the kitchen bigger and move the bathroom upstairs.

The door swung open, but not fully, the person inside not wanting to invite whoever was outside in or even give them a view of her house. Was it messy? Or was she in the middle of something and not wanting to be kept away for too long.

Peering around the edge of the door, a thin yet pretty twenty-one-year-old looked down at our faces from her elevated position. She wore her blonde hair pulled into a simple ponytail that hung between her shoulder blades and her face was bereft of makeup. It was hard to judge her height from outside since there was a step up to get into the house, but she was short at maybe five feet and two inches. Her brother was at least a foot taller and her features were dissimilar. It made me question if they were only half brother and sister.

Ashley held up his warrant card.

"Good morning, Miss French. I'm Detective Sergeant Long, this is Detective Sergeant Heaton. May we come inside, please? We need to speak to you about Craig Chowdry."

I was curious to hear what she might say in reply. She had to know about us from her boyfriend, so she couldn't pretend to be surprised to see us. Her eyes were darting around, never staying in one place for very long – a sign of nervousness, and she clung to the doorframe, her knuckles white as if it were the only thing keeping her up.

"Now's really not a good time," she tried weakly. "I don't have anything I can say to help you anyway."

Ashley wasn't about to be put off. "I doubt that will be the case. It's just a few questions, Miss French."

Shadow of a Lie

She turned around to look back into the house and the door shifted slightly. It revealed a little more of the woman inside and I spotted two things instantly. The first was that she was pregnant. Not that far along, but far enough for the disproportionate swell of her belly to show. The second was the bruise on her neck. The kind you get when someone grabs you hard and holds on.

"Is there someone here?" I asked, my tone a hushed promise of assistance.

She twisted back to face me, a questioning look in place. There was no one there, she just didn't want to let us in and was looking for an excuse that might convince us to go away.

Now that her eyes were on me, I said, "You have to talk to us, Sarah. There's no getting away from it. Craig deserves the truth to be known."

At my final remark, her cheeks coloured, and she tore her eyes away and down. When she spoke, her voice came out as a whisper, "That's not fair."

I kept my tone kindly when I said, "Fair doesn't come into it, Sarah. Let us come inside, please."

She relented reluctantly. Letting go of the door finally, her arms flopped to her sides in defeat.

Ashley wasted no time, stepping over the threshold and into her house as she backed away.

"I don't know what you hope to achieve," she muttered, leading us down the hallway toward the kitchen. "I don't know what happened to Craig and quizzing me about it again won't change that." She was setting us up to be let down, announcing her position before we could even pose our first question.

People about to be interviewed do this more often than the public realise. It never works. I expected her to have answers all lined up just like Daniel and Andrew, so

STEVE HIGGS

I chose to come at her from an angle she wasn't expecting.

"How often does Andy hit you?"

We were still filing into the dining room, Ashley turning left to go around to the far side of the small wooden table. Sarah had her hand on the back of a chair, about to pull it out, but her whole body froze upon hearing the question.

"Andy doesn't hit me." Her lie was instant and unconvincing.

"Yes, he does, Sarah, and I would like to know why? Is he just generally violent or has our arrival and the resurfacing of the Craig Chowdry case brought this on?" I motioned to the mark on her neck to make it clear what I was referring to. I had enough experience of domestic abuse to know the bruise I could see was probably a fraction of those that existed beneath her clothes.

"I don't know what you are talking about," she growled, frustration and embarrassment pushing anger to the surface.

I shot a quick glance at Ashley, checking he wasn't going to jump in to stop me.

"Sarah," I started, almost pleading with her to see sense, "you don't have to put up with this. There are lots of ways to get help. I can have someone here to talk you through your options in just a few hours if you wish."

"You don't know what you are talking about," she continued to protest.

I kept right on going. "Sarah, we know Andy was involved in Craig's disappearance. A conviction will ensure he never hurts you again."

This time she said nothing, keeping her lips shut to ensure she gave us nothing. It was another reason to believe she had also been coached.

Shadow of a Lie

Ashley spoke for the first time since entering the house, "Let's circle back to that, shall we?" The suggestion was mostly aimed at me, and he made sure to make eye contact with Sarah before he spoke again. "Sarah, we are here to talk to you about Craig Chowdry. I'm sure you know we have already spoken to your boyfriend, Andy, and to your brother, Danny. We will be speaking with Shane and Tim in due course and with the other persons who gave witness statements at the time of his disappearance."

Sarah snatched a chance to talk when Ashley took a breath. "Witness statements? How can there be witness statements when there was nothing to witness? My brother and his friends didn't do anything to Craig."

"How do you know that?" I seized upon what I thought was an opening. I believed she was lying, but her body language didn't reflect it. When she claimed Andy never hit her, the timbre in her voice was different … hesitant, and she struggled to make eye contact. In stating her brother and his friends were innocent, she delivered the words confidently and was glaring right at Ashley when she did.

Turning her head rather than her body, Sarah looked at me. I was to her right at the dining table though none of us had pulled out a chair to sit down yet.

"My brother isn't capable of killing someone."

I shot back a response to that claim easily enough. "It never ceases to amaze me what people are capable of that their loved ones never deemed possible. Do you have anything tangible, Sarah?"

"Do you have a body?" she replied. Once again, her answer was too cool, too confident. She, like her brother and his friends, knew there was no case without the body. Taking my pause as an opportunity to press home her advantage, she said, "I don't know what happened to

STEVE HIGGS

Craig. I didn't see him the day he decided to leave, and I cannot speculate on how his blood came to be on the grass in the meadow."

Silence ruled for a beat, neither Ashley nor I having any way to counter her claim. However, Ashley had more questions he wanted to ask.

"Your statement taken the day after he vanished places you in Whitstable on August 8th. You were there with a friend, yes?"

"Yes."

"What time did you get home?"

Sarah's answer came with a bored tone, the effect that of a person being quizzed on questions intended for a child to answer. She fired off response after response, giving answers that matched her statement from seven years ago each time. Some of them were word for word verbatim.

She knew how long the bus took to get from Whitstable to Goodnestone and which villages it went through. She remembered the number of the bus and could recall a description of the drivers that day for both journeys.

I knew from the case notes that both girls handed over ticket stubs from their trip. They paid cash which was clever because most people would have tapped a card and left a definite trail. Not that I suspected Sarah of being involved in Craig's murder, this was just another example of how well the witnesses had been groomed.

Only a few minutes in, I nodded to Ashley that he should wrap it up. Sarah wasn't going to give us anything and speaking to her was a waste of time.

"We're done?" she asked, relief very clearly evident in her voice. I was given the impression she'd felt under pressure to perform and was thankful to have come through the ordeal without messing up. Throughout, her posture and tone had altered depending on how confident she was

Shadow of a Lie

of her answer. One thing was obvious to me: she believed the four boys to be innocent.

I was surprised at that, and it gave me something to think about. It could be as simple as wholly buying into her big brother's lies. I didn't think that was it though.

Now that she was expecting us to leave and there was no good reason for us to stay, I had one final question. It was one she wasn't expecting.

"Why do you think Craig would run away?" I wanted to trip her up with something she might not have rehearsed. Ashley's questions had been about the facts of the case. This one was speculative – what did *she* think?

Her mouth opened and closed a few times. Sarah's nerves had been on display since she opened the door. She didn't want to talk to us and acted as though on trial the whole time. It gave her a guilty appearance, but what lie she might be hiding I could not yet guess.

"I guess he knew he was in big trouble for sleeping with me." Her cheeks coloured a shade. "I was underage, but you know that, of course. Danny found a condom wrapper under my bed and went nuts. I know they planned to beat Craig up and I begged him not to. I warned Craig to stay out of the village that day. I told him to stay at home, but they were never going to do anything worse than rough him up a little. It was you guys ... the police he needed to worry about. He would have been placed on the sex offender register for sleeping with a minor. I think that's why he ran away. To avoid the humiliation and embarrassment it would have caused his family."

Most of her answers had been truthful, but this one wasn't. Craig would have been in hot water, but the sex offender register? Probably not. She could have given a short, easy answer, but chose to embellish instead, thinking it would sound more convincing.

107

It didn't.

I could see Ashley was thinking the same thing and had new questions lining up because Sarah's answer brought to light new evidence: she warned him that he was going to get beaten up? That wasn't in the case notes. How did she warn him? In person? By phone? With a text message? She claimed to have not seen him the day he vanished, but her most recent statement seemed to contradict that.

I've faced tough interviewees before; people who had their story clear in their heads and stuck to it rigidly, so even though I knew they were lying, it was hard to find a chink in their armour.

But that was precisely what Sarah just showed us.

The sound of the backdoor opening startled our host, a look of shock registering on her face.

"Babe, where are you?" Andrew Curzon called out from the kitchen.

Her eyes wide, Sarah said, "I'm – I'm right here." The tremor in her voice and the stammer when she replied enough to confirm she was scared of her boyfriend.

His footsteps were coming our way and I thought about calling out to announce our presence. I chose not to, and held a finger up to my lips to keep Ashley quiet because I wanted to see how Curzon would react.

"Why can I see dirty plates in the sink?" Andrew growled. "Have you done anything today other than sit around on your lazy backside?"

He came through the door from the kitchen, a surly expression fixed to his face. It switched to one of surprise when he saw me and then Ashley, but only for a fleeting second. Almost instantly, he was raising his fists, rage sending adrenalin into his blood supply. It wasn't aimed at us though.

Shadow of a Lie

"What did I tell you about speaking to the cops, you dozy, fat cow!"

He had his right arm across his body and swinging upward to deliver a backhand slap before I could react. I was closer than Ashley, who was on the far side of the round dining table, but Sarah was the closest to the kitchen door and there was nothing either of us could have done to stop the blow from landing.

She didn't even try to duck. Perhaps experience dictated it was better to accept what was coming than to fight it and get even worse treatment for her troubles later.

The slap echoed like a thunderclap in the small room and Sarah cried out in pain as she fell away only to have her arm caught in one of Andrew's giant mitts.

He was going to hit her again, but two seconds had elapsed since his intentions became clear and that was all the time I needed to close the distance between us. Ashley, with age and fitness on his side, got there first.

I was half a second behind him and that was long enough for my partner to grip Curzon's arm, bend it behind his back and force him to the carpet. Curzon let go of Sarah the moment Ashley grabbed his arm, a cry of pain accompanying his descent to the floor.

"Andrew Curzon, you are under arrest for the crime of assault," Ashley recited Curzon's rights as he secured first one hand with a set of cuffs and then the other.

It happened so fast, and I was so out of practice, that I found myself left gawping at the scene. It was much akin to watching Chuck Norris or Jean Claude Van Damme in action. Ashley moved with economy and like lightning, no effort wasted on flamboyance or showmanship. One moment Andrew Curzon was upright and angry, the next he was enjoying a mouthful of carpet, his arms folded into an acceptable impression of a pretzel.

STEVE HIGGS

Ashley looked up at me, a curious eyebrow raised.

"You just going to stand there?"

Gathering my thoughts quickly, I shot back, "You don't appear to need my help."

Sarah had a hand clutching the injured side of her face, tears welling in her eyes, but not falling. Was that toughened resilience I was seeing, or did he hit her so often she no longer bothered to cry?

"I'm not pressing charges," she stated.

"Damned right you're not," Curzon growled.

I fired back, "Yet I think we'll process you anyway, Mr Curzon." We had enough reason to get social services involved and every justification to do so. Did Sarah really think this was a safe environment into which she should bring a baby? What if he proved violent to the child as well?

Of course, we were far from finished with her. If nothing else, I needed to explore her remark about warning Craig, but a knock at the door changed everything.

CHAPTER 17

I WENT TO THE DOOR MYSELF, TAKING CHARGE OF THE situation. Curzon was still on the floor and though I harboured some minor concern Sarah might do something silly, I doubted she would try to stab my partner to free her boyfriend.

The shadow on the other side of the frosted glass was dark, the person outside squinting in with their hands cupped around their face to blank out the sunlight. It looked like a man, but it wasn't until I got the door open that I realised I knew who it was.

Detective Sergeant Glenn Beckett wasn't pleased to see me and saw no need to hide it. His head was the same height as mine, and he was able to look right into my eyes, but he was outside where the surface was perhaps six inches lower; a stark reminder of how tall the man was.

"We got a call about a disturbance," he grumbled, his voice deep and gravelly like an orc from *The Lord of the Rings*. He looked around me to see my partner levering Curzon off the floor. "Seems that was accurate."

I squinted at him. "Why is it that I think you mean us and not the man now in custody for assault?"

STEVE HIGGS

A flicker of something passed behind Beckett's eyes.

"I'll take it from here," he volunteered and moved to get by me.

I held my ground, blocking his access with my body.

"Who called in the disturbance?"

"Anonymous," Beckett replied, his tone dismissive. "Do you mind moving out of the way. I actually work here, I'm not just in the area to dispute the work of others and question their ability to conduct an investigation."

Ah, so there was the reason behind the hostility. Not that it surprised me, but it was unexpected to hear him verbalise it so openly.

"That's not what we are doing," I stated, speaking in a reasoned and measured manner. "Nor was it our idea to go back over the Craig Chowdry case." Ok, so that last part wasn't entirely true, but getting assigned to the task force and picking the cases that were identified as possibles to investigate hadn't come down to either one of us.

Delaying Beckett gave Ashley the time he needed to get moving and he was coming down the hallway behind me, escorting Curzon who griped loudly and swore inventively.

"I don't want to press charges," Sarah repeated, her voice carrying over our heads.

Beckett shot me a victorious look. "The lady doesn't wish to press charges," he echoed, a smile teasing the corners of his mouth.

I leaned forward until I was close enough to smell cigarettes on his breath.

Speaking clearly, I said, "I don't care, Detective Sergeant Beckett. I witnessed an unprovoked assault, and he is going to be charged. Social services are going to be informed and consequences are going to occur. Perhaps you, in your capacity as a local police officer, should attend to the victim and see to it that calls to the appropriate

Shadow of a Lie

services are expedited." I raised an eyebrow, waiting for him to argue and knowing he couldn't.

He could hand the task off to someone else and probably should. Sarah might very well feel more comfortable in the company of a female police officer, but that was down to her. It hadn't escaped me that the incident resulted in our interview being terminated just when it was getting interesting.

Ashley was coming up behind me, Curzon in front of him, so I stepped out of the house, forcing Beckett to move to one side. I lost my height advantage in so doing and now had to crane my neck to look up at his face.

However, with Sarah at the door where she stopped to watch her boyfriend be taken away, I chose to quiz her anyway.

"Sarah, before we were interrupted, you told us you warned Craig the day he went missing. What did you say?" I wanted to know if she delivered the warning face to face, but asking her that would expose her error. I needed to give her room to expose her own lies.

"I – I don't know," she stammered, her confidence gone again.

Beckett chose that moment to demonstrate his superior size and strength. Walking around me to get to the door, he made sure to nudge my shoulder, jerking me off balance so I had to take a step to counter myself.

"Didn't you just say the lady had been assaulted?" he reminded me. "Hardly the time for an interview, wouldn't you say? In fact, what was it you said to me? Oh, yes. I should attend to the victim and make sure the appropriate calls are expedited." Gripping the edge of the door, he said, "I'll do just that," and slammed it in my face.

Numerous bad words echoed in my head while I gave myself a five count to fume. I could have rung the doorbell

STEVE HIGGS

and made a fuss, but Beckett could then report how I was harassing a witness in the aftermath of an assault. Heck, he would probably film it from inside the house and it wasn't like I could expect his boss, DCI Pascoe, to take my side, not if I was even half right about the cover up.

Turning away and wishing there was something I could kick, I aimed a swing at a garden gnome. I stopped short, convinced I would break my toes if I completed the strike. Telling myself all the excitement and adrenalin was good for me, I made my way out to the street.

"You want to follow?" Ashley asked, loading Curzon into the back of his car and locking him inside. "Or jump in?"

"I'll follow." Having brought my car out to Goodnestone, I had no desire to leave it in the street. Not that I thought it likely to get molested, but why risk it?

I honestly intended to follow him to the station, and was doing so when I saw something that distracted me.

CHAPTER 18

As the boss cop of the area, DCI Pascoe has the right to go where he wants. However, in the normal course of things, it would be typical for him to stay at the nick unless his authority was required at a crime scene. His little station would cover a lot of territory, but not a whole lot of people. The southeast of England, if one discounts London, is the most densely populated part of the country. Despite that, the part of it we are talking about is all farm-land and small villages. The majority of people cluster together in the cities: Canterbury, Maidstone, Tonbridge, Rochester, and more. Away from them it is possible to drive miles without going past a house.

Not that I'm suggesting it's like going to Canada where a person can drive all day and only see a moose, but the point is DCI Pascoe ought to have a relatively quiet life with little reason to be dragged out of his nice office.

Personally, I would rather not spend all my time indoors, and perhaps that was all I was seeing. Of course, in my case my excursions were to avoid work and ensure I had a semi-legitimate reason for a two-hour lunch. However, when the DCI passed me in his car, crossing

STEVE HIGGS

from left to right as I gave way at a junction, curiosity demanded I flick my indicator on and abandon my partner to handle Curzon on his own.

DCI Pascoe drove a black Audi A5. It was a sleek car and better than I could afford. Of course, I had no idea of his circumstances. For all I knew he'd married a lawyer, or a bestselling novelist and she brought in hundreds of thousands a year. Or maybe he was borrowing up to his eyeballs. I'd seen bright people do daft things like that plenty of times.

The car, like the money, was most likely insignificant to my investigation, and I pushed my idle thoughts to one side as I tried to guess where he might be going.

It was just after noon and my stomach rumbled, declaring its empty state as if I needed a reminder to eat. There was a packed lunch in my bag on the passenger seat. Mary put it together this morning while I was eating breakfast, but I knew what it contained: a pork pie, a rather nice ham and cheese sandwich with thick cut, fresh, white bread, a packet of cheese and onion crisps ... the list goes on. Mary moans about my waistline – it's certainly not what it used to be – but she's the one feeding me all the time.

I fumbled for the bag, needing to negotiate the zip to get inside where I would find the plastic lunchbox.

DCI Pascoe was ahead of me, and I didn't want to get too close. However, unlike on TV where the person tailing will always stay a few cars back, out here in the countryside there are no other cars. He wouldn't recognise the vehicle in his rear-view mirror, and I doubted he would be able to make out my face. Probably. I had to hope he didn't because I wanted to see where he was going and felt certain he would abort his mission (if he was doing something clandestine) if he spotted me.

Shadow of a Lie

His indicator came on and I left mine off. He was going right, taking another country lane to get to wherever he was going. I had my plug-in satnav on, the screen showing me the road layout though it was hard to see where each road went. For that I needed to zoom out, but my attention was already divided between driving, keeping Pascoe in sight, and trying to access my lunchbox from inside my bag which was proving harder to open than an average bank's vault.

I let DCI Pascoe take the turning, confident the road was a long straight one – that's what the satnav showed – and slowed before taking the turn to follow him. His car was out of sight, but if I was reading the map right, I could catch up enough to see which way he turned at the far end where it met a T junction.

Now trundling down the country lane and thinking it unlikely I would come across anyone coming the other way, I allowed my attention to stray. With a triumphant bark, I snagged the lunchbox from my bag and held it aloft like the Sword of Grayskull.

I got a scant half heartbeat of notice that I was going to hit a deer and snatched at the steering wheel. Heartrate spiking, I dropped the lunchbox, which hit the gearstick and burst open, showering the contents across both front footwells.

The deer vanished as fast as it appeared, somehow missing my car though I will never know how. Wrestling the wheel, I pumped the brakes, squishing something under my heel as I did.

The car skidded across the leaf litter and detritus at the side of the road and came to a wobbly stop. My pulse hammered in my head like an audible alarm, and I gulped in a breath unaware that I'd been holding it.

A check of my rear-view mirror confirmed I hadn't hit

STEVE HIGGS

the deer, and a quick look around my feet assured me I was going to need something else for lunch. The only survivor was the packet of crisps. The thing under my foot was the porkpie, driven into the carpet and utterly inedible.

Cursing my stupidity as images from a thousand police road awareness safety campaigns played through my mind, I set off after DCI Pascoe's car once more, confident I must have now lost him.

I had.

I reached the T junction at the end of the narrow lane without any sign of the fancy Audi. Left or right? It almost certainly didn't matter which way I turned because he would be half a mile and another three turns away even if I somehow managed to guess right at this one. Nevertheless, having come this far, I twisted the wheel to the left and set off that way.

The satnav showed me heading toward Rowling rather than back to Wingham. I might as well have flipped a coin. That the DCI chose to leave his office was nothing to be suspicious about. That he was in Goodnestone, though, that warranted a few questions. There could be dozens of legitimate reasons for his excursion, but I would learn nothing unless I caught up to him and could discover his exact destination.

That, largely, was why I went left and not right. Right led back to Wingham and were he to be heading that way, it probably meant he had already been where he wanted to go.

I drove for another mile, passing several side roads down which DCI Pascoe could easily have turned. I pressed on, slowing to scan each narrow path. Had he taken one? There was no way for me to know. Had there been rain the previous day, there might be puddles with tyre tracks indicating the recent passage of a car. However,

Shadow of a Lie

the roads were as empty as a politician's pre-election promises.

Ten minutes after losing him, I turned around and started back the way I had come.

My phone began to ring, Ashley's voice coming through the speakers when I tapped the button to connect the call.

He didn't bother with small talk. "Yet again I find myself asking where you are. Were you not right behind me? Were you not following me to the station?"

"I saw Pascoe," I replied, thinking that to be explanation enough.

A second of silence was followed by a question I could have predicted. "What was he doing?"

"Driving. Other than that I don't know. I didn't want to tail too close and I lost him." I couldn't be bothered to lie about it, I'm too old for all that nonsense. "I'm on my way to you now. Shouldn't be long."

I heard Ashley huff out a breath; he was still trying to figure out the best way to manage me and fighting the certain knowledge that he couldn't.

"Okay, well don't rush, there's nothing for you to do here anyway. I'll get Curzon processed as quickly as I can, but the investigation is going nowhere while I'm stuck here. Can you finish up with Sarah French?"

"I'll swing by, but if Beckett is still there, I'll leave it. There's nothing to be gained by a harassment charge."

Driving back toward Wingham, my eyes almost popped from my head. I hit the brakes while snapping my eyes to my rear-view to make sure I wasn't about to get rear ended. Ashley was saying something, but I rudely cut him off with, "I'll call you back!" Stabbing the button to disconnect the phone, I checked the road before performing a U-turn.

119

I didn't believe my eyes were deceiving me, yet could not be certain without checking.

Going back past an open gate – a large one designed to let tractors in and out – I took a closer look at the Audi A5 I'd spotted. It was DCI Pascoe's car all right. He wasn't in it, which meant he was somewhere in the area on foot, but what did that mean? I was close to Goodnestone still, but on the opposite side to Craig Chowdry's house and the likely site of his murder.

The gate led into an overgrown yard filled with weeds and surrounded by old barns and farmyard buildings. One building, made of wood, had a huge chunk of the roof missing. Elsewhere, a tree was growing inside a barn, a branch poking out through a hole in the side. The area looked derelict, but the gate was serviceable, pushed open to allow DCI Pascoe in. There was only one set of tyre tracks running through the old, dried mud, so if he was here to meet someone they were yet to arrive.

Assessing what I could see, I dismissed the possibility of a clandestine meeting. Had that been the case he would surely have waited by or in his car.

So ... what?

The answers running through my brain were both worrying and possibly correct: he was here to check the grave of Craig Chowdry. It looked like the kind of place a body could be stashed and not found. The police and volunteers might have scoured the village and surrounding countryside in 2016, but that didn't mean they looked everywhere.

I drove fifty yards further down the lane to find a space big enough to pull off the road and onto the grass verge. Nerves rose, a sense of trepidation and a touch of adrenaline telling me I should call in to let Ashley know what I

Shadow of a Lie

was doing. Stupidly, I ignored the voice of reason, unwilling to appear scared when I had no just cause to be.

DCI Pascoe could be here for anything and if he spotted me and asked why I was snooping around him, I would say I spotted his car and wondered if he was looking into the Craig Chowdry case again. He would probably believe me.

Fighting a rising sense of dread, I crossed the road and went through the gate.

CHAPTER 19

My heart banged in my chest loud enough that when I paused next to Pascoe's car to listen for movement, my vital organ was all I could hear. It reminded me of my teenage daughter abruptly discovering thrash metal in her early teens. The peaceful tranquillity of my Sunday mornings, a thing I had long cherished without understanding how lucky I was, exploded one day in a deafening cacophony of what I could only describe as demons screaming in agony.

Listening to my rapidly beating heart was little different and just as scary.

Yet again it comes down to lack of practice. Years ago nothing much bothered me. It wasn't that I had a God complex or thought I was unkillable, just that I believed I was equipped to deal with most situations. Plus, I have always worked in a sleepy seaside village where hardened criminals are not the norm.

Now though, so close to retirement, there was a certain Hollywood film extra vibe going around my head. The cop with a few days left to serve always gets killed, right?

Shadow of a Lie

Muttering under my breath, the comments all aimed inward, I rotated slowly on the spot. There were birds twittering in the trees, the sound of something scurrying in the undergrowth, and in the distance, a pneumatic drill cutting a hole in a piece of road somewhere.

Of DCI Pascoe there was no sign or sound.

The tyres of his car left faint tracks in the dirt, but his shoes had not. He was here, of that I felt I could be sure, but unless I explored, I would only see him when he returned to his car, and I had no idea how long that might be.

Returning to the worrying concept that he was here to check on Craig Chowdry's shallow grave, I set off.

First, I poked my head into the barn nearest to where he parked. It had doors and was the most intact of the three farm buildings in sight. The doors were open to reveal the empty interior and I stepped inside where the noise changed instantly.

Like all big, enclosed spaces, the barn suppressed the sound coming from outside and gave a hushed, eerie sensation that crept up my spine. To the left along one side, what appeared to be a stack of straw bales from a harvest many years earlier, had rotted in place.

How many years had they been there? Seven? Could they have been there that long? Covering the shallow grave of a teenage boy? How quickly do bales of straw rot? Regardless, I doubted this was the site. If it was, Pascoe wasn't here looking at it, so I moved on.

The other barns were much the same, the holes in them a clear sign they were not actively used and hadn't been for some years. Something skittered in a corner when I entered the one with the missing roof. A rat, I guessed, or something similar.

STEVE HIGGS

I stamped my foot, the noise it made echoing just a little in the empty space. The buildings all had concrete floors and there was no sign they had ever been disturbed.

I walked back to the centre of the overgrown yard and looked around, my lips pursed as I tried to guess where DCI Pascoe could have gone and what he was doing here if it wasn't to do with Craig Chowdry.

Unwilling to give up just yet, but thinking it might be a good idea to hide in a corner and watch for his return if I couldn't find him in the next few minutes, I aimed my feet at a gap between the barns. There were fields beyond rather than trees, and when I got to another gate, I could see they were in use. The field immediately to my front had been harvested already, only the denuded stubs of whatever crop had grown there this year remained.

It might have been corn or wheat or oil seed rape for all I knew, and it made no difference. The yard led to the fields and had to be part of the same farm. I made a mental note to find out who owned it. A simple check with Land Registry would get me that information.

Behind me, the sound of an engine starting snapped my head around. I couldn't see it, but I knew it was Pascoe's Audi – it was the only car close enough.

My right leg twitched. However, my instant reaction to run back and see him leave halted before I started moving. He wasn't going to have a body on the backseat and hadn't been here long enough to have dug one up. Shifting position slightly, I got to see the German car back up, angle its rear end around until the nose pointed back out the gate, and then leave, turning left to head back toward Wingham.

"What were you doing here, Sir?" I asked the wind.

Just for my own peace of mind, I went back to the yard to check there were no obvious drag marks: there were not,

Shadow of a Lie

and then spent a further five minutes nosing around the area beyond the barns. Wherever Pascoe had gone, whatever he was doing here, he left no obvious trace.

I trudged back to my car, not spotting the thing that was wrong until I got to it.

CHAPTER 20

"Yes, slashed. All four of them," I repeated.

"You think Pascoe did it?" Ashley was whispering, keeping his voice low because he was still at Wingham nick where he was becoming impatient with the pace of the desk sergeant processing Curzon.

Had Pascoe slashed the tyres on my car? I could speculate, but to do so was rarely helpful in an investigation, and there was no evidence either way. He was the only one around, but that hardly made him guilty, and anyone could have driven along the road and chosen to participate in a little light vandalism.

Heck, it could have been some 'green' nutter attacking my car for parking on a rare flower for all I knew.

I expressed as much to my partner.

"All right, look, you might as well call the AA and get them to come out to collect it. Let me know when they do, and I'll come to pick you up."

The call to the AA had already been placed, but I didn't like their ETA of seventy minutes, and I liked my lunch options even less. Unless I wanted to pick over the smushed pork pie or attempt to reassemble the sandwich,

Shadow of a Lie

which was undoubtedly coated in grit and fluff, all I had was a packet of crisps.

The crisps lasted all of two minutes. Wiping greasy fingers on my handkerchief, I settled in to wait on the passenger's seat with the door open and my legs stretched out on the grass.

With time to kill, I thought about the case and tried to do something proactive. Taking out the ordnance survey map again, I twisted it this way and that to get it orientated, then spent more than ten minutes trying to figure out precisely where I was.

Actually, it wasn't my location that interested me, but the site of the derelict farm buildings. I found them eventually and noted the grid reference. Picking up my phone, I called Doris back at the station in Herne Bay.

She answered on the first ring. "Tony?"

"Tis I," I replied brashly. "Can you do something for me, darling? I need to know who owns a farm."

She didn't sigh or complain, but I swear I heard her roll her eyes - addressing her as 'darling' flagged that I was going to ask a favour. As a civilian employee working out of Herne Bay nick for more years than she would like anyone to mention, she possesses a wealth of knowledge that cannot be underestimated. She performs all manner of helpful tasks and researching information is just one of them.

"Shoot," she invited after a second, the time taken to grab a pen and a notepad I imagined.

I reeled off the coordinates and confirmed what road I was on just to make it a little clearer.

"Can you check with Land Registry, please?"

"How urgent is it? I've got a backlog." She didn't tell me who was in the queue already and I didn't ask. If I

STEVE HIGGS

claimed it *was* urgent, she would drop anything that wasn't to deal with mine first.

"Semi," I replied, not wanting to unnecessarily overstate its importance. "Sometime today would be great." I was stuck here for the next hour anyhow.

Doris promised to get back to me with an answer as soon as she could, and I knew she was good for her word. The hour, however, turned out to be closer to two, the familiar and welcome sight of the bright yellow AA van unnoticed until I heard its tyres crunch on the gravel at the edge of the road.

Flashing lights on the roof of the cab warned drivers to beware, but I'd counted less than ten passing cars since I settled in to wait.

The AA man – his badge labelled him as Hudson – eyed me sceptically when he saw the cuts to each tyre.

"I'm a cop," I offered which, surprisingly enough, was enough to explain the damage.

I called Ashley while Hudson reversed my car onto the road and into position to be loaded onto his tiltable flatbed.

"Are you still waiting for the AA? I thought they boasted an average response time of thirty minutes."

"An average, yes," I pointed out the failure in his thinking. "They are here now. The 'man who can' is going to take me to Boxley Tyres in Goodnestone. I'm not much good without tyres and I'll need to collect the car before they shut for the day." I didn't say it, but that was likely to be five o'clock, less than two hours from now. "You want to collect me from there?"

"Yeah, I'm done here." There was subtext in his decision, mainly that I couldn't wander off without telling him for a third time today if I was in his car. "I'll meet you at the tyre place."

And that's what he did, pulling onto the forecourt

Shadow of a Lie

before I could exit the cab of Hudson's AA pick-up truck. The owner of the tyre place had the right size in stock, but apologised because he wasn't going to be able to get to it until the morning.

One flash of my warrant card was enough to change his mind. It always feels like abuse of position when I do that, but sometimes it's just necessary, and a cop rarely has to say anything. I think it's the worry that we might decide to look around if they don't comply with our wishes and that everyone has something to hide.

Thanking the tyre shop boss for his help and understanding, I confirmed I would be back before five to collect my car and slid into the passenger seat of Ashley's Mondeo.

"Where to?" I enquired, curious to hear if he'd learned anything in the last few hours. I'd drawn a blank unless you wished to count DCI Pascoe's continuing suspicious behaviour.

Ashley huffed out a breath that ruffled his lips. "I wanted to resume our chat with Sarah French. She was lying about what happened to Craig. Her answers were great, like textbook answers up until you asked her why she thought Craig ran away. Well done on that, by the way. I wouldn't have thought to go down that line."

He'd pulled off the forecourt and was heading in the direction of Sarah's house. It was two minutes around the corner from the tyre place.

I acknowledged his praise with a nod of thanks. He was trying to bridge the gap between us, building rapport and I was all for that since we were going to be working together for the foreseeable future.

To respond, I said, "I wanted to see what she would say when presented with an accepted 'truth' she knew to be a lie. Anyway, you said 'wanted'. You 'wanted' to resume our

129

chat with Sarah. I take it your use of the past tense means that is no longer the plan."

"Well, it's still the plan," he replied, pulling to the curb right in front of her house. "But she has absconded."

I raised my eyebrows. "Absconded?"

"She was gone before the social worker could get there to deal with the domestic abuse case I raised. I flagged it as a priority." We both knew the mention of her pregnancy was enough to up the ante and get people moving. "But she was gone. Beckett saw no need to let me know, so I'll be having a word with him next time we meet."

"He has quite the chip on his shoulder."

"He's going to have my foot up his arse if he interferes with my investigation again."

"I thought it was *our* investigation," I teased.

Ashley was getting out of the car, I made to follow but he waved for me to stay.

"Hold on a second, I doubt she's here." He knocked at her door and peered through the frosted glass much like Beckett had earlier. He knocked again before accepting defeat and returning to the car.

"She's not answering the phone?" I asked, knowing that had to be the case.

Ashley shook his head. "I left messages, but no response. I'll hang around outside her house if I have to. She'll come home eventually."

"Not if she's scared of her boyfriend, she might not. Any idea how long they will keep him?"

Ashley sighed again. "Not long would be my guess. If Sarah won't press charges, Curzon can expect to be out today."

We fell into silence. It was broken when my stomach reminded me that it was empty. It did so by making a noise

Shadow of a Lie

much akin to the groan one might get from a Labrador attempting complex mental algebra.

Ashley stared at me and uttered a profanity. "Was that your stomach?"

"Missed lunch," I remarked, not wanting to explain the details of my incident with the deer.

Ashley reached around to his bag in the footwell behind my seat.

"Here. I've got a protein bar."

My partner is lean and looks like the kind of person who visits the gym multiple times a week. He's not overly muscular though and I've always associated the existence of things like high-calorie protein bars with the body builders of the world.

"Chocolate, caramel and peanut," I read from the label.

"You're not allergic to peanuts, are you?"

I frowned at the label again. "It says this thing is six hundred calories."

He tried to snatch it back, and I had to whip my hands out of his way.

"I didn't say I wasn't going to eat it."

"You didn't say thank you either," Ashley pointed out.

He was right. I hadn't.

"Thank you," I mumbled around the chewy deliciousness of the chocolate and caramel mix. It was tasty, I couldn't argue that, but I could hear Mary's voice berating me for eating a chunk of my daily calorie allowance in the form of a chocolate bar.

"I keep a couple of those handy for when the day doesn't go according to plan. They last forever and they are really filling."

I knew what he meant. In my day it used to be a packet of digestive biscuits in the glove box of the car. As a detec-

STEVE HIGGS

tive, I have rarely worked set hours. You get called to a crime scene when you ought to be going to bed. You get stuck at a crime scene or interviewing witnesses when you ought to be going home. And God forbid you end up involved in a drawn-out court case. You can sit around doing nothing for days waiting to be called to the witness box for your testimony. Having some food in your pocket is a survival necessity.

Munching my way through the bar, idly killing time in the forlorn hope that Sarah French might reappear, I questioned when it was that I lost my touch. I was aware my effort levels had waned in recent years. That was only natural. That 'go-get-em' attitude is for the young, not those counting down the days until retirement. Still, I felt a little embarrassed to be so underprepared for this investigation.

Tonight, I would sort myself out, get some necessary gear together and be set for tomorrow.

My jaw ached from all the chewing by the time I got to the end of the protein bar, but I was no longer hungry.

We waited in the car for a while; sometimes silent, but mostly talking about the case. We agreed it warranted reopening with a superintendent as SIO and a full team behind them. It needed the authority a superintendent would bring, but to make that happen we would have to produce a tangible reason to justify the request.

If any one of the witnesses were to state their testimony was doctored or led by one of the investigating officers. If we could find any kind of evidence that Craig was indeed murdered, we could justify staffing our concerns up the chain of command. However, without one of those two things or something equally damning, the mere suggestion that DCI Pascoe's original investigation was anything less

Shadow of a Lie

than thorough would land us both in a disciplinary meeting.

You just don't accuse your fellow officers. Not unless you know for certain you are right and can prove it.

When the clock ticked around to half past four, I announced my intention to walk back to the tyre place.

"I'll drive you," Ashley offered, reaching for the ignition.

I grabbed the door handle and pushed it open, the cool October air slipping in to kiss my cheek and chill my neck.

"Nah, stay here. If you leave for five minutes, it will be when Sarah reappears."

Ashley let his hand drop back to his lap. "I'm going to stay for a while then, see if she does come home. What's your plan?"

"Head home, I think. Get some sleep and be fresh for the morning." I thought Ashley was going to argue or make a point about wanting to start early, but he yawned instead, stretching out in his seat like he needed to relieve the ache in his back.

"Okay," he replied, and I thought that was all he had to say until I was out of the car and he called my name.

I ducked my head down to see what he wanted.

"Do you really think DCI Pascoe could be the reason no one was ever charged with Craig's murder?"

I had to offer a shrug. "I think someone in the investigating team was. As SIO, Pascoe was best placed to manage the flow of information and make sure the boys said the right things. He would have been involved in controlling the search for Craig's body and could have steered them away from the grave, and he was the only one we talked to when we arrived at Wingham nick. Thirty minutes later, Andrew Curzon was ready for us." Ashley said nothing but displayed the worry he felt in his eyes.

STEVE HIGGS

"Look, we don't have anything yet, but I think we have to keep going. You wanted a big headline-making case to crack – this is it." Pushing the door closed, I offered final words of wisdom, "Don't sweat it too much. You have a list of other cases. If it gets too tense here, we can always walk away."

Walking down the street, I genuinely wondered if I could.

CHAPTER 21

BY THE TIME I HAD WALKED THROUGH GOODNESTONE IT was six minutes to five and the chaps at the tyre shop were clearly getting ready to close for the day. I imagined for a moment what it must be like to have a steady nine-to-five job. The chaps working here were bound to live in the local area.

To highlight that belief, two of the chaps ducked under a closing roller door with a shout to whoever was inside. They were walking home, lunchboxes tucked under their arms.

My car was parked facing outward across the forecourt, the two tyres I could see were brand new as expected. I had a bill to pay which my wife wouldn't like to hear about, but I was stuck with it either way.

I winced at the price, paying more than I would normally because all the man had was premium brand and I hadn't wanted to wait twenty-four hours for him to get something cheaper in.

He asked what happened to my car, saying he'd never seen a tyre get slashed before and he'd been running the business for almost forty years.

I gave a noncommittal answer; what else could I do? I didn't *know* who was behind it. The lights went off in the workshop area to my right, separated from the customer area by an old wooden door stained to black all around the handle by years of grimy fingerprints.

A man in a ball cap came through the door, a backpack hanging off one shoulder.

"We're all locked up, Jim. See you tomorrow."

From behind the counter, the owner, Jim, replied without looking up, "See you tomorrow." He stapled my receipt to the invoice and handed it over along with my keys. "You're all good to go. Thanks for the business."

In my head it was a sassy thing to say since he knew I didn't want to pay over the odds for the tyres he had in stock, but I had no snappy comeback to offer. Instead, I thanked him for getting it done and pushed through the exit door to head back outside.

I used the key to open the driver's door of my car and slid inside, folding the invoice neatly to show Mary when I got home. Ashley and I worked late last night and though we were making progress and there existed the tantalising suggestion of leads to follow, I felt no inclination to get home late and miss dinner two nights in a row.

I turned the key and that was when I saw it.

Stuck under the driver's side wiper blade was a yellow Post-it note. There was no chance it was there when I went into the office to pay for the tyres, I would have seen it for sure. Leaving the engine running, I opened my door and levered myself out enough to snag it. It took two attempts, and I would have been better served to have got out and gone around the door to retrieve it.

Nevertheless, I slumped back into my seat with the note in my right hand and an odd sensation creeping up my spine again.

Shadow of a Lie

'*Meet me at the clay pits on Cave Lane at six o'clock. Shane.*'

Shane had to be Shane Travers, one of the four boys involved in the altercation outside the village convenience store on August 8th, 2016, and subsequently brought in for questioning in connection with Craig Chowdry's disappearance.

He wanted to talk to me, and I had to quell my instant excitement. It could be a big lead. Heck, it could even be the case getting blown wide open. If Craig was murdered, it wouldn't have been at the hands of all four boys. Most likely it was one of them, and witnessing first hand his propensity for violence, my money was on Andrew Curzon.

That being the case, it wasn't much of a leap to imagine Shane Travers, the smallest and probably weakest member of the group, being coerced into corroborating the story the other three gave. Maybe it never sat right with him. Maybe he wanted to tell the truth now rather than continuing to live with the lie that was probably eating him up inside.

Criminals want to confess, that's something few civilians realise. Not the professional ones, of course, I don't mean them, but the ones who did something awful or stupid in the heat of the moment. They try hard to stick to their story, telling themselves they can go back to their normal life if they can just convince the police they are innocent. But the pressure of the lies they tell builds and builds, overwhelming them so that in the end they feel nothing but relief when they finally admit the truth.

On the flip side, a quick search on my phone showed me the location of the clay pits on Cave Lane. It was a classic place to kill someone. Miles from anywhere, far away from the nearest houses where violence would not be

STEVE HIGGS

heard. The question I had to ask was whether I was being lured to my death or not?

Someone had already slashed my tyres today; that sort of thing can put a person on edge, yet I already knew I was going to go despite my desire to avoid getting home late for a second time in as many days. The only question was whether I ought to tell Ashley first. The answer was a resounding 'yes', so I phoned his number but had to listen to it ring. After a few seconds, it went to voicemail.

It was twenty past five and the sky was beginning to darken. I had enough time to swing by Sarah's house once more, so I did that, coasting to a stop where his car was no longer parked. Perplexed, I tried to call him again and when it went straight to voicemail once more, I sent him a text message explaining what I was doing. Best guess was that Ashley needed the loo and had gone in search of one. That probably meant the local pub, the Fitzwalter Arms. Stakeouts are crappy things to do at the best of times and when you need to 'go', you have to go somewhere.

Using the loo would also explain why he wasn't answering my calls, but not why he hadn't immediately texted back. His absence and my inability to reach him left me with a dilemma: Go meet Shane and risk walking myself into a dangerous situation, or leave it and risk him getting cold feet?

Ultimately, I knew I couldn't ignore the opportunity and told myself the likelihood I was heading into a trap was slim. If Shane Travers intended to clear his conscience, we could wrap the whole case up in the next hour, and that alone was reason enough to ignore the potential danger.

I flicked my eyes to the clock on my dashboard: 1733. It would take me ten minutes to get there, so I would be fifteen minutes early. I didn't see that as a problem. I could

Shadow of a Lie

check the area to ease my concerns and wait for Shane to arrive.

The sky had darkened another shade. An hour from now it would be pitch black, and with twilight coming on, I wanted to get moving.

By 1744 I was pulling into the turning for the clay pits. Having never been there before, I had no idea what to expect, but the picture in my head was about as far removed from what I got as could be. I thought it was going to be a big quarry with a gate and carpark and safety fences to keep people out.

It was none of that.

In a gap between the trees where a dirt path ran, a steel pole had been mounted horizontally between two concrete posts to form a barrier. It was secured in place with a hefty padlock and while a determined driver in a reasonable sized truck would be able to batter their way through, the pole looked sturdy enough to stop my car.

"I guess I'm going the rest of the way on foot," I muttered. Not wanting to block the road, I pulled onto the grass to the right. It felt slick beneath my tyres which slid and skid across what I thought was a solid surface.

Outside of the car, I could feel how spongy the ground was when I stepped on it. I didn't think my car was going to bog in, and if it was then I was already too late to stop it happening.

The dirt path, wide enough for one vehicle going in one direction, went under the canopy of trees five yards from the barrier. It was far darker with the branches blocking out the remaining daylight. There was a large bank to my left. I couldn't exactly see it in the dwindling light, but where I could see patches through the trees ahead and to my right, to the left there was only black.

Unwilling to acknowledge my own sense of trepida-

STEVE HIGGS

tion, I pushed on, not for the first time in my career wishing British police were permitted to carry sidearms.

There was enough light under trees that I didn't need to use a torch to see, but I stumbled on rocks or tree roots a couple of times before I came to a clearing. It was only fifty yards from the road, and I had been able to see the brighter patch of light ahead before I got halfway through.

Bathed in moonlight, the clearing measured fifty yards by perhaps seventy-five, longer left to right than across. It dipped into a bowl where water reflected the moonlight back up at the sky.

I could smell the mud, a damp, almost rotten scent. However, that was ahead of me where the stagnant water sat. The ground under my feet was still the gravel of the road which bent around to the left now to an empty parking area.

A check of my watch confirmed it was very nearly six o'clock now and there was no sign of anyone waiting for me. A glance confirmed no car had arrived back at the gate and since the clay pits were not walking distance from Goodnestone or anywhere else, if Shane was coming and planned to be on time, he would have to appear soon.

Cursing that I should have waited by the car, I jolted when a zippo cigarette lighter flashed into life fifty yards away on the other side of the clearing.

CHAPTER 22

"SHANE?" I CALLED OUT, MAKING SURE MY VOICE WAS confident in spite of the nerves I felt. I never used to be this skittish. "Shane Travers. I'm Detective Sergeant Tony Heaton. There's nothing to be afraid of." I was hedging my bets that I was right and he wanted to come clean. "Please come out so we can talk."

The zippo lighter had only been alight for a second, the person holding it using the tool to attract my attention before extinguishing it once more.

"Shane, I'm not going to hang around. Either come forward or I'm leaving."

A quiet voice came back. "Were you followed?" I'd never met Shane Travers, so couldn't tell if I was hearing his voice, but the mousey, insecure timbre it carried matched his photograph. It had a nasal twang to it, making me think he had a cold.

The figure stepped out of the shadows for a moment, revealing their outline. I knew Travers to be five feet seven inches and slight of build. However, the person I could see, quite indistinctly in the gloom, was wearing a dark hoody.

The gathering darkness hid all other details. I could have been looking at anyone.

"Were you followed?" he repeated, obviously concerned about his safety. Inside my head I was calculating probabilities and guessing how things might have happened. Shane Travers was the weak one in the group and he knew it. He wouldn't stand up to the others and when they killed Craig, whether accidentally or with deliberate malice, he was given no option other than to go along with their cover up. He was most likely guilty of nothing more than being a coward.

"No," I called out, raising my voice to make sure it would be heard above a gust of wind unexpectedly blowing through the small clearing. "You are safe, Shane, but you should come with me. I can protect you better in custody. Let me take your statement and ..."

The snap of a branch to my right whipped my head and eyes around. I could see nothing inside the treeline to suggest someone was there, but at the sound Shane bolted like a startled rabbit.

Squinting, I thought I saw movement, but I lost any hope of hearing them when Shane kicked a dirt bike into life. It roared in protest, the engine growling as he let the clutch go and the back wheel bit into the soft earth.

He was making good his escape, convinced there was someone else with us while I remained rooted to the spot, staring into the dark. A primeval sense at the back of my brain flared into life, flashing an urgent message that I was in deep trouble a moment before I saw a ray of moonlight glint off something metallic.

A word to describe the shiny object appeared in my brain: gun.

I knew I needed to duck and run, to make myself into a moving target, but the shot went off before the message

Shadow of a Lie

could reach my muscles. I've read spy novels and war stories where the soldiers describe their ability to tell how close the bullets are. It has to do with the proximity of the snap when it passes you or something like that. Well, I have no experience on which to base a comparison, but the thing that whipped past my face felt close enough that it could have planted a kiss if it had lips.

I wasn't moving before, but I sure was now. My legs pumped and my heart raced, adrenaline delivering the ability to move faster than I had in years. A second shot came almost an instant after the first, this one sounding less close than the previous when it carved a path through the air behind my head.

A stolen glance to my left revealed the figure, a man for certain, coming out of the trees. He was running, which I knew worked in my favour for the accuracy of his shots, but the knowledge provided no relief to the panicked fear now ruling my emotions.

I had to get back to my car and be far enough ahead of the shooter to be able to get it started and moving. Otherwise, I would land in the driver's seat and present a perfect target to be shot.

However, the path to get there was a straight line under the canopy of trees and running down it would create a wonderful silhouette against the patch of dim light showing at the far end. I had to take the path to reach my car quickly, but I couldn't because I would get shot long before I made it. Sensing the paradox before it got me killed, I aimed away from the path and through the woods to the right.

I was already out of breath, cursing my lack of fitness for the umpteenth time today. Another shot rang out, the bullet smacking into a tree trunk some yards behind me. Could I stay still and blend into the darkness? Would he

STEVE HIGGS

find me if I did? Or would he worry his shots would bring someone to investigate?

The latter was unlikely, I decided. Out here in the countryside, anyone hearing the shots would assume it was nothing more than a little game shooting. Even I knew twilight was the perfect time for it.

Keeping low, I continued through the trees, making best speed but not running for fear I would trip and fall and make too much noise. Pushing onward and away from the path, I met what I had earlier guessed to be a bank of earth, but turned out to be a craggy rock face. It was chalk, that much I could see, the sedimentary rock abounding throughout the county. Covered in small plants that clung to the vertical surface, I tried to climb it, but my first attempt spilled me straight back to the ground – it was too crumbly to hope hand and footholds would sustain my weight.

Picking myself up, I held my breath for a moment to listen.

The shooter was yet to speak, perhaps aware to do so might give away his identity. Was it someone I had met? Was Andrew Curzon already out? I knew they wouldn't keep him long, but surely they hadn't processed and released him that fast.

I stopped, crouching behind a fallen tree to get my breath and check to see if the gunman was visible. If I could spot him, perhaps I could double back to get behind him, or simply slip away. If I could get enough distance, I could use my phone to call for help – attempting to do so now would highlight my position the instant the screen lit.

Of course, while I was doing my best to be quiet and spot my attacker, I failed entirely to consider that phones work both ways.

The sound of it ringing in my coat pocket was like a

Shadow of a Lie

brass band starting up. Swearing loudly, for it wasn't like I could give my position away any more completely, I tore at my clothing to find it.

Another shot rang out. Whether it was the fourth or fifth hardly mattered because this one found its mark.

Well, sort of.

The bullet hit the rock face, slivers of stone flying off to pepper my face and prove it wasn't just chalk. It shocked me, stopping my heart momentarily. Then the pain hit, but I was running again already, my hands still fumbling to get hold of my phone and silence it.

Another shot, this one high and wide as the gunman chased me through the woods.

Finally, with the phone in my hand, I aimed my thumb at the red button to kill the call, but saw the name and answered it instead.

"Ashley!" I gasped, aiming for a bellow, but unable to get enough air into my lungs for that. "I'm being shot at!"

I had more to say, but with the light from the phone ruining my night vision, I failed to see the low branch before I hit it. Mercifully, and because I am ecologically conscious and had no wish to damage the tree, I struck it with my skull and bounced off, the unyielding bough laughing at my pathetic attempt to smash through it with my forehead.

Running as I was, the rest of my body kept going while my head stayed still. The resulting equation of force and inertia compelled my legs to leave the ground as I performed something close to a backflip.

The back of my skull hit the ground first, snapping my neck awkwardly so my chin hit my chest. They say you see stars, and I can confirm that is true. You also taste blood, apparently.

STEVE HIGGS

"Tony!" Ashley's voice filtered through the mushy fog that was now my brain. "Tony!"

I rolled, lifting my right hand and registering surprise when I discovered it still held my phone.

Woozy and disorientated, I managed to mumble, "Get to the clay pits on Cave Lane and bring an armed response unit! Just don't hang around!" My tongue felt too big for my mouth. My brain felt too big for my skull.

Only when another shot tore past my face did the fear of death wrench back control of my limbs to get me moving once more.

Ashley was yelling questions. I wanted to give him answers and a small voice at the back of my head insisted this was my only chance to have someone carry a final message to my wife. Ignoring that voice, I left the call connected and launched my phone into the trees to my left. Let the gunman follow it in there.

CHAPTER 23

I HAD NO IDEA IF HE WOULD TAKE THE BAIT, BUT I COULD hear him coming my way, his legs thrashing through the undergrowth. In many ways I was lucky it was dark now; in the daylight I would have been easy to spot and kill. Then again, in the daylight, maybe the gunman wouldn't have risked it.

Veering away from the rock face, I skirted around a clump of nettles, but stumbled on a root because there was blood flowing into my left eye. I used my coat sleeve to wipe it away, the garment coming away with rather more slick, bright liquid on it than I was expecting. There was a cut to my head from the shards of rock that peppered me; that was the source of the blood, but while it stung, I allowed myself to believe it wasn't a terrible wound.

Compartmentalising my injury and labelling it as something to worry about later (if I survived), I pushed on. The sound of running feet stomping through the undergrowth had stopped, the gunman no doubt listening to hear his quarry, so I stopped moving too.

Peering through the undergrowth and around the trees, I couldn't spot him. I heard it when he chambered another round though. Should I make a break for it? I was halfway back to my car now. How quickly could I cover the remaining twenty something yards? Certainly a lot slower than I used to be able to.

I glanced, like a batsman at the crease checking the position of the slips, and was ready to put my head down and run when a set of headlights swung into view. They were turning off the road!

Highlighting my car when it obscured the dual beams of light, I was coming out of my crouch when the driver's door flew open, and I heard Ashley shout my name.

"Tony! Tony, are you here?"

My lips twitched, my mouth opening to yell my reply only to hesitate. How close was my assailant? Would he risk trying to get one last shot and then escape through the woods?

"Tony!" Ashley's car door slammed shut, but his lights stayed on, and the engine was running.

If I could get to him, we could both escape, returning later with armed police. The gunman would be long gone, of course, but the incident had to be investigated and I wasn't coming back here without a platoon of commandoes led by Arnold Schwarzenegger.

I bunched the muscles in my legs, getting ready to sprint the remaining distance. I *could* make it. I wouldn't slow down, and when my lungs began to burn, I would just keep going.

The thrashing sound of legs running through the undergrowth gave me pause, my heart rate increasing yet again though I would have been willing to bet such a thing was not possible without it exploding inside my chest like a potato left too long in a microwave oven.

Tensed behind a tree, my brain assured me I could hear the gunman going away, not coming closer. I sagged a

Shadow of a Lie

little, wanting to believe it, but hardly daring to. A few seconds later when I could be sure the danger had passed, I breathed a sigh of relief.

"Here!" I called out, slumping against the trunk of a tree. "Ashley, I'm over here."

Ashley found me quickly enough, using the torch on his phone to help him from falling as he homed in on my voice.

I guess I must have looked about as bad as I felt because he swore loudly the moment he saw me.

"Are you hit?" he demanded to know, checking out my face while constantly scanning around for my attacker.

"Ricochet," I replied. My breathing, which had been laboured and, in my head at least, could probably be heard in parts of Scotland, was slowing, my heart rate returning to something resembling normal. With a jolt to force myself away from the tree I had been using for support, I told myself to get a grip. I was shaken, yes, and that's fair enough, but now it was time to act like a seasoned professional and show the youngster how us old gits do it.

Coming to upright, I gently pushed Ashley's hand away – he was cupping my shoulder as though he might be the only thing keeping me upright.

"Whoever it was has gone. Thank you for your timely arrival, by the way. I might have been a goner otherwise." Turning, I pointed back through the trees. "He went that way. I didn't get a good look at him, and he didn't speak, but I would guess the man I saw to be over six feet tall and broad across the shoulders." I paused to check my thoughts before saying, "It might have been Andrew Curzon. The size was about right. He'll have to have some form of transport with him, a dirt bike or a quad perhaps – all the farmers have them, I'm sure, so roadblocks probably won't work."

STEVE HIGGS

"Okay, let's get you back to the car, Tony. You're covered in blood."

"It's nothing serious," I insisted, genuinely worried about the amount of blood dripping off my chin. I gave my face another wipe, the sleeve of my coat coming away with a sheen of dark liquid on it once again. I kept my concerns to myself, focusing on the opportunity to show I was tougher than a bear with a black belt, harder than a girder made from Royal Marines.

"Well, it looks bad enough. Units are coming. We need to be back at the car to meet them."

Ashley moved to herd me, using an arm around my shoulders again to steer me out of the trees and onto the path.

"I'm fine, dammit," I growled, twitching my shoulder to shake his hand loose. I wasn't though, I soon discovered, when my vision, which I thought was blurry because of the blood, went fuzzy and sparkly and then stopped altogether.

So much for the tough guy act.

CHAPTER 24

ASHLEY LONG WATCHED THE AMBULANCE PULL AWAY. THE paramedics were adamant DS Heaton's condition wasn't life threatening and that his blood loss looked worse than it was. A small piece of flint had wedged in his skull and was keeping a vein there open, so it leaked without healing. The bigger concern was his probable concussion. There was a lump the size of an egg in the centre of his forehead, and he was unconscious.

They suggested he would be kept in overnight and would commit to nothing beyond that.

Ashley's concern was more than simply professional – the way anyone would react to the injury of a colleague. Tony was his partner. Okay, so they'd only been together a day, but there were several immutable truths, some unshakable laws that went with being a police officer, and right near the top was, 'Never let anyone mess with your partner'.

The armed response unit took only thirty-seven minutes to get to the clay pits from Canterbury, the primary hub for police in this part of the county. Their boss took over the scene, quizzing Ashley only long enough to ascertain how little he knew. With the gunman almost certainly well clear of the area, they were there only to secure the scene and ensure the safety of those who would follow.

DCI Pascoe arrived shortly thereafter, zeroing in quickly on DS Long for a debrief on the event. The local head cop had been at home relaxing as he ought to be, but was back in his suit and tie and looking very much the man in charge.

Someone had tried to kill a police officer in his territory, and such things were not allowed to pass without a full investigation. Oddly, Ashley knew, had Tony been killed, the attention given to the incident would be many times that which he was seeing. The Chief Constable for Kent would have made an appearance most likely, though not until the morning when there was something to learn. It didn't do to get involved too early; that just upset the equilibrium of the hierarchy and made senior people question and second guess their movements.

Very much the fifth wheel, Ashley chose to hang around to see what was found. DCI Pascoe's entire force appeared to be in attendance, and he heard Pascoe arguing with the boss of the armed response unit about calling in additional help - he had his own forensics team, and they could manage to find a set of tyre tracks in some woodland.

DS Long's report that Tony had been at the clay pits to meet Shane Travers, one of the four boys formerly accused of involvement in Craig Chowdry's disappearance, met with a barrage of questions.

"He came by himself?" DCI Pascoe snapped.

"I learned about his intentions after the fact," Ashley replied calmly. "He was unable to reach me." Ashley chose not to reveal that his phone had run out of battery and

Shadow of a Lie

he'd sought an evening meal in the local pub so it had some time to recharge. He usually kept a power bank in his bag in case such events arose, but had found it to be absent. "Signal around here is a little patchy," he added because he knew it to be true.

Pascoe spat, "Damned fool. Where is Travers now? Was he the shooter?"

"I was only able to obtain minimal information from DS Heaton before he lost consciousness, Sir. However, he described the gunman as at least six feet tall." Ashley debated passing on Tony's suggestion that the assailant could have been Andrew Curzon. However, it sounded tenuous at best when Tony said it.

"Not Travers then," remarked Beckett, standing in his boss's shadow.

Speaking over his shoulder to address his subordinate, DCI Pascoe said, "Have a unit pick him up anyway. I want to know why he was out here. Coming here means he was avoiding town and thus avoiding people who know him."

"You mean French, Curzon, and Botterill," DS Long questioned. He got an eyebrow lift and no comment from either Beckett or the DCI.

"Why didn't he call for local support?" DCI Pascoe asked a question of his own.

Ashley tried to void all expression from his face. How could he answer that? Tony didn't let Wingham nick know in case DCI Pascoe found out. Maybe Pascoe wasn't behind the cover up seven years ago, but that was kind of the point: they didn't know who they could trust.

Covering his inability to give a straight answer, Ashley said, "I would guess there was too little time."

"Utter rubbish," spat the DCI, Beckett doing nothing to stifle the grin forming on his face. "Anyway," he continued, "How did he know to meet Travers here? Did

153

STEVE HIGGS

he receive a text? Something we can use as evidence, man?"

Ashley told them about the last thing Tony said before he passed out: the Post-it note.

"So where is it now?" Beckett challenged.

Ashley could only provide the truth, "That I do not know."

"Helpful," Beckett snorted.

Rounding on him, DCI Pascoe snapped, "I don't see you being any more useful, Beckett! Go check the man's car. Maybe it's in there."

DS Long observed the exchange without comment. There seemed to be no love lost between them, but that was no indication of anything unusual.

Turning his attention back to DS Long, DCI Pascoe said, "So you don't know anything, and you didn't see anything."

Ashley didn't rise to the bait. "I received a text message from DS Heaton in which he claimed to have received a note from Shane Travers. He did not, however, say where the meeting was set to take place. When I called him, he answered immediately to report that he had been shot at, believed he was being pursued, and needed an armed response unit. When I arrived here, I was able to find him, and it was then that he provided the description for the gunman."

"Did you see anyone else here?"

"No, Sir."

"Did you hear a vehicle departing the area?"

"No, Sir."

DCI Pascoe huffed out a breath and looked away. It was clear to DS Long that the senior man was choosing not to voice his thoughts. Thus far there was no sign of anyone having been here, but the armed response team

Shadow of a Lie

only arrived half an hour ago; long enough to sweep the area and declare it safe, nothing more.

If Tony had been chased through the woods by a man shooting at him, there would be spent shell casings. There would be footprints too, or possibly not because it hadn't rained for weeks, and the ground was hard.

"The weapon," DCI Pascoe prompted when a new question presented itself. "Was DS Heaton able to provide any indication what sort of weapon it was?"

"A rifle or handgun, Sir. Not a shotgun."

"He said that?"

"No, Sir." To deflect the inevitable next question coming his way, Ashley explained, "DS Heaton's head wound came from a ricochet. Pieces of flint came off the rock face when a bullet struck it close to his head. A shotgun would not produce that effect."

Truthfully, a shotgun probably would have killed Tony, the greater spread of the shot far more likely to strike home than a single round. Winging him might have slowed him enough for the gunman to catch up.

It was moot now.

Spotting his forensics van pulling off the road, DCI Pascoe dismissed DS Long, but had a final word, "Don't go too far, DS Long. I will have more questions. You pair have stirred up a right mess and I'm going to have to be the one to clear it up."

The DCI hurried away before Ashley could respond. Not that he was going to. The task force was always going to be unpopular; they weren't looking into other coppers' failures or trying to show the world where they went wrong, but that was how it would be perceived.

With a nod to himself, Ashley realised why Tony was so protective of his old case. He could understand the reluctance a little more now, but that did nothing to change his

155

desire to solve it. Whether they could solve the riddle of Craig Chowdry's disappearance or not, he was going to investigate what happened to Bruce Denton and nothing Tony could do or say would change that.

He was about to wander away, thinking his next logical move was to follow Tony to the hospital – his partner was injured, not going sent a strong message about their relationship – when he heard the DCI instructing two uniforms to collect Shane Travers.

CHAPTER 25

WHETHER SHANE TRAVERS WAS A WILLING PARTICIPANT IN this evening's attack or genuinely wanted to speak with Tony, and the shooter was there as a coincidence (which Ashley didn't buy), he would not find out until Travers was brought in for questioning. Of course, Ashley recognised the advantage presented by having one of the four boys in custody.

Travers would be there to answer questions about tonight's incident, but no one would be able to argue his right to question him about how it linked to Craig Chowdry's disappearance. Questioning Travers under caution inside a police interview room was vastly different to conducting the same interview anywhere else.

Inside the station there is far greater pressure and being under caution lent weight to the possibility of being arrested and incarcerated. Ashley needed the opportunity to quiz the group of suspects' weakest link and there might never be a better time.

Late in the evening, the roads were empty, and it took almost no time at all to get to Wingham, Ashley's brain barely registering the miles as he chewed over the latest

STEVE HIGGS

development. Pulling into the station and parking around the back in the same space his car occupied yesterday, Ashley took a moment to message his fiancée, Tanya.

'Sorry, babe, I'm going to be late home tonight. Later than yesterday. The case is hotting up. Love you XX.'

He didn't expect an immediate response, but his phone started ringing before he could get out of the car. Ashley closed the door with him still inside and tapped on the button to connect the Facetime call.

"Babe."

The screen swam into focus to the sound of water moving: Tanya was in the bath. Ashley couldn't stop the broad grin that broke out on his face. Tanya was holding the phone with both hands above her face as she lay in the water. Ashley could see the steam rising from the surface.

"Working late again? What's the case?"

He sighed, "Ugh, babe, you know I can't talk about that stuff. It's always boring anyway."

"Only to you, Mr Police Officer." She liked to tease him and also liked to have him do police stuff in the bedroom which, to be perfectly honest, he was fine with. It's why she was employing her sultry voice and calling Ashley 'Mr Police Officer'. "You must be able to tell me something. Is it a murder?"

"Yes," he relented, then saw a need to correct himself. "Well, not officially."

She frowned, the expression pulling her eyebrows together.

Sceptically, she asked, "How can someone be murdered unofficially?"

"When there is no body," he replied in a macabre tone. "I really can't say anymore other than we think we know who did it and we are definitely making them nervous." They were making someone nervous, that was for certain.

Shadow of a Lie

"Oh, yeah, your partner. How's that going? Any better today?"

Ashley wasn't going to make her worry by revealing the truth of tonight's incident, so what was the right way to answer? His relationship with Tony wasn't any better. At least, Ashley didn't think it was. Tony turned up late this morning, then went off to do his own thing, then got into trouble and his tyres were slashed and after that someone shot at him. Tony had endured a tough day, but could be blamed for most of what he befell.

To answer Ashley said, "We're still figuring things out. He knows his stuff, but he's weeks from retirement and he's not what one might call keen."

"He's not you then."

Ashley shook his head, but said, "I think maybe he used to be. That's what I am hearing, anyway. Maybe I will be like him when I have only a few weeks left to go."

"Surely you'll be Chief Constable of England by then," she joked though she knew how serious her intended was about his career. She also knew his determination and drive to succeed and climb the ranks had been imbued from an early age. His family were coppers. All of them. Successful ones too, which made it all the worse. Ashley had one cousin ten years his senior who was still a constable. The family never invited him to any of their gatherings. He was the black sheep and Ashley knew he had to make it to the higher echelons of the service to be considered anything other than a failure.

Laughing, Ashley said, "There's no such rank, babe."

"Then you'll have to invent it when you make it to the top, darling. Now, when can I expect you home?" she asked, her bedroom voice returning. "I'm missing you." To prove a point, she tipped her phone to angle it down and lifted her torso out of the water just enough for her twin

STEVE HIGGS

peaks to break the surface, water sheeting from them invitingly.

Ashley's breath caught the same way it always did when he saw her naked and he realised his eyes must have dilated because when she brought the camera back to her face she was laughing at him.

"Goodness, you are an easy mark. It will all be waiting for you when you finish the case, Mr Police Officer. Now go catch some bad guys, I'm taking a bath." She made a big kiss at the screen and ended the call.

The car park was silent, but only for a moment. Pulling in behind Ashley was a squad car with Shane Travers in the back. A second car followed it in, this one driven by DS Beckett.

Ashley pushed thoughts of Tanya from his mind, especially the naked ones, and exited the car into the cold, crisp October air.

It was time to get some answers.

CHAPTER 26

SHANE TRAVERS WAS BEING LED TO THE STATION BY THE two uniformed constables DCI Pascoe sent to get him. They were both men in their late twenties. Detective Sergeant Beckett was half in and half out of his car, collecting something from within before following the others into the station.

Ashley tagged along, positioning himself so he arrived right after the guys escorting Shane. He wasn't restrained, but if he agreed to come willingly, there would be no reason to use cuffs.

Aiming for a collaborative approach, Ashley waited for Beckett and said, "Hey, it's Glenn, right? Ashley."

Beckett looked down at Ashley's hand as though he was being offered something unpleasant to touch.

With a snort of bored amusement, Beckett sneered, "What? We're friends now, are we?"

Ashley dropped his hand and narrowed his eyes. "Very well. You don't like that we are here digging over an old case of yours. Tough. It doesn't thrill me to be doing it, but Craig Chowdry was murdered, and no one ever got

STEVE HIGGS

charged with it. That ought to make you want the case reopened."

"Craig Chowdry ran away," Beckett repeated the party line. "There was never any evidence to suggest otherwise."

Ashley sighed, "Come on, man. Surely, you can see there is something wrong here? We arrived yesterday and already my partner has been shot at in an incident that we know involved one of the original suspects."

"So he says." Beckett delivered his response with a nonchalant shrug. "You said there was a Post-it note, but you never saw it yourself and it wasn't with your partner or in his car."

"You didn't find it?"

Beckett didn't bother to answer. "According to you he was shot at, but from what I hear, the team searching the woods around the clay pits have yet to turn up any brass."

Ashley could have argued that finding a few spent shell casings in woodland at night would be fraught with difficulty, but that went without saying and Beckett knew it.

Instead, he asked, "What are you saying?"

Beckett smirked again and went around Ashley to get to the station. Over his shoulder he remarked, "I think you have nothing, and your partner chose to make stuff up so it wouldn't look like you were utterly wasting everyone's time. Shane Travers has an airtight alibi. He was nowhere near the clay pits this evening and he doesn't own a dirt bike on which your partner is alleging he escaped. I only brought him in to take an official statement."

Guessing what answer he would get, Ashley posed an obvious question, "Who is providing his alibi?"

Beckett stopped walking and stared at him, his expression somewhere between amused and bored.

"Daniel French, Andrew Curzon, and Tim Botterill.

Shadow of a Lie

All four have been watching the Manchester derby, eating pizza, and drinking beer at Shane's house."

Ashley shook his head, straining to believe Beckett was so blind.

"The boys arrested seven years ago in conjunction with Craig Chowdry's disappearance provide an alibi for one of their own when they are most likely behind what happened tonight? Travers lured my partner into the woods and one of the others tried to kill him. They should all be in custody. Travers should have been read his rights, and he should be interviewed as a suspect until such time as it can be proven he was not involved."

Beckett's response came as he went into the nick, "That's how you would do it in the big city, is it?"

Ashley was about to question Beckett's sanity when he spotted Shane's face. He was in the custody area, his face cast down and his eyes locked on the floor. When one of the constables asked him something and he looked up for a moment, Ashley got to see how fat his lips were. Travers also sported two black eyes, the rings of colour mild, yet given the obvious recent nature of his fat lips, the shiners were probably still developing. They would look worse by the morning.

"Has he been offered medical treatment?" Ashley enquired, his voice filled with concern. He considered Travers to be a suspect in tonight's firearms incident regardless of what Beckett said, and it wouldn't do for his solicitors to later suggest he was withheld the right to see a medical professional.

One of the constable's replied. "Yes. He refused, says he walked into a garden rake."

"I did walk into a garden rake," Shane Travers mumbled, his eyes still aimed at the floor.

Taking everyone else out of the equation, Ashley spoke

STEVE HIGGS

directly to Shane, "Do you feel you need to have your injuries assessed? You may have a broken nose." Ashley did not for one moment believe the story about a garden rake, but also knew now was not the time to question it.

Shane shook his head, still refusing to make eye contact.

Beckett stepped between them, his back to Ashley.

"We just need to take your statement, Shane. Then I'll have one of the boys drop you home."

Ashley had to go around Beckett's bulky frame to get in his face.

"He is not being dropped home. Someone lured a fellow police officer into the woods this evening where he was shot at. It's pure luck we are not investigating a murder charge. Shane Travers is a prime suspect."

"Are you stupid?" Beckett asked. "I already told you he has an alibi. Three of them, in fact. I'm not letting you waste his or anyone else's time with your silly nonsense, or do you think the rest of us cannot see that this is a thinly disguised attempt to quiz him about Craig Chowdry?"

Beckett stepped into Ashley's personal space, using his height and girth to intimidate the smaller man. It might have worked on someone else.

Ashley tilted his head right back to look up rather than talk to Beckett's chest, and was both calm and self-assured when he said, "You will stand down, Beckett. Like it or not, my investigation into the Craig Chowdry case not only precedes yours, it also has the backing of the Chief Constable for Kent. Regardless of that, I intend to interview the *suspect*," Ashley heavily accented the word, "about the attempted murder of a police officer this evening."

To hammer home the point, Ashley spun around to face Shane Travers and began to read his rights.

"Shane Travers I am arresting you for the crime of

Shadow of a Lie

attempted murder …" Ashley expected Beckett to interrupt him or maybe even try to stop it from happening, and was relieved to get to the end of the rights. Having finished, he addressed the constable standing next to the now shocked looking Travers, "Take him to an interview room. I will be along shortly."

The uniform twitched his eyes across to check with Beckett. Ashley expected the local DS to counter his order, but Beckett gave an almost imperceptible nod that he should comply.

"On your head be it," scoffed Beckett, walking away with a chuckle. "Just don't blame me when the DCI tears you a new one. He told me to send Travers home."

Ashley watched him go, certain his next move would be to call his boss. Would DCI Pascoe involve himself? Tony fingered Shane himself. He had to be questioned. Only a fool would think otherwise.

Beckett was right about one thing though: Ashley was going to be questioning Shane about Craig as well. How could he not? Tonight's incident and the teenager's disappearance seven years ago had to be linked. He didn't need to see the Post-it to believe in it. The questions he had were all to do with who put it on Tony's windscreen and what the desired outcome might have been. It looked very much like Tony was being lured to his death.

However, Shane looked and sounded like the weak link in the gang of four boys. Both Ashley and Tony agreed on that point and waiting outside Sarah French's house earlier, they had discussed the possibility that he played no part in Craig's murder. If his friends killed Craig, did Shane take part, or was he just too weak to run home and tell the truth when he saw what the others did? Perhaps he wanted to meet Tony because he felt compelled to confess now that there were new detectives trawling over the old case.

Ashley intended to find out. Soon, if possible, just in case Beckett was right and DCI Pascoe chose to intervene. Were he to do so, it would go a step closer to showing he was the force that kept the boys out of jail.

The why of it, though, that was just as big of a mystery. Why would a DCI want to protect four adolescent murderers?

Ashley found the interview room just as the uniformed constable was coming out.

"He wants a lawyer," he advised, closing the door.

With a nod of acknowledgement, Ashley offered his hand. "DS Ashley Long. Were you here when Craig Chowdry went missing?"

"Den Blackburn." The constable returned the shake with a strong grip and a cocked eyebrow. "No, I was still in school."

"With Shane Travers?" Ashley hedged.

He shook his head. "No, I was the year above them." He gave no opinion on the case or what was happening now.

Knowing he could do nothing until the lawyer arrived, Ashley said, "Thanks for your help." With a nod at the door of the interview room, he asked, "Are we talking about the duty solicitor ..." he left the question hanging, not feeling he needed to explain why he was asking. If it was a duty solicitor, they would arrive within a couple of hours. Otherwise, if Shane Travers somehow had his own lawyer, he would almost certainly have to wait until the morning to question him.

"Yeah. DS Beckett made the call already. They usually pitch up within a couple of hours."

Okay, so it was good news and bad. Ashley was going to suffer a later night than he wanted, but he'd already warned Tanya not to expect him at a decent hour. There

Shadow of a Lie

was no point going anywhere and he had already eaten. The nick in Wingham felt hostile – Beckett had a surly attitude and was only too happy to show it. His boss was professionally polite, but Ashley was poking into a case DCI Pascoe failed to solve, and while he wasn't being obstructive, it was very clear he would not offer help beyond the bare minimum required.

With time to kill and plenty to do, Ashley headed for the incident room – DCI Pascoe had given them that at least, though Ashley questioned what they would have got if the DCI had an ongoing investigation that required it.

The wall of whiteboards was still as devoid of thoughts and ideas as when Ashley first walked in yesterday, but that would change. He thought about starting to chart the case now. He could lay out a timeline, identify the key persons, but there was no chance he could annotate any of his thoughts regarding how well coached the suspects acted and his suspicions regarding the case's original SIO. There was just too much chance someone else would let themselves in.

With that in mind, Ashley chose instead to conduct some research. Expecting Travers to be prepared just like Daniel French and Andrew Curzon, Ashley wanted to catch him off guard with something he didn't expect anyone to know – a little trick he'd learned from Tony, he acknowledged silently.

Opening his laptop, he navigated to a social media platform. The wonders of modern online interaction made it easy to delve into the lives of others. Despite that, more than an hour after starting to poke around in the boys' Facebook profiles, easy because they each had set them to 'public', Ashley was getting bored and irritated.

That was when it happened.

CHAPTER 27

FACEBOOK IS A TREASURE TROVE OF INFORMATION, OF THAT there is no doubt. Unfortunately, it can also be a time suck that yields no results. The latter happens far more often than the former.

Prompted by the sight of Shane's battered face, Ashley chose to dive into their online profiles to look for photographs. Specifically, any picture taken shortly after Craig Chowdry went missing. If his 'friends' coerced him into taking part in the cover-up, did he have similar bruises back then?

He was with the other boys when they accosted Craig outside the Shop Ryte, and the police brought him in for questioning after they found the missing boy's blood. Involved again tonight, he showed up having clearly taken a beating, but was that also what happened to ensure his silence and cooperation all the way back in 2016?

Looking at photographs taken after Craig went missing, there was no sign that Shane was beaten into toeing the party line. He looked relaxed and happy in the pictures. However, when scrolling through his online albums, Ashley's eyes caught something that caused him to stop.

His heart beat hard, itching to confirm he hadn't imagined it. There were several pictures of Shane with his friends and what were probably family members. The photographs were taken inside a house at a party, but it took Ashley a while to figure out it was Shane's mother's birthday party. She was turning fifty. He saw no sign of a Mr Travers in any of the shots and he wasn't behind the camera because most of the pics were selfies.

The pictures of the party were irrelevant except that they showed the thing that was missing. It was five days after Craig went missing, which meant the boys were brought in for questioning, held for almost two days, and released only the day before the party. It was hardly the time to be celebrating, though Ashley suspected a fiftieth birthday bash would have been planned months earlier.

Leaping from his chair, Ashley ran over to the wall where he'd pinned the six by four photographs of the prime suspects and key witnesses yesterday. They were far from the greatest pictures, each of them whatever the families deemed of so little value they were happy to hand them over to the police.

Shane's picture was of him in his house. The angle was slightly different from the selfies taken at his mum's party, but none of that mattered. What stood out was the thing he was standing on: a rug.

Ashley darted back to his laptop and Shane's Facebook profile. His mum's fiftieth party took place on August 13th, 2016, five days after Craig vanished never to be seen again. The rug was gone by then. It presented a key question: how long since it was there?

Shane was wearing the same top and looked the same

age in the picture stuck to the wall, the one Ashley took from the boxes of evidence. The picture bore no date, but scrolling back to the album prior to his mum's birthday, Ashley found a handful of pics taken a week earlier.

There was a rug on the floor.

It sat atop the polished wooden floorboards, an old, patterned thing. Ashley thought the style was called oriental, but wasn't sure and it made no difference to the fact that it was there before Craig Chowdry went missing and was not there a few days later.

It was slim and certainly circumstantial, but he suddenly had a rug - the perfect thing in which to hide a body - missing from the home of one of the suspects in the Craig Chowdry case right around the time he vanished.

He continued to search for more of the same – little clues that might tell him something or provide information he could use.

When another hour ticked by without his research bearing further fruit, Ashley pushed back from the desk to give his eyes a break.

His watch showed four after ten, the evening already gone. Interviewing Travers might take an hour or three, depending on what he had to say. Best case scenario was that he'd revealed the truth to his lawyer and was going to confess everything. Ashley doubted he was going to be that lucky, but couldn't deny the sense of hope.

He paced the room for a bit, willing his brain to consider that which had not yet occurred to it. Who had done what, and how was he going to prove it? How would he extract a confession from the four boys who must be behind Craig Chowdry's murder?

Yes, the suspects responded to questioning more fluidly and confidently than any Ashley had ever interviewed, and

Shadow of a Lie

yes, he could believe they had been coached and had a hand from someone to help them evade justice. It was a long stretch from accepting those things as facts to believing DCI Pascoe could be the one behind it.

Nevertheless, and angry at himself, Ashley sat back down behind the desk and started a new search, this time looking for Hector Pascoe. Like most cops, especially the older ones, he had no social media profile, but a quick search revealed his wife's name and she did.

The decorated detective chief inspector had a successful career, a wife and kids, and nothing to suggest there could be any reason why he might not want to catch Craig's killers. There was no visible link between him and any of the suspects or their families and nothing to suggest he was in debt or had other problems someone might be able to use to leverage his help.

It was perplexing, but it was not surprising. Tony's gut reaction that the DCI was hiding something was unlikely in the extreme. There was no actual evidence to support such a wild and dangerous accusation and even if he were keeping a secret regarding the Chowdry case, it wasn't going to be that he was instrumental in covering it up.

A knock at the door made Ashley's heart skip, and he slammed the lid of his laptop closed when whoever was outside chose not to bother waiting to be invited in.

Den Blackburn poked his head through the gap.

"Solicitor is here. You can get started with Travers if you like."

He didn't wait for a response, ducking out but leaving the door open a crack when he retreated down the hall. As Ashley's pulse slowly returned to normal, he reopened his laptop, closed the browser tabs, and cleared his history. No one was going to look at his laptop to know he'd been poking into the DCI's life, but it made Ashley feel less on edge to remove the evidence.

Leaving the room, he questioned whether Shane Travers might just choose to come clean. Either way, he was going to get some answers.

CHAPTER 28

"WHO HIT YOU?" WHEN THE PRELIMINARIES WERE OUT OF the way, Ashley fired that off as his first proper question.

Shane hadn't expected it and his forehead wrinkled when he said, "No one. I'd had a few and went to put the chickens to bed. I stepped on a rake and got the handle right in the face."

Ashley did nothing to keep the incredulity from his voice when he confirmed, "You stepped on a rake?"

Shane laughed, but it sounded fake and forced. "Yup. Just like a cartoon. Wham!" He used his right arm to act out the scene.

Ashley leaned to one side to examine Shane's busted lips.

"It looks like a knuckle mark beneath your nose." It didn't, but Ashley needed to make it clear Shane's story wasn't going to wash. If he was innocent of direct involvement in what happened to Craig Chowdry, as he believed him to be, Shane was the one guy who had a chance to get out of the mess without serious jail time. Pressing on before Shane could respond, Ashley asked, "What did you plan to tell my partner this evening?"

STEVE HIGGS

He was ready for the question. "Nothing. It's a mix up. I heard there was something about a Post-it note?" He did a decent job of sounding like it was all news to him.

Ashley stayed quiet, waiting to hear what Shane would say next. Would he have the nerve and good sense to stay quiet? Ashley didn't think so. Shane's eyes were darting this way and that, never settling on his interviewer's face for more than a second or so at a time. His hands were clasped in his lap and his right leg jiggled constantly.

He rewarded Ashley's patience in under five seconds.

"I was at home this evening. The guys came around when I got off work. Man City played Man United tonight, I don't suppose you know the score, do you? I missed the second half."

Ignoring the question, Ashley asked, "You work at the bakery, don't you?"

Shane nodded.

"For the recording, please."

"Yes," he gave a verbal response. "I work at the bakery."

"Which is just a few yards from Boxley Tyres, isn't it?"

"How is this relevant?" the solicitor cut in.

Ashley kept his eyes fixed firmly on Shane's.

"After you put the Post-it note on my partner's car ..."

"I didn't," Shane protested.

"... how did Andrew Curzon and the others find out what you had planned?"

Shane gave no response, but his solicitor leaned in to whisper in his ear, and Shane's eyes continued to dart around the room.

"How did they find out you were going to spill the beans about what happened on August 8th, 2016?"

The solicitor fielded that one. "Shane was brought here to answer questions about a shooting incident that

Shadow of a Lie

occurred earlier this evening. An incident he played no part in and has no knowledge of." He turned to address Shane Travers. "There are no charges to answer, Shane. You do not have to answer any further questions and you have grounds to file a complaint for wrongful arrest. Please say nothing further."

The solicitor lifted his briefcase from where it sat next to his chair and placed in on the desk to pack his items away.

Flicking his eyes up to look at the detective sergeant on the other side of the table, he said with confidence, "We are done here. I shall be filing on behalf of Mr Travers in the morning."

It was always a risk that Shane would fail to comprehend the avenue of escape being presented, so Ashley laid it out for him as plainly as he could.

"Look Shane, I don't think you killed Craig Chowdry. But I believe the other boys did and they have forced you to play along with their lies. You can get out from under it all. You don't have to be a part of it any longer."

The solicitor's irritation increased by the second. He talked over the top of Ashley, advising Shane to keep his lips firmly shut.

Shane would be gone soon, out of the station and back to his 'friends', so Ashley carried right on talking.

"Shane, I can help you. You can live without fear and be free of the weight hanging around your neck. They won't hit you again. All you have to do is tell me what happened to Craig Chowdry. His family deserves to know where his body is hidden. Let him have a proper burial. Don't leave him wrapped in the rug from your mum's living room."

Knowing the use of the rug was nothing more than an educated guess, Ashley watched carefully to see Shane's

STEVE HIGGS

reaction. The seemingly offhand remark was timed to perfection.

Shane's head shot around to look at the detective sergeant, his mouth slightly agape. It only lasted for a second before he gathered himself and fought to resume his innocent expression. It was too late, though, and he knew it. Ashley was looking right at him when the shock registered.

"If they forced you to help, Shane, if they made you play along, the courts will take that into account. Tell me what happened!" Ashley snapped out the words, trying hard to jolt some sense into the fool sitting opposite.

The solicitor got to his feet and started ushering Shane to the door.

Ashley implored Shane with his eyes, urging him to do the thing that would set him free.

Shane paused in the doorway, resisting when his solicitor tried to push him out. Looking directly at DS Long, Ashley's heart beat out a double tap of expectation when Shane's tongue darted out to wet his lips; it was clear he had something to say.

Barely daring to breathe, Ashley listened.

"We didn't kill Craig Chowdry."

It was the opposite of what he hoped to hear, and Shane Travers was gone almost before he finished delivering the line, shunted through the doorway by his impatient solicitor. Ashley could have followed, but was still reeling from what Shanes Travers said.

It wasn't so much the words as the inflection. He didn't say, 'We *didn't* kill Craig Chowdry'. What he said was, '*We* didn't kill Craig Chowdry.'

CHAPTER 29

Choosing to leave Wingham nick minutes after the interview with Shane Travers abruptly ended, he ducked a potential dressing down from DCI Pascoe. Nevertheless, before leaving the building he got an exaggeratedly friendly wave from Beckett that went well with his smug grin. It was much the same as saying, 'Don't let the door smack your arse on the way out.'

He chose to bite his tongue, embarrassed that he'd made such a mess in his desire to see results. Worse yet was the realisation that Beckett tricked him into the arrest. Ashley would not have taken that step had Beckett not made such a show of his intention to release Travers. Yes, Shane had alibis, but given the circumstances, they could hardly be taken at face value. They were investigating the attempted murder of a fellow officer, for goodness sake!

Beckett didn't seem to care about that, though. He saw the task force's investigation as interference and was going to do what he could to undermine them. Had he been involved in the original investigation, Ashley might have questioned if he was the one who influenced the outcome.

Arriving early the next morning, Ashley parked outside

STEVE HIGGS

Wingham nick and waited in the car. He knew the call from his boss was coming; it was quite inevitable. The only way to control his situation was to get ahead of it, so he called DCI Harris himself, hoping he would catch him before the news reached his desk.

He didn't.

DCI Harris answered on the first ring. "Ah, DS Long."

Ashley closed his eyes. His mother always used to address him formally when he was in trouble. Usually it was Ash, but when she believed he'd done something he ought not to have, it was always Ashley Patrick Long.

"Sir, I ..."

"I'll stop you right there, Detective Sergeant. You made this call in the hope that you would seem more responsible, yet I've been around too long to be fooled by such tactics. It doesn't matter what excuse you might have concocted."

The calm and measured tone made Ashley wince. He was going to get both barrels shortly and wished Harris would just get it over with.

"It doesn't matter if you thought you were doing the right thing, or if the injury to your partner last night made you believe your actions were justified. What does matter, Detective Sergeant Long, are you listening?"

"Yes, Sir."

"Is that I just got a call from the deputy chief constable of Kent!" The sharp change from calm to bellowing was loud enough that Ashley had to move his phone away from his ear. "You arrested a man inside a nick after being advised he had an alibi that cleared him of any involvement in last night's attempted murder of a police officer! You then proceeded to interview the man and, according to the duty solicitor appointed to his counsel, badgered him mercilessly about a crime completely unrelated to the

178

Shadow of a Lie

one for which you chose to arrest him! Are you completely mad?"

Ashley wasn't sure if he was expected to answer the question or not, and waited to hear whether his boss was going to launch into a fresh tirade of expletive loaded, and wholly accurate, statements.

When DCI Harris failed to say anything, Ashley ventured, "I believe I can solve the Craig Chowdry case, Sir."

A beat of silence passed, and Ashley felt his world closing in.

"You're investigating the Craig Chowdry case?"

Ashley winced again. "Yes, Sir."

"The Craig Chowdry case we discussed and labelled as unworthy of any attention because no body was ever found. That Craig Chowdry case? The same case that I downgraded from amber to red on your traffic light system?"

Deflating in the driver's seat of his car, Ashley recognised the hubris that led to his current predicament. Changing the case to green before he let Tony see it had been a mistake. He was a good investigator. A determined detective. A police officer willing to throw himself into his work at the cost of almost every other part of his life. More than that, he had a family reputation to uphold and was being watched and judged by his father, his uncle, and others. He was expected to win and had allowed the pressure to justify his rash decisions.

Getting the chance to act as Senior Investigation Officer as a DS was unheard of. Ok, so they were all old cases with a low probability of success, and he had no support staff. But he knew that if he was able to solve any of them, it would be his name listed on the paperwork. That would be something, but if he was able to close a case like Craig Chowdry's disappearance, not only proving he was indeed murdered, but also bringing the killer to justice, well that would change his landscape forever.

Public recognition. Making his boss look good and probably getting a pat on the back and a commendation from the chief constable himself. Those were the drivers behind Ashley's choice to go after the hardest cases, that and their public nature. People remembered Craig Chowdry's name, just as they would Bruce Denton's if he could solve that one after so many years.

There was no point in defending his actions. To do so would prompt more angry words. Instead, he said the one thing that would stop his boss dead in his tracks, "I think DCI Pascoe helped to cover up Craig Chowdry's murder, Sir."

The moment the words left his lips, he knew he had gone too far.

DCI Harris took a moment before responding, his calm, measured tone back in place when he began talking.

"Now listen very carefully, Detective Sergeant Long. If I ever hear you accuse another officer, senior or otherwise, without irrefutable proof to back up your claim, I will see that your career is ended on the spot. Do you have such irrefutable evidence?"

With his eyes closed, Ashley admitted, "No, Sir."

"Your behaviour is unexpected, DS Long. Unexpected and unacceptable. Ditch the Chowdry case and focus on the one with the French tourist."

"Michelle Canet, boss."

"Yes, that one."

"I can close the Chowdry case, Sir. We have the killers spooked. Last night's incident proved it. They know we are on to them, and they are going to make a mistake, boss."

Shadow of a Lie

That was all it took to get DCI Harris shouting again. "Did you not hear anything I said!"

Ashley finally got off the phone two minutes later thinking himself lucky he hadn't been pulled from the task force. Why the heck had he mentioned DCI Pascoe? Panicking in the moment and trying to find a way to defend his actions, he'd blurted what he currently believed was the stupidest thing he'd ever said in his life. He had done it now and couldn't take it back. DCI Harris wouldn't repeat it to anyone, so it stopped with him, but that was hardly cause for celebration. When Harris wrote his next report, he would remember it and only producing a major win would fix things.

Unless DCI Pascoe is guilty.

The little voice echoed deep inside Ashley's head, hope blooming for a second, only for the bubble to pop just as swiftly. Ashley knew he had no easy way to prove DCI Pascoe had done anything. DCI Harris had ordered him to drop the Chowdry case, clear out of Wingham, and concentrate on Michelle Canet, a French tourist stabbed to death in Whitstable three years ago. If he did anything other than precisely that, Ashley knew his boss would bounce him out of the task force with a big black mark against his name. It would set him back years.

Or worse.

A vision of Tony swam into Ashley's head. He screwed up once. Just once. His boss at the time chose to make sure he carried the can, which Tony probably deserved, though he ought never to have been in such a position to screw up that badly. However it came about, it ended his career.

Imagining the same awful scenario for himself was enough to give Ashley an icy shiver. It ran down his spine like a cup of cold water, making him squirm.

DCI Pascoe pulled into the carpark, his Audi cruising

past the nose of Ashley's car. Ashley's heart quickened, nervous guilt impacting his pulse. He shouldn't feel guilty, he was the good guy in all this, the one seeking the truth. Yet Ashley also knew he was in the wrong. He should never have chosen the Craig Chowdry case. Or, at least, he ought not to have focused all his energy on it. Restarting his engine, he eased back onto the road and aimed his wheels at Canterbury.

He felt untethered; adrift on conflicting emotions, and in need of something to help clear his head. He also recognised that he had to visit Tony. The fact that his partner had been injured and was in the hospital was enough to demand that he check in with him, but he also felt it would be better to explain the change in status, the order to drop the Chowdry case, and switch to investigating Michelle Canet's murder in person.

More than anything, Ashley wanted to hear what the older man had to say on the matter.

CHAPTER 30

"DON'T DRINK TOO MUCH TEA, TONY," MY WIFE NAGGED. "You know too many cups make you jittery."

Okay, so she was right, but stuck in a hospital bed waiting for the doctors to tell me I could go was boring, and the breakfast they served was awful. The tea was passable, so I was making the most of it. I was about to offer an argument when Ashley popped his head around the door. His eyes lit up in recognition or relief that he had found the right room.

I lifted a hand in welcome and mentally acknowledged the shift in our dynamic. I had been hostile to the kid since I first met him barely twenty-four hours ago. He caught the brunt of my ire not because he had done anything wrong, but because he was the only one around for me to target. I was happily cruising through the last days of my career when Bruce Denton's name crashed back into my world, bringing old emotions back to the surface.

However, when he came to my rescue last night, the way I viewed him changed. Without intending to, I now saw him as a partner. A junior partner with too much confidence and not enough experience, but a partner no

STEVE HIGGS

less. This was a good thing, because we had inadvertently kicked over a hornets' nest in Goodnestone and I needed help now if I was to catch Craig's killers.

"Ashley, I'm glad you're here. I've got some thoughts about our next steps."

The apologetic look on his face was enough to stop me in my tracks.

Narrowing my eyes, I encouraged him to speak. "What?"

Two minutes later I was shouting.

"Calm down, Tony," my wife frowned at me. "You'll give yourself a headache."

Still responding to my young partner's revelation about his change of assignment, I growled, "Not a chance!" from my hospital bed. "We get close enough to the truth that my tyres get slashed and someone tries to kill me, and your boss thinks we are just going to drop the case?"

"He wasn't asking," Ashley pointed out.

"I don't care if he offers me money or points a gun at my head. Pascoe is involved. I told you right at the start he was lying about the case." I leaned forward, aiming an index finger at Ashley. "My entire career has been about solving cases and bringing criminals to justice. Some even said I was good at it." I knew I was good at it but didn't wish to blow my own trumpet too hard. "In all that time, I have never once come across a dirty cop. I mean, sure, there have been some who would play it a little loose with the rules, maybe even take a bribe, not that I ever had any evidence, or I would have turned them in, but Pascoe is up to his neck in Craig Chowdry's murder, and I am going to prove it."

Ashley gawped at me. "How? We're off the case. My boss has reassigned me to the Michelle Canet murder. I'm to start that investigation immediately. Maybe you want to

Shadow of a Lie

check, but your boss assigned you to work with me as local liaison and I've no reason to believe that situation has changed."

Before I could say another word, the fact that my wife was narrowing her eyes at me demanded I acknowledge her desire to give input.

"You have something you wish to say, dear?" Thirty years of marriage have taught me many things. One of those is to let my wife speak before she interrupts; trying to prevent her from voicing her thoughts has never worked out well for me.

"You suffered a head injury last night and the doctors said you had a concussion. You are going nowhere today, dear, other than home with me."

Ashley mumbled, "I can manage by myself for the next few days, obviously." Like most men, he would argue with a colleague until he was blue in the face, but wasn't about to challenge a colleague's wife.

I swung my legs out of bed, grumbling, "There's nothing wrong with me. I got a knock on the head, nothing more. I feel fine and there's no chance I'm letting this case go. Not when we have clearly come so close to the truth of it."

However, Mary wasn't wrong about the current state of my health and, annoyingly, was in the room last night when the doctors were explaining my condition and advising that I should 'take it easy' for the next few days.

My superintendent was there too, saying all the right things even though he meant none of them. I could be sure of his true feelings for he chose to voice them when the doctors left and Mary set off to fetch coffee.

"Leading your new partner astray already, I see." He smiled at me, pleased to be in the position of power. "Too much to hope that his attitude might rub off on you instead of the other way around." Pausing in the door to aim one last insult at the man with the splitting head, he sneered, "Try not to ruin his career the way you ruined your own."

To be fair I was ready to ignore his orders and do what I knew to be right long before he goaded me into it. Now though I had to ease Ashley into the same way of thinking.

"Do you think we can close this case and catch Craig Cowdrey's killers?" It was a direct question with only two possible answers and we both knew which one he had to pick.

"Yes, obviously," Ashley grumbled. "I wouldn't have started if I thought there was no chance of success."

"So do you want to be a good little robot blindly accepting your orders without questioning them? Or shall we show a little backbone and take down the ring of killers and liars behind a teenage boy's murder?" I was laying it on thick, especially with the stab about courage, but my boss is an idiot, just like most people his rank. Ashley's boss sounded little different, both too interested in their next promotion to do their current job the way it ought to be done.

Bright enough to know I was manoeuvring him, Ashley's expression was filled with warning when he asked, "You intend to directly disobey your instructions regardless of the consequences?"

"Yup."

Ashley blinked. That was not the answer he expected.

Pushing on, I said, "Look, we got close enough to scare them. From where I sit, we already know who the guilty persons are. Half the work is done. Sarah slipped up and when we finally get to question her again, I believe we will expose a corner of the lie that has protected Craig's killers for the last seven years. In so doing we will discover how

Shadow of a Lie

and why the SIO for the original investigation in 2016 chose to make sure the four boys got away with it."

Ashley shook his head. "We can't go after DCI Pascoe. You said it would be career suicide."

"For you perhaps." My retort came automatically, and I saw there was a need to quickly follow my comment with something more. "There are a few things I omitted to tell you about DCI Pascoe."

Ashley folded his arms across his chest, his expression a mix of curiosity and accusation. His eyebrows encouraged me to keep talking.

"When you called me yesterday to see where I had gone ..."

"When I was on the way back to Wingham nick with Curzon in my car?"

"Yes. Well, I omitted to tell you that I found Pascoe's car."

Ashley frowned. "You told me you lost him."

"I did. Then I found him again. Pretty much by accident. Now," I raised my hands, using the left to fold out my right index finger, "he was at a derelict farm on the far side of Goodnestone. Second," I folded out another finger, "he's the one who slashed my tyres. You're going to ask me how I can be sure, and I can't. However, there were no other cars around. I waited two hours for the AA to turn up and a grand total of ten cars went by. Pascoe stuck a knife in all four of my tyres just to slow me down."

Mary blinked. "Your tyres got slashed?"

Bother.

"Yes, dear," I replied, hoping I might be able to skip over it.

"You got them fixed?"

"Yes, dear."

"And this Pascoe fellow paid for them."

STEVE HIGGS

"Not exactly."

Mary flared her eyes and I held up both hands to slow her down. She can be a little fiery at times.

"Can we circle back to that, sweetheart? It genuinely isn't top of the list right now." Turning my attention back to Ashley, I said, "I think he was there to check on the grave. Make sure it hadn't been disturbed."

Mary's eyes went so wide I thought they might fall from their sockets.

Ashley was equally surprised by my words, but had a question.

"Why? Why do you think he went there to check on a grave?"

"Because it looked like a great place to hide a body for a start. We know the police did a thorough search in 2016, but as SIO he would have been able to steer the search teams. Even if he couldn't, it would be easy enough to cover the body in straw or seed or whatever they might be harvesting at that time of the year. I have Doris back at the nick in Herne Bay looking into the property's ownership. She'll have an answer by now. In fact, the answer is probably on my phone already. Did they find it?"

Ashley shrugged. "It wasn't mentioned, and I wasn't going to ask. Anyway," Ashley continued, a sceptical look aimed my way, "so he poked around some derelict farm buildings. Maybe he's looking to buy them. Did you see him near anything that actually looked like it could be a grave?"

I had to admit I hadn't.

"I didn't really see him at all. His car was there, but I got back in it and drove off while I was still trying to find him." I slid off the bed to the floor where I found the tile about a hundred degrees colder than anticipated. "Good

Shadow of a Lie

Lord, do they chill the tile to keep the patients in their beds?" I danced around looking for my socks and shoes.

"Here," Mary pulled a pile of clothes from a bag next to her chair. "I brought you fresh stuff to wear. There was blood, dirt, and goodness knows what on your clothes from yesterday. I put them in the laundry last night."

I accepted the clothes with thanks.

Ashley mumbled something about giving me a minute and I realised he was trying to exit the room mid-conversation.

"Good grief, man, I'll go behind the curtain." I gave it a yank, shutting off his view of me when I dropped my pants and donned the fresh ones Mary brought from home. I continued talking while I used the can of deodorant to mask my odour. I needed a shower, truth be told, but it could wait. "Listen, the way I see it, we have a duty to keep digging into this case. You can get started on the next one, but I've got sick days, and no one will question what I am up to."

Ashley mumbled something that wasn't exactly agreement, but couldn't be categorised as argument either.

"I can find out who owns the derelict farm buildings and maybe that will lead me somewhere. I can nose around a bit more and find where Sarah French went. I can also visit an old pal of mine who just happened to be involved with the case at the time."

"Gary Hunt?"

That's right. I had already told Ashley about him.

"Yes. He's retired now and lives within easy driving distance. Hopefully he'll be able to shed some light on how Pascoe was acting when the case was live."

"You still think Pascoe was involved?" Ashley's tone was more hopeful than anything else.

"No." I yanked the curtain back so I could see the

189

bewildered look on Ashley's face. "I *know* he was involved. He lied both times I asked him questions about the outcome of the case and he's poking around at derelict farms in the middle of the day. The only real question I have yet to figure out is why. That one remains a mystery, but when we know why he helped the four boys cover up Craig's death we will know everything."

Mary made a tutting noise with her tongue. "You're supposed to rest, Tony." It was quite clear she expected me to obey the medical advice.

Ignoring my darling wife for just a moment, I accentuated my plan by jabbing my finger into the air.

"You get started on the next case just like your boss expects, but drag your feet a little. We are all set up in Wingham, so let's just leave them hanging. That will give me a few days to uncover what I can."

"All by yourself?" Mary asked.

Now, was she seeking confirmation, or trying to point out a flaw in my plan?

"After you had your tyres slashed and almost got shot, you want to go back to the place where that happened, but this time without backup?"

"There are local police if I get into any bother."

"Yes!" she cried out. "Local police you currently believe to be complicit in a murder!" I guess she kind of had a point.

"Not all of them," I argued, somewhat weakly. "Just their boss."

"Who controls what all the others do!" She wasn't letting this go without a fight.

I looked at Ashley for help, but he said, "Don't look at me. I think she's right."

I looked from him to her and back at him, questioning the plan in my head to see where it failed to meet their

Shadow of a Lie

needs. It looked and sounded fine to me. In fact, I thought it was close to genius, just like me.

Flapping my hands at Mary's concerns, I said, "It'll be fine, love." She clearly agreed because she rolled her eyes and stormed from the room to celebrate my incredible brilliance.

"You need to go after her?" Ashley asked.

I cocked an eyebrow. "What for?"

"Um, because she seems upset?" he questioned as though that alone was enough reason.

I sniggered. "It's obvious you haven't been married for thirty years."

CHAPTER 31

MARY WAS NOWHERE TO BE SEEN WHEN I LEFT THE hospital room, and I couldn't call her because I didn't have my phone. You might think I ought to know her number and could use a landline, but I haven't had to type it in for years. There was a seven in it for sure and it definitely started with a zero. Beyond that I had no clue.

I was supposed to wait for the doctors' rounds so they could discharge me, but I was not inclined to delay my departure. Honestly, I hadn't felt this invigorated in years. It was as though the blow to my head had removed the cobwebs that slowly formed over the last decade. The years were stripped away, returning me to my former youthful glory.

I mean, obviously I was still fifty pounds overweight with bad knees and a trick back, but mentally I was raring to go.

In the car on the way to Herne Bay where I planned to ascertain from Doris the name of the person who owned the derelict farm, Ashley told me more about his encounter with Shane Travers.

Was there anything to read into the way he said, 'We

Shadow of a Lie

didn't kill Craig Chowdry?' Ashley thought so, but what did it mean?

If the four boys didn't kill Craig, then who did? Ashley also told me about the rug missing from Shane Travers' house, and how he'd looked into DCI Pascoe via his wife's social media account but found nothing of interest.

Would DCI Pascoe know we'd been bumped off the Chowdry case? He would have spoken to my superintendent and probably Ashley's boss last night following the shooting incident and today would be up to his eyeballs in that case. There would be questions for me to answer of course. Had I hung around at the hospital, someone like Beckett, or maybe Pascoe himself, would have shown up to take a statement.

Of course, the need to provide a statement gave me reason enough to return to Wingham. Ashley was reluctant to go back there, not that he had a choice, but having made such a mess of things last night, he was understandably uninspired at the prospect of showing his face again today. Regardless, he was going to have to suck it up sooner or later.

Impressing me, he decided to deal with it head on.

"I think I'll follow up on that rug," he announced unexpectedly.

We were just coming into Herne Bay along the seafront. The pier was ahead of us, stretching into the water like a bony finger. On our right, the murky, grey sea lapped at the pebble shore. The tide was out, and the breakers fitted long ago to help fight longshore drift were exposed. I could see a pair of old ladies picking winkles for their tea.

Nodding along, I said, "I think that's a good idea." Truthfully, I thought he ought to get started on the Michelle Canet case; his boss would check in and expect to

STEVE HIGGS

hear he was obeying his orders. I was not, however, going to dissuade Ashley from pursuing a case I believed we could solve. Besides, what he was proposing wouldn't take long.

"I can do it on my way to Whitstable," Ashley added.

A frown formed as I pointed out, "It's in the opposite direction."

Ashley shrugged. "My boss doesn't know that."

I liked that. I liked that a lot.

Arriving at my hometown nick a few minutes later, I checked the superintendent's parking spot to see if his car was there. It was, which meant I might run into him. Not that doing so was necessarily a problem, I just didn't want to. He would ask what I was doing, since he expected me to be taking a few sick days, and he would know by now that we were investigating the Chowdry case and had been ordered to stop.

He was the sort who would make a big point of confirming that I was going to do precisely as ordered. Although, to be fair, that's probably because I have a tendency to do what I want instead.

I threw a wave at Mike on the dispatch desk, and pushed through the door to access the ground floor offices. There I found Doris exactly where I expected her to be. She had a cup of tea steaming on her desk – a proper cup, not a mug. It even had a matching saucer. Halfway to her mouth when I sailed through her open door was a digestive biscuit, the kind with a coating of chocolate on one side.

Spotting the packet, I swooped.

"Morning, Doris."

My fingers were closing over the packet of biscuits when her spare hand swatted it.

"Get yer own," she mumbled through a mouthful of crumbs, too late because I was already thumbing one out.

Shadow of a Lie

The moment I put the packet back on her desk, she snatched it up and dropped it into her drawer.

Smiling sweetly, I said, "Thank you, Doris."

She shot daggers with her eyes. "Here, what happened to your face?" she asked, noticing the two steri-strips next to my left eye for the first time.

She got the vastly abridged version. "I had a fight with a tree." Doris wouldn't have heard about the incident last night and there was no good reason to bore her with it. Moving things along, I said, "That enquiry I sent you yesterday. Did you manage to find out who owns the land?"

Doris squinted at me. She'd finished her biscuit and wasn't going to risk taking another from the packet until I was gone. "I messaged you yesterday before I finished work."

"No doubt you did. I, um, lost my phone though while I was fighting the tree."

Doris rolled her eyes, rubbed her hands together to remove lingering biscuit crumbs, and turned her attention back to her computer screen.

"Let me have a look," she remarked to herself, nudging the mouse, and clicking to find that which she sought.

"Mathew Anderson," I read from her screen, having to get the distance right to avoid fishing out my reading glasses. I got Doris to print the page as it provided the owner's address. I was disappointed the farm didn't belong to DCI Pascoe, but hoped to discover a link between him and the owner.

Handing the page to Ashley, I asked, "Can you find time to explore this?"

He held the sheet of A4 up to read it. "This is the farm where you saw ..." He almost said the name of the DCI from Wingham, but caught himself before he aired our suspicion, "... him," Ashley concluded, his cheeks tinging

STEVE HIGGS

with red. "Sure, I can find a few minutes to find out who Mathew Anderson is."

"Thanks. I'm going to go back over the case notes again. I need to talk to Sarah French still and I think I might find the friend she was with that day, see if she can remember the details that went into her statement." Essentially, I wanted to test whether Sarah's friend could recall that day's events from memory. If she gave a true account seven years ago, it would be clear in her mind. If not, then she lied in her original statement and that introduced a whole new line of enquiry.

Ashley hovered in the doorway to Doris's office, his feet twitchy because he wanted to be elsewhere. His boss expected him to go to Whitstable, and Ashley wanted to be able to report his compliance.

I got it. There was a time when I cared what my boss thought about me.

Thanking Doris once more, I nodded my head in the direction of her window, making her look that way when I asked, "Whose flashy new car is that?"

The distraction technique worked, but her top drawer squeaked when I opened it to steal a second chocolate biscuit and I almost lost the tips of my fingers when she slammed it shut. Giggling like a fool, I danced out of swiping range and escaped her office just before a stapler flew through the space my body occupied only a moment earlier.

Insults followed, but they only served to strengthen my desire to raid her snack supply.

Ahead of me down the corridor Ashley shot his cuff, making a show of checking the time.

"I'm coming," I held up my hands in surrender. "Drop me at Wingham and get going. Unless you're still planning to find Mrs Travers and quiz her about the rug?"

196

Shadow of a Lie

Ashley pursed his lips, considering which course of action he ought to pursue, but nodded after a moment.

"I can spare the time for that. If my boss calls I can say I'm breaking down the incident room in Wingham nick and clearing up the details after last night. I need to give a statement too."

Good lad. Nothing like a little rebellion to stir the blood.

CHAPTER 32

Arriving at Wingham nick felt like returning to the scene of a crime. We were not wanted here, that much was certain, but it was more than that. The outward hostility from Beckett notwithstanding, the fact that I suspected the top guy made the station feel like an enemy fortress into which I was about to sneak.

I spotted my car as Ashley pulled into the carpark. It looked none the worse for wear though I noted the grey muck dried onto my tyres and around the wheel arches – the clay from the clay pit. At least they didn't leave it there.

When Ashley parked, I got out to take a look.

"Good luck getting that out of your clothes," he remarked. "I'll have to put my suit from yesterday in to be dry cleaned and I think it might stain even so."

I crouched to examine the icky grey mud. It was stuck to my tyres and coated the inside of the arches where it was still damp. The same grey mud had got all over my clothing when I ran through the trees. In the dark I failed to notice, and Mary hadn't said anything this morning or last night. She never was one to make a fuss.

Shadow of a Lie

I had my spare keys from home just in case, but left the car as it was for now and headed into the nick.

Coaching Ashley, I said, "Keep your head high. You messed up, but you're not the first and you won't be the last. Beckett will probably have something smart to say, just don't rise to his taunting."

Ashley huffed at me, "I can manage to be professional, thank you." He didn't feel he needed advice from a passed-over-for-promotion has-been.

Inside the station, a young man was being processed. It sounded like he'd been caught swiping Amazon parcels from doorsteps though I only caught a snippet of conversation between the custody sergeant and the arresting officer.

Ashley took me through to the incident room to show me the photograph with the carpet.

"It's here in this shot, but it's gone just five days after Craig Chowdry goes missing."

I thought about Jane Wallace, the woman who saw the four boys crossing the B2046. "They were carrying it," I murmured.

Ashley shot me a blank look.

"Jane Wallace saw the four boys late in the afternoon on the day Craig went missing. They had Craig's body with them, and it was wrapped in that rug."

Ashley pulled a doubtful face. "That's quite the leap."

I shrugged. "I'm lining up the clues. Craig lived in a big house outside the boundaries of Goodnestone. There's a row of them, all costing way more than a million at today's prices." I moved across to the map Ashley had pinned to one wall. Pins identified key points such as the Shop Ryte, Craig's house, the houses of the four boys, and the site where officers found Craig's blood.

Ashley got involved, sweeping his right hand over the area to the west of the B2046. "They searched all around

STEVE HIGGS

these woods. If they moved the body, they would have needed to cross the road." He tapped the pin showing where Jane Wallace claimed to have seen the boys. "Her statement says nothing about a large roll of carpet."

"No," I agreed. "They put it down to make sure the road was clear before attempting to cross."

Ashley poked out his lips and made a face – he wasn't convinced, but he also wasn't arguing.

I continued to theorise. "If they bury Craig in the woods, he will be found. Knowing this, they head for the village."

"The village was searched too," Ashley pointed out.

"Ah, but you and I both know there are always places to stash a body and maybe what they were aiming for was a car or a van. Get the body far enough away and the search radius will never reach it."

Ashley shrugged a shoulder, neither agreeing nor disagreeing. "How does that help us?"

"It doesn't," I admitted. "However, I was right there yesterday," I jabbed the map right on the crossing point. "The church is easy to access."

Ashley flipped his eyebrows. "You looked into burials around that time and said there was nothing to find."

"That's right, there were none that week. However, the church is overshadowed by trees and on a Monday in August, there wouldn't be anyone around. If they were going to load the body into a car, that's where they would do it."

Ashley frowned deeply, not seeing what I was saying. "Why take the body to the car when the car can come to them?"

"Because the blood was less than half a mile from Craig's house. To get to it, they would have needed to drive by all the houses there and park at the edge of the woods.

Shadow of a Lie

Then they would need to carry the body out and load it into the car. If one person saw them loading a thick roll of carpet into the back of a car, do you think we would be having this conversation now?"

Ashley blew out a slow breath. "No, I guess not. They had to go the other way, or they would have been caught. Someone would remember seeing the car even if they did manage to hide what they were doing." He sucked on his top lip for a second before pointing out the obvious flaw, "This still doesn't help us, Tony. It's nothing more than a theory unless we find the rug and Craig's body wrapped inside it. If they did load him into a car, he could be anywhere."

I could offer no argument. "That's why we need to talk to Jane Wallace again, see if her memory can be jogged. They were all too young to drive, but they could easily swipe the keys to a parent or older sibling's car."

"No older siblings," Ashley reported, showing his superior knowledge of the case again, "and the parents' cars were all searched at the time. No forensic evidence to suggest Craig had ever been in any of them, alive or dead."

Refusing to be defeated, I said, "Then they used someone else's car."

Ashley straightened and looked at me, our eyes locking before we both said, "Pascoe."

CHAPTER 33

WE TOOK SO LONG DISCUSSING CRAIG'S POSSIBLE whereabouts that Ashley changed his mind and left the rug for later. He felt certain his boss would check up on his movements, so at the very least he needed to make an appearance at the nick in Whitstable. He would get to the rug once the boss in Whitstable, a DCI called Jacob Tanner, had seen him.

Splitting up, he left me behind in Wingham, where I made my way to Pascoe's office.

That Ashley and I both uttered his name as the person most likely behind Craig's unfindable body strengthened my conviction. Whichever way I looked at the case, and trust me, I'd been bending my head to view it from alternative angles, I could not see how the four boys could have escaped justice without the help of someone inside the investigation. Especially since they now presented themselves in a calmer and more confident manner than anyone I'd ever interviewed.

In theory, it could have been anyone, but the guilty person had to be someone near the case, not a uniform and not one of the forensics team. Add to that DCI

Shadow of a Lie

Pascoe's willingness to lie about key facets of the case and his unexplained excursion to a derelict farm in Goodnestone ... well, let's just say I wasn't looking at anyone else. The four boys killed Craig Chowdry and DCI Pascoe helped them to get away with it.

Annoyingly, I still had no idea why.

Politely, I knocked on the frame of Pascoe's open door and waited outside.

His eyes flicked up from his computer screen, meeting mine over the top of his reading glasses.

"DS Heaton? I'm surprised to see you this morning. I sent Beckett to the hospital to check on you and to get your statement provided you were up to it."

I was pleased to hear Beckett had a wasted trip.

"Mind if I come in?"

DCI Pascoe lifted his chin, inviting me to come forward.

"You are feeling well enough to work?" I could hear the doubt in his voice.

"Yes, but we've been pulled off the case." I made the announcement, watching keenly for his response. Expecting to see relief, I did, though he worked hard to mask it.

"Oh? I hadn't heard. Is there a reason?"

"DS Long's boss, the SIO for the task force, considered Craig Chowdry's case too unlikely to yield a result. He wants us to concentrate on other cases. DS Long has already departed, in fact. We need to break down the incident room still. Will you permit us a day or two? I need to make sure the case file and all the evidence is correctly accounted for. We wouldn't want to ruin the chain of evidence should there be a development years from now."

DCI Pascoe nodded his agreement, but said, "I'll need

STEVE HIGGS

it cleared out soon. You have the bigger room and physical evidence is already arriving from last night."

"Well, I thought I had better let you know I am fit and well. I need to record a statement about last night, of course. Any leads?"

"You'll be kept informed." Pascoe's response was dismissive, he had no desire to discuss the incident. Was he now trying to cover that up too? "Beckett will take your statement when he gets back from Canterbury. He ought to have checked your status before he set off." Pascoe's tone betrayed how he felt about Beckett's error. "You can wait for his return?"

"Of course. I have work I can busy myself with, Sir. I will remain in the area." Pausing in the doorway like I was Columbo, I turned back to face the DCI and waited for him to look up.

"Is there something else, DS Heaton?" There was no mistaking his wish that I would leave him to get on with his work.

"Mathew Anderson, sir?"

I got a small shake of his head – displaying that he didn't understand the reference. "Is that name supposed to mean something to me?"

"I guess not," I smiled, but I stayed where I was and tried a different line. "Just a thing that's been bothering me about the Chowdry case, Sir. The whole thing with the body. I stumbled across some derelict farm buildings yesterday."

A flash of something lit up his eyes for a moment. I took it to be that he understood what I was asking and what it meant: that I was on to him.

"The barns were filled with all manner of abandoned farm machinery and rotting bales of hay. I couldn't help thinking it would be a great place to hide a body. Under

Shadow of a Lie

the concrete which is then covered over by … well, whatever really. How deep would a search team look?"

"I can assure you they were very thorough." DCI Pascoe didn't exactly growl his response, but it wasn't friendly either.

"Anyway, that's why I mentioned Mathew Anderson. I wondered if his name might have come up before. In the original investigation, I mean. Or since."

His eyes never left mine and the tension in the room ratcheted up several notches. DCI Pascoe knew full well I observed him at Mathew Anderson's property yesterday and I was certain he slashed my tyres to hamper me. This was a standoff, a classic challenge to see who would blink first.

He knew I knew something, but by the same token, he could be confident I had nothing actionable. His cards were close to his chest, his secrets daring to believe they could remain just that.

Pascoe's desk phone rang, the sound cutting through the wall of silence like a hammer smashing glass. Snatching it up, he placed a hand over the receiver and looked my way once more.

"We already had this conversation, DS Heaton. I cannot say what might have happened to the body, or even be sure there ever was one. All we know for sure is that Craig lost some blood and vanished."

Conversation over, I left Pascoe's office and then the building after stopping to enquire about my car keys. They were being held in the dispatch office, the constable working there briefed to expect me. He also had my phone, the screen of which was cracked, I noted to my annoyance. But it still worked and someone had even gone to the trouble of charging it.

Surprised, yet pleased that every copper in the nick

STEVE HIGGS

wasn't against me, I thanked the constable and left the building.

With foreboding grey skies overhead, and a cold breeze that threatened rain, I started my old jalopy and aimed it at Goodnestone.

CHAPTER 34

I COULD HAVE TAKEN MYSELF TO THE INCIDENT ROOM AND started the process of finding a connection between Anderson and Pascoe. Or between Anderson and one of the four boys' families. Finding pay dirt there would help immensely, though it would require a lot more than a connection to convince a forensics team to examine an area for signs of a body.

While a fresh grave can be an easy thing to detect, a grave several years old is far harder. Harder, but a long way from impossible. Decomposing flesh releases compounds containing nitrogen which are detectable using a gas called ninhydrin. Forensics teams can use it to find the nitrogen compounds because one gas reacts with the other to cause a colour change. It's a bit like being able to see farts.

Or they can bring in specially trained cadaver dogs that will sniff out a body's location.

Both these methods, and the use of ground penetrating radar, become exponentially more difficult and less accurate if the body is encased in concrete or buried under a slab of rock. Then the team is forced to dig or drill holes.

None of that was going to happen unless I could show

STEVE HIGGS

unquestionable reason why I thought Craig Chowdry's body was in a particular place. Right now I had nothing to go on and finding the connection between Anderson and Pascoe ought to have been my highest priority.

However, knowing I would need to return to give my statement and not wishing to hang around when there was no way to know when Beckett might return, I opted to see if Sarah French had returned home.

On the way there, I called Gary Hunt again.

"Tony."

He must have pounced on the phone he answered it so swiftly.

"Gary, are you going to be around today? I'd like to visit if I may."

"Sure thing. I'm retired, old boy. Nothing much to do except watch TV and go fishing. This is still about that missing teenager?"

"Yeah, sorry, I wish it was social. Maybe when I retire next month you can help me land a pike."

"That sounds great. What sort of time are you thinking? Just so I can let the missus know. She'll want to bake a cake if we are having a visitor."

"No need to go to any bother."

"Ha!" Gary spat. "She's tearing her hair out with me at home. Keeps looking at me as though I ought to be working. Giving her something to do will take her mind off murdering me for five minutes."

I've talked to lots of retired people in my life and they seem to fall into two distinct camps: those who fail to adjust to life without a job and drift along helplessly like flotsam, and those who dive into their next adventure, using their sudden abundance of time to explore and enjoy all the things working life denied them.

I planned to be the latter. Mary and I were already

Shadow of a Lie

planning a cruise for next year and I had a dozen garden projects lined up. I'd even given some thought to taking language classes. I could learn Italian and then we could take a driving holiday one summer. There were endless options.

Letting Gary know I would aim to be there after lunch and before two o'clock, I explained I might get delayed and would try to let him know if I was going to be much adrift. The call lasted most of the journey to Goodnestone where the village looked green and inviting again today; a complete contrast to how it felt last night when I was running for my life.

Birdsong greeted me as I stepped out of my car in front of Sarah's house. Was she here? Truthfully, I doubted it. She wasn't answering her phone or responding to text messages. She left before the social worker arrived yesterday, and I would not blame her for choosing to stay away. However, I worried something might have befallen her.

Was she simply choosing not to answer me, or was she unable to?

I knocked on her door, doing so in a gentle manner, not like a thug looking to break down the door. There was no camera doorbell that I could see, so if she was in, perhaps she would think it was the postman or a neighbour.

A shadow fell across the patch of light inside the house, a figure moving my way. I knew instantly from the gait and height it was Andrew Curzon and not Sarah. Involuntarily, I tensed, certain the man we arrested less than twenty-four hours ago was going to have something to say about me being back at his door.

Not that I thought he would attack me, but were he to do so, his arrest would come later because I doubted I could overpower him.

He yanked the door open, a piece of toast hanging

from his mouth. Using his right hand, he removed the toast without taking a bite.

"You again," he observed, the timbre of his voice menacing yet calm. Yet again, it presented me with the notion that someone was operating him. The hot head willing to slap his girlfriend was the authentic version. The man I met at his father's farm and the one before me now were the fakes.

I said nothing, but then I wasn't looking at him. Not his face, at least. My eyes were tracking his right hand.

"Nice bruise," I smiled up at him. "How many times did you hit Shane?"

Curzon's brow furrowed. He had not expected the question.

"Did you beat him to make him leave the note and lure me into the woods when he didn't want to? Or did you find out that he was planning to tell the truth and give him the beating after you stopped him from meeting me?"

Curzon let a disappointed smile tease his lips. "You're barking mad."

"Tell me," I persisted, "Was it you who shot at me? The rifle used sounded like a semi-automatic .22. It won't take me long to check which one of you owns something like that."

He sniggered, "This is farm country, old man. Everyone has a hunting rifle. Now get off my doorstep," he commanded, using his right arm, still holding the toast, to point back toward my car. "Go on. You've already been kicked off the case. You've no business here."

Now it was my turn to grin, a knowing expression that unnerved my youthful rival.

"Now how would you know that, Andrew?"

His expression froze, a haunted look filling his eyes.

I took a step toward him, crowding his personal space

Shadow of a Lie

even though he had a good six inches height advantage and was standing inside the house, which made him about a foot taller in total.

"How could you possibly know about that unless someone at the nick elected to tell you?" I left the question hanging in the air, waiting for him to say something. Yet again, he showed a calmness I have rarely seen, staying quiet when ninety-nine percent of people would have felt pressured into talking.

Getting even closer, though I knew I was pushing my luck now and could feel my heart starting to hammer in my chest, I delivered a final line, "The noose is tightening, Andrew. It might have taken seven years for justice to catch up with you, but it's coming. Enjoy these last moments of freedom."

His mouth twisted into an angry grimace, his eyes displaying the anger he worked hard to control. It came as no shock when he took a step back and slammed the door in my face. I'd come to speak with Sarah, but if she was home, I wasn't getting to her and there was no reason to hang around. I could return later if I wanted to. Right now, it was time to withdraw and observe.

Curzon was kind enough to not make me wait too long.

CHAPTER 35

I COULD FEEL CURZON'S EYES ON MY BACK WHEN I WALKED back down his garden path to the street. Of course, it could have been my imagination, but I suspected he was watching through a window and refused to glance over my shoulder to check. Whether he was or not didn't matter so much as seeing what action my words might provoke. It was what he would do next that I cared about.

Pulling away from his house, I drove down the street – it was important that he believe I had left the area. However, at the first corner, when I reached a side street a hundred yards down the road, I turned the car around and parked out of sight behind a plumber's transit van.

Using that for cover, I watched Curzon's front door. He came out of it less than a minute later, jabbering animatedly into his phone. His free hand made exasperated gesticulations – he wasn't hearing what he wanted.

He calmed a little, but doing my best to lip read, I saw him end the conversation with a terse expletive. Stuffing the phone into a back pocket, he hoisted a motorcycle helmet into the air, the kind they use for rallycross, and vanished around the back of the house.

Shadow of a Lie

The sound of a motorbike engine catching replaced the quiet village air like a chainsaw starting up during a church service. Birds took to the sky, leaving their perches in the nearby trees and a moment later, Curzon powered out of his garden and onto the road.

On a dirt bike.

He turned away from me, heading in the rough direction of his father's farm, though his destination could be any one of a thousand places. I wanted to know where he was going, but there was no chance I would catch him in my car and suspected he would head through the abundant countryside when he inevitably noticed me following.

Instead, I walked back to his house and crouched, my knees clicking in protest, to examine the grey dirt the bike left behind.

Defence counsel would argue the clay, for that was what it was, could have been on the bike's tyres for weeks and that the clay pits were a haven for off-road bikers. I knew this, but the clay left behind was still damp and squishy: it was quite clearly new.

I took some pictures and a sample.

Following the trail of grey clay back up the driveway, I found a clump that still possessed the tyre tracks. I photographed that too, fairly certain it would match tyre prints taken from the clay pits last night.

I still couldn't be sure it was Shane's nasal voice I heard across the clearing last night. Not until I heard it again, but suspected it was because Ashley told me his nose was busted. Whether coerced or a volunteer, he lured me into the woods and one of his friends tried to kill me. They then escaped on Curzon's dirt bike.

"Are you the police?" asked a wobbly old lady voice from behind and to my right.

I used a hand on the driveway to fight against the resis-

STEVE HIGGS

tance in my knees and forced myself upright while turning to offer a smile. The voice belonged to Curzon's neighbour, a woman with wispy grey/white hair on both her head and her face. No doubt she plucked her facial hair for many decades, but had long since given up the practice. At five feet and maybe two inches, she was short, but had undoubtedly shrunk in later life. She wore a gold wedding band alongside an emerald and diamond engagement ring and an eternity band. I guessed her age to be around ninety, that she was widowed, and that she saw and heard everything that went on around her. She was so frail and thin a good breeze might pluck her from the ground.

"Yes. Good morning. I'm Detective Sergeant Tony Heaton. You are …"

"Edna Byrne. Are you going to arrest that one?" She angled her walking stick at Curzon's house.

"Do you think I should?" I posed the question in a conspiratorial way.

Edna gawped at me and shifted her upper set around in her mouth before saying, "I reckon that one knocks his girl around. Should be his wife, of course, her being in the family way and all."

I felt there was a need to head her off before she strayed too far from the subject.

"Have you seen Sarah today?"

"Nah, she's taken off again."

"It's not the first time?"

"Hah!" Edna scoffed at the notion. "Those two are at it hammer and tongs half the time. You should hear the language that comes through their windows. The names they call each other. She ought to leave him for good and be done with it."

"Any idea where she might have gone?"

Edna shrugged.

Shadow of a Lie

"Does she have family in the village?"

"A father, not that he's of any use. Her mum died of cancer way back when the kids were little. Her dad used to be a builder, but he took up with another woman a few years back and she cleaned him out before vanishing. He was a fan of the booze." Edna mimed upending a bottle into her mouth. "I'm not sure Sarah has anything to do with him."

I wasn't getting the answers I wanted, but this was good stuff, nonetheless. Like many small villages, the reduced population and the fact that rumours have less distance to travel means people know more than they ought to about everyone around them.

I tried another question. "Did you hear Andy's bike last night at any point?"

"Coo, yes. More than once, to tell the truth."

"Could you estimate when that was?"

Edna grinned at me, a sign that she was about to show off how clever she was.

"I can tell you exactly when I heard it. The first time was just after five o'clock. I can be sure of that because Harry, that's my husband, was arguing about what to have for dinner. I told him he needed to make his mind up because it was gone five already and he likes to eat at six."

I was wrong about her being widowed.

"I had to say it twice because he," she angled her head at Curzon's house, "was revving his stupid bike and Harry couldn't hear me. He returned at seven thirty, and I can be sure of that because *Coronation Street* was just finishing."

There it was. Shane's alibi for last night was exposed for the lie it was. Feeling like I was on a roll, I took out my phone.

"Can I show you a couple of pictures?" I asked,

STEVE HIGGS

fumbling through the infernal device to find what I wanted.

"Are they grisly?" Edna wanted to know, her tone hopeful.

She got a wry smile in return, her attitude amusing me.

"I'm afraid not." Turning the phone around to show her the screen, I showed her Shane Travers. "Do you recognise this man?"

"That's June's boy, Shane."

Of course she knew him. I rephrased the question.

"Have you seen him here recently?"

Edna shrugged. "Yes, I suppose. He's here all the time. Him and his two mates, Danny and Tim. The four boys have been tight as anything ever since that boy went missing." Her expression froze for a second, Edna jolting as she realised why I was asking questions. "Here, are you looking into that again? I never did believe he ran away. I said to Harry, I bet those boys did for him."

I chewed on my cheek, taking a moment to choose my words.

"I'm afraid I cannot comment on that, Mrs Byrne. I do, however, have one more photograph to show you though." I turned the phone around again. "Have you ever seen this man speaking to any of the four boys?"

Edna squinted at the picture, but shook her head. "No, I don't know him. Should I?"

My bubble burst. If she had said 'yes' everything would have changed in an instant. But she hadn't. The picture of DCI Pascoe, a recent one, showed a face she didn't recognise. That didn't mean I was wrong; only that he was careful.

I thanked Edna for her time, gave her my card, and asked that she call me if Sarah reappeared at her house.

Shadow of a Lie

Edna promised she would, and it felt good to have someone in Goodnestone on my side.

With my questions exhausted, I made my way back to my car. There were still people to talk to, but the web of lies surrounding this case were slowly falling apart. I would deliver the news about Shane Travers' alibi when I got back to the nick in Wingham.

DCI Pascoe would be angry that I was muscling in on his case, and would likely demand to know why I was still poking around when he knew I had orders to drop it. I was playing a dangerous game and had to hope I could win before someone else did by finishing what they almost achieved last night.

The very thought sent a shiver down my spine and made me rotate slowly on the spot to check I wasn't being watched. I couldn't see anyone, but I wasn't fool enough to think that meant I was safe.

CHAPTER 36

IN A CAR PARKED DOWN THE STREET, A MAN WATCHED DS Heaton when he left Andrew Curzon's house. Too experienced to make a sudden move – nothing catches the eye faster than movement – he remained still, watching to see what Heaton would do next.

His heart thumped out a quick staccato when Heaton looked right at him. Had he been spotted? His presence was explainable – delivering an excuse for idly sitting in his car wouldn't be too difficult. It proved unnecessary though, Heaton continuing the final yards until he got to his rusty, blue Vauxhall Astra estate.

When he drove off, the man in the car chose to wait long enough that he wouldn't be noticed pulling out behind the annoyingly persistent cop. Then he followed, sticking far enough behind that he could see where Heaton was going without the risk of being spotted.

Long before Heaton stopped again, the man in the car knew where the over-the-hill detective was going. There was only one person connected to the Chowdry case who lived in this part of the village. He considered it both good and bad that Heaton planned to speak with her.

Shadow of a Lie

There were holes in her story, but a visit just yesterday reinforced her need to get it right or to say nothing at all. She would be home, he knew, tending to her one-year-old. The baby had made it easier to lean on her – she had so much to lose, and the lie was an old one now, one she had lived with for years.

All she had to do was keep things straight in her head and she would be fine.

Wishing he could stay, the man in the car knew his presence would be missed if he didn't return to the nick soon. Reluctantly, he kept going at the next junction, leaving Heaton to do his worst and confident the holes had already been plugged.

Berating himself, he muttered, "It would have been so much easier if I hadn't missed last night."

CHAPTER 37

TRUDY LAWRENCE KNEW TO EXPECT A KNOCK AT HER door. Initially, when she was warned there were new police officers looking into Craig Chowdry's disappearance, she thought about taking a trip to visit her gran in Aberdeenshire.

The advice when she suggested it was to stay put and ride the wave. All she had to do was remember the story she gave the first time and reinforce that it was accurate. Under no circumstances could she withdraw her statement or suggest it was anything but the whole truth.

Trudy knew it was the wrong thing to do and that embracing the truth would result in arrests, but would that lead to convictions? If it didn't, the people she exposed would be thrust back into the same small community in which she lived, and even if they did go to jail, she would be left with their families and friends, all of which were happy with things the way they were.

To tell the truth now, so many years after being convinced to lie, would mean having to leave her home, never to return.

When the knock finally came, it occurred less than a

Shadow of a Lie

minute after she received a text reminding her to keep her mouth shut. There was subtext to the message, and it was anything but subtle.

With Millie, her thirteen-month-old baby on her hip, she padded barefoot to the door, pausing before the mirror to take a deep breath and attempt to reassure herself she could get through the next few minutes.

That's all it will be, Trudy told herself.

CHAPTER 38

"Good morning," I hit Trudy with a smile and held up my warrant card. "I'm Detective Sergeant Heaton. Miss Trudy Lawrence?"

"H-hello," she stammered, looking more nervous than a person ought to unless they had drugs or a body stashed in their house. "Are you here about Craig Chowdry?"

Her question came as no surprise. In such a small community, word would get around and her connection to the case likely ensured someone messaged her with a warning.

I gave a nod of confirmation. "Can I come in, please? I just need to ask you a few questions; nothing difficult and nothing to be concerned about. Won't take a minute." I started forward, lifting my left foot and placing it on the doormat. It was a move intended to make her back away, and it worked as it almost always does.

"Would you like a cup of tea?" she asked, demonstrating manners I rarely witness.

"That would be lovely, thank you."

Trudy retreated down her hallway, leaving me to close

Shadow of a Lie

her front door. She occupied a small terrace house, not dissimilar to the one in which Sarah French and Andrew Curzon live. It had been modernised at some point, the stairs ripped out and placed against a wall to allow the dining and living spaces to be joined. It made the downstairs into one big room that was more practical for a family.

Trudy lowered her daughter into a bouncer next to her small dining table and proceeded into the kitchen.

"Little lady not walking yet?" I called through.

"She is," came back Trudy's response. "That's the problem. If I'm not with her, she'll climb up the sofa or onto the table. She started walking at ten months."

"Impressive," I replied. The preliminaries were over, Trudy sounded calm, so it was time to hit her with the question no one ever expects. Moving to the kitchen, I leaned against the wall in the doorway and waited for her to look my way.

Trudy had filled the kettle and was hooking two mugs from a cupboard at head height.

"I forgot to ask how you take it." She paused with mugs in hand for me to supply the information.

"Why did you lie in 2016?"

Trudy's jaw dropped open.

"You are going to want to lie again today, Trudy. I would imagine that whoever helped you to perfect your stories in 2016 has visited you again in the last couple of days to make sure you remember all the details. You will be able to recall the number of the bus you took to get to Whitstable and what the driver looked like. Heck, you might even be able to tell me which traffic lights you got stopped at. The problem you face, Trudy, is that Sarah already let slip that she saw Craig that day. In 2016, she stated that she didn't see him and that she was with you all

STEVE HIGGS

day. So, to keep things short and simple, why don't you tell me where you really were?"

This interview, which wasn't an interview at all, but policy dictates we shouldn't call them interrogations, would have been much better carried out at the nick. Any nick. I couldn't do that though. I was off the case, just like Ashley. Taking Trudy in for formal questioning, where I could record her confession, would get me into deep water and end any chance I had of solving Craig's murder. Her confession, if I got one right now, would likely be inadmissible, but that wouldn't matter too much provided I could use her words to lead me to the next clue. I didn't care that Trudy lied when she was fourteen, she was of no interest. I wanted the boys responsible for Craig's death and the chance to bring down a corrupt DCI.

This was high stakes stuff and although I was bluffing with a handful of bad cards, there was still a good chance I could win.

Trudy might have no idea what actually happened with regards to Craig, Sarah, and the four suspects that day, but she would be able to confirm she wasn't with Craig's underage girlfriend and that would chip away another piece of armour from this ironclad case.

Trudy opened and shut her mouth twice, her cheeks burning bright red before she managed to stammer, "I-I don't know why you would think I lied. Everything Sarah and I said was true. We went to …"

"You went to Whitstable, yes, that's what you told the police. But you didn't, did you? I don't think you saw Sarah at all. Maybe you were supposed to. Maybe the pair of you planned a day out, but Sarah's brother found a condom wrapper under her bed and her focus was on trying to stop Danny from beating up Craig. Am I close?"

"Not even a little bit," Trudy lied to my face. She was

Shadow of a Lie

close to tears, the wrong reaction for an innocent person. She ought to have been getting angry and demanding I leave, but that was yet to occur to her.

"Trudy, the lies that were told in 2016 have done well to have lasted this long, but it is a house of cards you wish to hide inside, and it is all going to come crashing down on your head!" My voice was starting to crescendo, the abruptness of it jolting Trudy.

"I- I'm not … That's not what happened," Trudy part wailed part whispered, a tear rolling down her left cheek.

Lowering my voice, I put warmth behind my words, so they came across as something close to a verbal hug. "Then tell me what did happen, Trudy. Tell me who helped you to perfect your story." I desperately wanted to name DCI Pascoe, so sure was I that it had to be him behind the cover up. If I saw her eyes snap up and register shock when I named him, I would know for sure I had the right man, but there remained a chance I was wrong and I wasn't quite ready to lay it all on the line.

Trudy's eyes were locked on the linoleum floor, her head bowed when she whispered, "I don't know what you are talking about."

"I'm talking about an innocent boy being murdered, Trudy. I'm talking about the parents and family of that boy who moved away from the area to escape the memories that surrounded them. I'm talking about how the perpetrators were helped to cover up his death and were allowed to lie on record to make sure the case against them had to be dropped. The evidence was made to disappear, Trudy, and you helped it happen."

"No, I didn't," she sobbed.

Millie, silent since her mother placed her in the bouncer/walker thingy, let out a wail. Trudy sobbed, but the

STEVE HIGGS

mother instinct kicked in and she shoved by me to get out of the kitchen where I'd hemmed her in.

Twisting around, I watched mum lift the child and pull her into a cuddle. Trudy made shushing noises though Millie continued to bawl, upset by some unknowable circumstance.

Turning to face me, a more defiant look on her face, Trudy said, "I think you should leave. I'm not going to answer any of your questions. The statement I gave in 2016 stands, so unless you plan to arrest me, I have nothing further to say."

The change from one state to the next was stark. One moment she was whimpering and afraid. Now she stood tall and in control. I'd caught her off guard with my initial volley, that was all. Like all the other witnesses, Trudy had been coached on what to say and how to defend her lies. I was probably lucky she didn't know I was off the case. Had she done so, I doubt I would have got past the door.

I blinked.

She didn't know I was off the case. So far, everyone in the small circle surrounding Craig's case seemed to know everything almost as it happened. Had Pascoe slipped up in forgetting to alert Trudy?

I didn't know the answer to that question, and it troubled me.

"I asked you to leave," Trudy repeated herself. The distinct wobble of tearful horror was yet to leave her voice, but she believed I was going to do as she demanded. And she was right.

I wanted to grab her shoulders and shake some sense into her. She knew enough that if she confirmed what I already believed to be true, I would be able to force them to let us finish the case. One statement admitting she lied,

Shadow of a Lie

and we could justify arresting Sarah. That would lead to Sarah confessing what really happened seven years ago.

My hands twitched, but while there are times when you can push the boundaries, this wasn't one of them. Trudy held her baby to her chest, her eyes aiming for defiant as she did her best to stare me down.

I gave it one last go.

"Trudy, you are going to lose. I'm close to the truth and the people involved know it. You can go down with them, or you can be the one to cut a deal."

Her top lip trembled, words forming only to be dismissed before they left her mouth. She was tempted to say something, I was sure of it, but either she believed I was bluffing and their web of lies was too well spun, or she was more afraid of speaking out than she was of being arrested.

Ultimately, I didn't get to find out.

Outside on the street a few moments later, I leaned against my car and sighed. The lack of energy was back. The burst of indignant righteousness that fuelled me this morning had waned and the need to rebel against those who would command my actions had more or less run its course. Maybe they were right. Maybe I was no good anymore.

Knowing the truth and proving it have always been very different things, and despite how nervous our activities were making the guilty, we were no closer to catching whoever was behind the crime. Was there any point in continuing to fight? I could just let it go, do what I had been doing for the last few years, and dodge the work.

Slumping into the seat of my car, I put the key into the ignition, but my hand fell back into my lap without turning it. Pondering life – mine, not life in general, I thought about my imminent retirement. Would I care about any of these cases once I was no longer a police officer? Would they ever resurface in my dreams?

Would it matter if they did?

Like Bruce Denton, Craig Chowdry was dead, and nothing was going to change that. With another heartfelt sigh, I coaxed the old Vauxhall's engine into life and made my way back to Wingham nick.

CHAPTER 39

BECKETT WASN'T AT WINGHAM NICK WHEN I RETURNED TO give my statement. I didn't know whether I'd missed him, or he was yet to return, and I didn't care much either way. If Beckett didn't show before lunch, which was only forty minutes away, he was going to have to chase me. I knew I ought to be more interested in seeing last night's shooter brought to justice, especially since whoever it was cared not one bit about trying to kill a cop, but I simply wasn't. I was so close to none of this being my problem that finding the effort to give a stuff proved beyond me.

Shutting myself away in the incident room, I flopped into one of the chairs, folded my arms on the desk, and laid my head on them. I wasn't getting anywhere with the witnesses – Trudy Lawrence knew well enough to keep quiet, and though Andrew Curzon's neighbour was a useful source of information that could ruin Shane Travers' alibi for last night, it was not directly connected to the Craig Chowdry case.

Unless I could prove it was and that would take more energy than I was feeling.

My phone rang, the abruptness of it making me jump

STEVE HIGGS

in the quiet room. Pulling it from my inner jacket pocket I saw Ashley's name displayed.

"What's happening?" I asked, moving my index finger up to hit the speaker button then thinking better of it. "Are you in Whitstable?"

"I am. I'll be leaving soon though, heading back to Goodnestone. How did you get on this morning?"

Now that I was asked to talk about it, even though I had nothing exciting to report, I had to admit I felt better. It had been years since I'd worked with anyone that I could call a partner – that's an American thing anyway. Here we operate as part of a team, but over the years there have been officers I spent more time working with than others, and I'd forgotten how it feels to have someone to confide in.

I told him about Andrew Curzon, the dirt bike, the clay, and his neighbour.

"That's Shane's alibi shot to pieces then," Ashley remarked.

"Yes, but it doesn't place him at the scene and if I tell DCI Pascoe, or anyone else for that matter, why I was quizzing Curzon, they'll be quizzing me about that, not him about last night." Obviously, they would get around to re-questioning Shane, but I would be getting hauled over the coals at the same time, and I didn't need the grief. "The point is that if I tell them how I know Shane and his alibis were lying, my option to continue investigating Chowdry's disappearance will evaporate. I want to stick with it a while longer."

I really did, which came as a surprise. Two minutes ago, I was ready to cash in my sick excuse and take the rest of the week off. Like a switch being flicked, Ashley's endless energy had somehow reignited me.

230

Shadow of a Lie

"Anything else? Or did talking to Curzon take up the whole morning?"

"No, I went to see Trudy Lawrence as well. Don't bother getting excited though, Pascoe got to her first. Or whoever it is," I added a caveat before Ashley could pull me up for the conclusion I'd already formed. "I thought she was going to cave at one point, but she remembered her lines and kicked me out."

Ashley muttered an expletive.

"Look, I haven't given up. Not just yet. I'm going to see if I can find a connection between Pascoe and that Anderson chap. If it's there … well, I don't know what that might mean, but I think I can annoy a couple of the forensics guys I know into doing some tests off the books. If there is a body at that farm, they will find it."

"Worth a shot," Ashley agreed. "Look, I'm about done here. I had a chat with the local governor, got him to allocate me an incident room, and let him know we would be out and about nosing into the dead French tourist case. It's before his time; he transferred in last year on promotion and sounded genuinely pleased to have some help. I'm going to see what I can get from Mrs Travers, ask her about the rug and see what she says. You want to meet in Goodnestone? Or back at Wingham nick?"

"Neither. I promised Gary Hunt, the …"

"Family liaison officer from 2016," Ashley completed my sentence.

"Yeah, that one. I'm seeing him at two this afternoon. He lives in Essex now, near Dagenham, so it's a solid hour plus each way. I'll let you know if he has anything helpful to tell me, and if I can get back here at a sensible hour, I think we should get together and decide if we keep going off the books, or let it go."

I could almost hear Ashley scratching his head. Our

STEVE HIGGS

position was an odd one. Not one I'd ever been in before or could remember hearing any other cop suffering. Ashley wanted to solve at least one of the cold cases thrust upon him and even though I belittled him for choosing this case, I genuinely believed we could crack it. Or could have, if we'd been left alone.

"Yeah, let's give it one last day and see what we can uncover, eh?"

"That's the spirit."

Feeling significantly more invigorated than I was five minutes ago, I tapped into the database and started to explore. From the comfort of my chair, my next task was to find how Mathew Anderson fitted into everything. All I needed was enough to throw doubt on Pascoe's original investigation. If I could do that, they would have to assign more officers to reopen it properly, not the half-arsed clue hunt I was on with Ashley.

Some time later, my stomach rumbled, prompting me to check my watch. It was almost one and I needed to get going if was going to keep my meeting with Gary. He wouldn't care if I ran a little late, but I would. The Dartford crossing can be murder at peak times, so I wanted to be done with Gary and get back across the bridge before the London rush hour traffic clogged it to make my journey home twice as long as it needed to be.

Trying to find a connection between Mathew Anderson and either DCI Pascoe or one of the four boys had drawn a zero result so far. Of course, finding such a tenuous thing can be difficult at the best of times unless one has an inkling what it might be.

I folded down my laptop, checked my pockets and snuck back out of the station just in case Beckett was around. I wanted to give my statement earlier and was surprised that the DCI didn't want to do it himself just to

Shadow of a Lie

get rid of me. Now, though, I was heading north to pick Gary's brains. Sure, I could do that over the phone, but there is nothing like watching a person's facial cues to know what they are not saying.

Truly, I doubted this trip would reveal anything, but you never know …

CHAPTER 40

ASHLEY WASN'T USED TO BEING A MAVERICK. HE WAS A rule follower, a straight-A guy who toed the line and could be relied upon to make sure others around him did the same. Not that other cops were all engaged in dodgy practices – nothing of the sort – but Ashley recognised that he was something of a boy scout.

Until today. Well, actually, until he chose to pretend to misinterpret DCI Harris's instructions and pursue the Craig Chowdry case when he knew he was supposed to do anything but. That was three days ago, and his decision had backfired in a more combustible manner than he could ever have imagined, yet here he was still doing it.

He knew why. It was because they were close.

Except somehow, they were not, and therein lay the conundrum.

What they had at this point, a mere two days into the investigation, was essentially nothing. Regardless, someone thought they were on the right track, as evidenced by the slashed tyres and attempted murder. So they were close, but they were yet to figure out where or how.

Only persistence would reveal that which they were yet

Shadow of a Lie

to realise had made their quarry nervous, and that was what brought him back to Goodnestone.

Mrs Judy Travers, fifty-seven, worked in a hairdressing salon. A small, privately run thing located near what could be loosely described as the village centre. She was neither owner nor partner, but the third full-time person employed by the other two.

Expecting to find her at work, Ashley was rewarded with a full house of ladies in chairs being cut, coloured, crimped, and curled, a lineup of other ladies waiting to be seen, and two more set off to one side with their heads stuffed inside giant helmet looking things he suspected to be hairdryers.

Every single face looked his way when he entered the premises.

Raising his warrant card, he introduced himself and aimed his eyes at Judy Travers.

"Can I have a word in private, please?"

"Is this about my Shane and what happened last night?"

"Yes," Ashley replied automatically upon hearing the expectation in Mrs Travers' voice.

"Good. Someone needs to lose their job over that debacle. You'll have to wait though. I'm halfway through Mrs Davies' highlights. Shouldn't be more than another half an hour."

Mrs Travers turned back to her customer, pulling a clump of hair to then slather it with mauve coloured muck. Ashley watched, fascinated to see her then wrap it in tinfoil and move on to the next clump.

"What did I miss?" asked Mrs Davies, her eyes searching for those of her hairdresser. "Did something happen to Shane?"

Ashley stayed quiet, listening to the conversation as

STEVE HIGGS

Mrs Travers told the trapped salon audience all about how her poor boy had been wrongly arrested for involvement in some kind of shooting incident when he had, in fact, been sitting on the couch watching the footie with his mates. He'd appeared this morning with two black eyes. The result of police brutality, she claimed.

The ladies in the shop all looked Ashley's way at that point, putting the young detective on the spot.

Clearing his throat, he said, "Any allegation of heavy-handedness will be investigated, and charges levied against the perpetrators if found guilty. Such things might have happened in the past, but that is where they belong." What he really wanted to say was that Shane arrived at the station with the black eyes and most likely received them at the hands of his 'so called' mates.

With the ladies still remarking about how deplorable it all was, Judy had to wait for it to die down before she could bring the focus of attention back to where she felt it belonged – on her.

"Yes, well, that nice Detective Sergeant Beckett said that it wasn't one of the local cops who arrested him, but some clever clogs from London who wants to reopen that nonsense about Craig Chowdry going missing."

Her announcement prompted more comments, and the conversation continued until Judy had coated the whole of Mrs Davies' hair with the mauve gloop. The process made Ashley glad his hair required nothing more than a fortnightly cut to keep it stylish. Seeing that Mrs Travers was finishing up, he moved toward her.

She handed Mrs Davies a magazine. "Right, love. You need ten minutes, then I'll be back to start taking it all off, okay?" She washed her hands, dried them on a towel, and looked expectantly at Ashley's face.

In a back room among shelves stacked with bottles

Shadow of a Lie

upon bottles of hair-related products, he finally got to pose some carefully worded questions. Convinced she would clam up or possibly go nuts if she for one moment suspected he was the one who arrested her son last night, he started with a broad-spectrum apology.

"I'm sorry to hear about what happened to your son, Mrs Travers. Have no fear, there will be an enquiry."

Reading the subtext of his words, she said, "That's not what you are here for though?"

"I need to ask a question about a rug, Mrs Travers." He watched her face to see how she reacted. If she knew her rug had been used to conceal Craig's body, she showed no sign.

She pulled a confused face. "A rug?"

Prepared for the moment, Ashley withdrew the photograph of Shane in her living room. This was going to go one of two ways: she would either realise the significance of the date when the rug left her living room and become agitated, or she would not. Like Tony with Trudy Lawrence, Ashley knew he would be much better positioned to pose his questions under caution in an interview room and wished it were an option.

"This rug, Mrs Travers." He held the photograph so she could easily see it. "The one Shane is standing on. Can you tell me what happened to it? This could be important for Shane. There are some detectives looking into the Craig Chowdry case again and it is best to be ahead of any discrepancies they may seek to exploit." There was no need to mention he was the one looking for the discrepancy.

Her face pinched, her eyebrows descending as she gave thought to the question.

"It got burnt," she replied after perhaps five seconds to consult her memory. "Shane had some friends over and ... well, Shane never said it, but I think it was that Andy

237

STEVE HIGGS

Curzon who did it. He smokes," she uttered the word like it was an accusation of criminal activity. "I was always telling him off for it because even when he went outside the smell of smoke would drift back in. And it lingers," she complained. "Anyway, that's what Shane told me. He was most apologetic, but then he usually is when he messes up. He said it was ruined and had taken it to the tip already."

Ashley tucked the six by four back into his jacket. The answer told him everything and nothing at the same time.

"Can you recall, Mrs Travers, what day of the week it was when you came home and the rug was gone?"

If it vanished the same day as Craig Chowdry, the likelihood it was used to conceal the boy's body would increase exponentially. However, there were five days between Craig disappearing and the photograph in which the rug no longer appeared. Unless she said the 8th, he was nowhere.

Again, Mrs Travers gave the question some thought, her eyes rolling up and to the left as she engaged the memory portion of her brain. Few people know how to read the facial cues, but police officers are trained for it. Her actions, involuntary and automatic as they were, told him she was likely to answer truthfully. Had her eyes gone up and right, she would be engaging the imagination centre of her brain, an indication that her response was likely to be a lie.

"I'm not sure," she murmured, still thinking. "I know I was annoyed about it because we had a houseful of guests a few days later for my birthday. I ordered a new one from Argos, but it didn't come in time."

"Would it have been early in the week or the previous weekend?" Ashley attempted to prompt her memory.

She huffed a breath through her nose, her lips skewed to one side.

Shadow of a Lie

"No, I don't recall. I'm sorry. It was seven years ago. Is it important?"

"It could be."

"Well, if I was forced to guess, I would say it was either the Monday or the Tuesday."

Ashley gave a small nod of his head to acknowledge her response and wrote it in his notebook. It was good enough. The rug vanished right around the same time as Craig. It wasn't evidence as such; they would need to have been seen with the rug for that, but it was another little piece of the puzzle. If he got enough pieces, they could solve the whole thing.

Except he wasn't on the case and would struggle to find just cause to bring any of his suspects in for questioning.

Thanking Mrs Travers for her time, he said, "You'll need to get back to Mrs Davies, yes?"

She flipped her arm over to check her watch, Judy being one of those persons who wears it so the face is under her wrist not on top.

"Goodness, yes." She hurried from the storeroom, leaving Ashley to follow.

He was halfway through the door, his hand reaching back for the handle to close it behind him when he heard Shane Travers' nasal whine.

"Oh, hi, love," said Judy in greeting. Her voice showed she was not expecting his visit. "We were just talking about you. Trying to clear up that awful business from last night."

Ashley saw her turning around to include the person she thought was behind her. He reversed fast, getting back inside the storeroom before Shane could twist his neck to look that way.

Cursing, Ashley fought against his need to cower out of sight. Criminals were supposed to hide from him, not the other way around! Taking a deep breath, he placed his

STEVE HIGGS

hand back on the door handle. Shane would start shouting the moment he saw Ashley's face and he would have to deal with the jeering and accusations from all the ladies in the salon.

Readying himself, Ashley almost changed his mind when Mrs Travers described the police officer she had been talking to and Shane screeched in rage. However, he would not be found skulking in a storeroom and was damned if he would climb out of the window to escape the situation.

Snatching the door open, his plan to confront Shane Travers and the lies about his black eyes went instantly sideways.

Outside the door wasn't Shane Travers, but all four boys. At the back, Shane Travers was almost lost from sight, his body all but eclipsed by the taller men in front.

Ashley opened his mouth to demand they step aside, but Curzon's right fist lashed out, catching his solar plexus to drive the air from his lungs. Instinctively, Ashley went with the blow, moving backwards while keeping his feet beneath his body.

Gasping for air, he got only a moment to reset himself – Curzon was already advancing, flanked on both sides by Botterill and French. He was hemmed in with no avenue of escape, but Ashley had a long history of martial arts and knew how to defend himself at close quarters.

"You don't know when to leave well enough alone, do you?" Curzon sneered as he lined up to deliver the next blow.

Ashley watched Curzon draw back his right arm, telegraphing the punch to let his opponent know it was coming. As a practiced fighter that was all the time he needed and more. Bringing his left arm up to block the swing, Ashley folded the same arm around Curzon's,

Shadow of a Lie

holding him in place to deliver a stiff palm to the bigger man's throat.

Squeals of alarm came from the salon, the ladies far from entertained by the sounds of a brawl breaking out.

Curzon fell back, gasping for breath. That made room for French and Botterill to move in. Neither looked all that confident, but they came together, both with their arms raised in classic boxer poses.

Though still winded from the first punch, Ashley twisted off his left leg, feigned a side kick to French's core, then grabbed his arms when French tried to make his whole body swerve in panic.

Turning the elbow joint of French's right arm against itself, Ashley levered him around and into Botterill when he came forward to throw a punch.

Deep inside his head, Ashley acknowledged that he was having fun. He sparred most weeks as part of his training, but there was never any real threat of injury and the people he fought against were all distinguished martial artists. Coming up against four idiots with no fight training was a joy.

His moment of mental jubilation ended when an industrial sized bottle of conditioner caught him full in the face. It shunted Ashley's head back with its five-kilo weight. Curzon had thrown it. Down, but far from out, the biggest of the four men showed good fighting sense in choosing to employ that which fell to hand.

The blow stunned the detective, his fingers losing their grip on Danny French's arm. He could have overpowered all four, called for backup and had them all arrested. It would have caused a big headache since he wasn't supposed to be in Goodnestone asking questions, but the situation went beyond such minor concerns the moment Curzon threw his first punch.

STEVE HIGGS

His skull buzzing and his vision fuzzy, Ashley gritted his teeth as the four men bundled him to the floor. They were killers, he knew that already, so when the back of his head smacked into the unyielding surface and he tasted blood in his mouth, Ashley questioned which one of them might be carrying a knife.

CHAPTER 41

"Tony! How are you, old boy?" Gary greeted me with more enthusiasm than I expected. It made me wonder if he had much contact with members of the old firm. Moving out of the area must have killed his circle of friends, and if he was as stay-at-home as he made it sound, then he probably hadn't made many new ones.

I stuck out my hand only to have him slap it to one side and pull me into a hug.

I returned it, unsure what else I could do, and was thankful he let me go a second later.

"Sally!" he called over his shoulder, gesticulating with one arm that I should come in. "Sally, Tony is here." I'd never met his wife, so wasn't sure why he thought she would find the news so exciting. "Come in, come in," he insisted. "Don't worry about taking off your shoes. The dog doesn't wipe its feet."

No dog had barked, but I saw why a moment later. Looking through his house, I could see all the way to the back where patio doors showed his garden. There, pawing at the glass, was a young spaniel.

I brushed my shoes on the mat outside his front door

STEVE HIGGS

and again on the one inside, though I was confident my shoes were clean.

Sally appeared in the living room, coming from the kitchen, I guessed. Like Gary, she was just the wrong side of sixty, but wearing it well. Where Gary's middle was a good few inches rounder than the last time I saw him, his wife showed no sign of middle-aged spread. Her hair was a light blonde though undoubtedly coloured, and sat around her head in a neat crown that fell to below her jawline but did not reach her shoulders. At five feet and seven inches tall in flat shoes, she would have towered over Gary had she worn heels when they were younger, and I idly wondered if she had stuck with less elegant shoes due to that fact.

I offered her my hand, and was thankful that she didn't also try to pull me into a hug.

"Hello, I'm Tony."

"Sally," she replied. "Can I get you a tea or a coffee?"

"Tea if it's no bother."

"It's no bother." She about turned to head back into their kitchen, leaving me with Gary.

"There's cake too," Gary added, calling after his wife, "Don't forget the cake, love."

Her voice echoed back, "How could I after you insisted I bake it?" There was an air of criticism in her tone that went right over her husband's head.

"Have a seat, old boy," Gary offered me an armchair and reversed into its twin set at an angle that forced us to sit diagonally across the seat cushions to face one another. "How are you? How are things? Looking forward to retirement?"

I afforded Gary a few moments to do the necessary catch up – this was a social call as much as it was a business

Shadow of a Lie

one. Old friends are precious things not to be dismissed lightly.

Sally brought tea in a teapot on a tray along with cups and saucers, a matching jug filled with milk, and a matching bowl filled with sugar cubes. There was a tiny pair of silver tongs for the sugar, tiny spoons to stir the tea, and an eight-inch round Victoria sponge filled with jam and cream. There were plates for the cake and a knife to cut it.

She set the whole lot down on a low table set between the two armchairs and backed away. Sally played the role of hostess to perfection, my swirling thoughts about how to steer Gary onto the subject of Craig Chowdry taking a momentary detour to question what their marriage was like.

Mary would never wait on me like that. I felt privileged when she brought me a cup of tea. Gary had enough sense to echo my words when I thanked his wife, but I think he genuinely wouldn't have said a word had I not prompted him.

Sally's departing comment of, "You're welcome," caused a lull in our conversation and I seized it.

"Craig Chowdry."

Gary dropped his smile, replacing it with a suitable sombre expression.

"Yes. You said you wanted to ask me a few questions about the case. You've been assigned to a task force sent to reopen a stack of old, unsolved murders?" He wanted to check his understanding.

I gave him an abridged version of what led to my inclusion.

"You think you got the job because of Bruce Denton?"

I shrugged, not wanting to discuss the case, but felt I had to say, "Maybe. It's more likely I got the job because

245

STEVE HIGGS

I'm weeks from retirement and there's no point giving me anything else. I'm little more than a local guide slash mentor for the youngster they've teamed me with."

"But you're actively pursuing a solution to Craig's disappearance?"

"We are."

Gary decided the tea had been left to infuse for long enough, so gave the teapot a swirl in the air and poured a test sample into his own cup. Happy it was dark enough, he filled my cup and then his own.

"Help yourself to cake."

When I failed to seize upon the chance to do precisely that, Gary used the knife to slice a large wedge from it. I thought it was for himself, but he handed the plate to me, along with a small fork that was dwarfed by the cake in the same way that a teaspoon is a poor tool for excavating a grave.

He took a second equally gargantuan slice for himself and simply bit into it, crumbs spilling back to the plate.

"So, what do you want to know?" he mumbled around a mouthful of spongey, delicious goodness.

And that was the question really. What did I want to ask? I chose to not beat around the bush.

"Do you think they did it?"

"The four boys?"

"Yes."

"Yes."

There it was. Plain and simple. Gary was the family liaison officer at the time of the case. Assigned to handle Mr and Mrs Chowdry, their needs, the press where it pertained to them, and to be a singular face they could trust through the terrible ordeal.

"How did they not get caught?" I forked a piece of the cake into my mouth, refraining from using my hands

Shadow of a Lie

to avoid getting them greasy. My tastebuds lit up instantly, and I had to rally my senses to focus on Gary's response.

He swallowed his mouthful. "Well, there was no body for a start. That would have made conviction all but impossible as you know. They hid it well and they were able to keep their stories straight through their questioning. Not that I questioned any of them, you understand, but that was what I heard, and it was evident in the daily reports there were doubts about their guilt right from the start."

"But *you* think they did it?"

"Yes."

"Why?"

Gary's arm paused halfway to his mouth, the cake moving around in the air as he used his hand to accentuate his next point.

"There was no one else in the frame for it. They tried to get him to fight earlier that day and were heard threatening him. On the day he went missing, a witness saw the boys returning to the village from the direction of Craig's house." Gary frowned for a moment. "I don't recall the name of the witness who saw them ..."

"Jane Wallace," I supplied.

"Yes, that's right. I remember thinking it was a breakthrough at the time, especially when they discovered Craig's blood between his house and the point where they were seen crossing the road, but it didn't lead to anything. No body means no murder. They accounted for their time and each of the boys, when interviewed individually, managed to keep their stories straight. I recall at the time I thought it odd. Even when witnesses or suspects are innocent, their stories never line up."

It was the prompt I'd been waiting for. I could have

introduced the subject of suspect coaching myself, but it was far better that he'd arrived at it independently.

"Gary." I made sure I had his attention. "Could the boys have been helped by someone inside the investigation?" Surprise, or possibly even shock, registered in his eyes, and I pressed on before he could respond. "They are just as well rehearsed now. Seven years later, their stories line up and they know precisely what to say to deflect our questions. When they were being interviewed, could someone have made sure they knew what to say? Could someone inside the investigation have helped them cover up the murder?"

Gary's eyes flared. I had waited until his mouth was full of cake before asking the question, knowing he would need time to chew and swallow before he could answer. Now I waited to hear what he wanted to say.

His automatic response was to shoot me down, but in choosing my moment, his delayed reaction gave him time to think. By the time his mouth was clear, the cogs had turned, and his startled face was gone. One of horrified recognition replaced it.

He not only knew I was right, he knew who had done it. The blood drained from Gary's face, his eyes taking on a haunted expression.

I fixed him in place with flint-hard eyes. "Who was it, Gary?"

CHAPTER 42

In Goodnestone, when the cops arrived at the hair salon with lights flashing and sirens wailing, the fight inside was long over. Having knocked the detective down, the four boys retreated, vacating the storeroom so they could lock it from the outside.

That left Ashley the time he needed to recover from the dizziness he felt. The bottle, large as it was, had been thrown with force. Had it collided with his nose it would have squashed it flat. Instead, it hit to the side of his left eye, right on the temple, snapping his head to the side and back in a whiplash effect. Then his head hit the floor just as hard, jarring his skull. His head hurt, but the throbbing was beginning to subside.

His neck felt bruised or strained, overextended might be a better word, but whatever it was, Ashley doubted he would visit the dojo in the next couple of weeks.

Demanding the door be opened and reminding everyone outside that he was the police officer and had just been assaulted by four men, he was surprised to find not only that his assailants were still there, their taunting voices echoing through the wall, but that Mrs Travers was willing

249

STEVE HIGGS

to back them up. She wasn't letting him out and claimed to have called 'the real cops'.

Mercifully, Ashley didn't have to wait long for the local cops to arrive, but that was where things went from bad to worse.

According to his assailants, who gave their account first while he was still trapped behind a locked door, he initiated the fight, attacking Andrew Curzon in a bid to get to Shane Travers. Most of the ladies in the salon had no view of the storeroom door, located as it was down a corridor leading from the back of the shop. However, those who did, stated either that they could not see who threw the first punch, or that they thought it had to be the man locked inside the storeroom.

When the uniforms approached the storeroom announcing their intention to enter, Ashley identified himself and had his warrant card open and ready when they finally opened the door.

Obviously, he countered the claim that he started the fight, but the officers were acting on the orders of DCI Pascoe. Once they'd informed their boss who they had in custody, Ashley knew what had to follow and made no attempt to resist when the constables demanded he accompany them back to Wingham station.

The officers cautioned Curzon, French, and the other two of their need to remain available for questioning but showed no interest in arresting them despite Ashley's assurance they had jointly assaulted a man they knew in advance to be a police detective.

He wasn't cuffed, there being no requirement for him to be restrained, but had to sit in the back of their squad car when the two officers drove him back to Wingham.

In the quiet solitude of his own thoughts, Ashley asked himself what this would mean when his boss found out.

Shadow of a Lie

He'd known better, that was the real kicker. His boss gave a simple order: go to Whitstable and investigate the Michelle Canet murder. He chose not to, and his current situation was the result.

Feeling morose, he uttered not one single word all the way to the Wingham nick where he knew DCI Pascoe was going to tear him into strips before contacting DCI Harris so he could do the same.

They would both see this afternoon's incident as a further example of him disobeying orders, and worse than that, might view it as harassment of a witness. That's what Shane Travers alleged at the scene. Given the likelihood that Ashley faced a charge of wrongful arrest that occurred only a few hours before and that he lied to Mrs Travers about his reason for visiting the salon, the only thing working in his favour was the ability to claim he had no idea Shane would appear at the same location.

They would believe him, but ultimately it wouldn't make a whole lot of difference.

Staring at the countryside flashing past his window, Ashley Long hoped Tony might have fared better.

CHAPTER 43

"TONY," I MUTTERED TO MYSELF, GLANCING DOWN AT MY speedo to make sure I wasn't going too far over the speed limit, "you have a knack for getting yourself into bad situations."

For the fourth time in as many minutes, I thumbed the button to call Ashley and listened to it ring without being answered. Why the heck wasn't Ashley answering his phone? It was just like last night when I needed him. In hindsight, I should have waited for him or called someone else for backup, but at the time I believed I was doing the right thing.

Nevertheless, here I was again, unable to raise my partner and questioning who else I could possibly call.

Gary only needed to say the name of the man most likely to be behind the cover up, but he did more than that, he also told me why. It wasn't something that appeared in any of the reports, case notes, or anywhere else, and it wasn't known by the general population or the other officers working the case.

In fact, Gary only found out when he asked DCI Pascoe why he wasn't handling the interviews himself.

Shadow of a Lie

DCI Pascoe is the godfather of Shane Travers. Such a relationship won't show up on a database anywhere. It's not recorded electronically or written down, other than possibly at the church where a child is christened, and there is no way to search for it.

I knew Shane's father was out of the picture, but hadn't read far enough to discover he was dead. More importantly, he died in the line of duty many years earlier and joined the police on the exact same day as Hector Pascoe.

I recalled my training; it's not the kind of thing one forgets. You forge bonds enduring tough circumstances and clearly that happened between Pascoe and Shane's father.

Appointed as the senior investigating officer for what soon proved to be a high-profile case, DCI Pascoe would have been overjoyed to gain such exposure when the SIO would otherwise normally be a superintendent.

Craig Chowdry's disappearance wasn't listed as a murder. That was how Pascoe managed to snag the appointment, but should have turned the case down the moment he realised he was directly connected to one of the primary suspects. No doubt at the start, he saw the shining lights of a promotion to superintendent on the cards, and the case, beaming straight into peoples' homes via the medium of television, was just what he needed to raise his own profile.

However, when he discovered his own godson was in the frame for Craig Chowdry's murder, instead of holding up his hands and having someone else take his place, he kept quiet and made sure the charges couldn't stick. Maybe he just didn't think it through. Maybe he panicked. Goodness knows what went through his head, but once he'd started, possibly telling Shane what to say and how to act, he realised he would have to get all four of them off.

No. I shook my head. It had to be worse than that. If

STEVE HIGGS

DCI Pascoe spoke to his godson and learned it was one of the other boys who killed Craig, he would have made him confess, convinced Shane to come clean so he would walk free. That he hadn't done so meant Shane was the killer, and since I didn't buy that, it meant they all were.

The second option made sense too. If it was any one of them who did the deed, the others would have cracked during interview and chosen to save themselves. Instead, whoever went first made the other boys take a turn, each of them stabbing Craig - I guessed a knife would be the murder weapon purely from the prevalence of knife crime in the UK. They were all equally guilty and motivated to keep the truth hidden.

To protect Shane, Pascoe had to bring the other boys into his conspiracy to protect his godson, but it went even deeper than that. The boys hid the body, and the police never found it. I would challenge any teenager to pull that off. It takes brains, knowledge, plus access to the right equipment, and a location to make a body disappear. That or a fat helping of luck.

Pascoe must have found out where the boys stashed Craig's body and moved it. He would have needed to do it all himself; he couldn't bring anyone else in to help.

I'd suspected he was lying from the start, but still found myself reeling now that I knew the how and why.

Gary discovered the truth about Pascoe's connection to Shane after the investigation collapsed. Teams of officers roamed the countryside around Goodnestone for more than a week, combing the land shoulder to shoulder looking for traces of ... anything. With no body to prove they were investigating a murder and no physical evidence such as blood on any of the suspects, there really was no case.

There were no other suspects and though the boys

Shadow of a Lie

were watched for some time after the case against them was abandoned, there remained no actionable reason to believe they were lying.

Gary hadn't taken part in the interviews. As family liaison officer, his work was elsewhere, but not long after, when he was tasked with breaking down the incident room and sending it all to general registry, he noted his boss had stringently avoided interviewing Shane Travers. Every single time Shane was questioned, it was someone else asking the questions.

Gary was friends with his boss outside of work, the two meeting semi-regularly for a few pints or a game of golf. Feeling courageous one particular evening, Gary asked why Pascoe avoided the interviews and got an answer, something Pascoe clearly regretted once he had sobered up because they never went out for a drink again and shortly thereafter Gary discovered he was being transferred out of Wingham to work at another nick.

Guiltily, Gary admitted he'd wondered once or twice if there was something untoward about the case collapsing the way it did, but never felt inclined to pursue it.

I was running when I left Gary's house, my tea still warm and untouched in its fancy cup. Doing more than eighty down the M2 on my way to Wingham or Goodnestone – I was yet to decide which – I continued to call Ashley without success.

Did I call my boss instead? I wasn't exactly on his best side. And what would I tell him anyway? I still didn't have any evidence to prove DCI Pascoe aided the boys to get away with murder. Knowing he did it isn't even close to being the same thing. The situation required a plan of action and that started by linking up with my partner.

Together we could get ourselves put back on the case. Now that we could show DCI Pascoe had an undivulged connection to a primary suspect, they would have to endorse our request for the case to be formally reopened. Not this penny-pinching paperwork exercise to appease the chief constable, but a real investigation with a new SIO.

I wouldn't be involved. At least I doubted I would. Ashley might though, ensured a position of worth in the team because of his knowledge of the case. That would be good enough.

Agitated by Ashley's lack of response, not even a text to say he couldn't answer the call, I continued to argue my next step all the way back to the Kentish countryside.

Reaching the outskirts of Wingham, I pulled off the road to think. It was twenty to four which meant I hadn't heard from Ashley in almost three hours. Yesterday someone shot at me and that thought resounded like a death knell in my head.

Was he okay? Could his lack of response indicate he was in trouble? I didn't want to leap to any conclusions, but if Pascoe could feel us closing in, what desperate measures might he be willing to take? It had to have been he who shot at me last night, he who scared Shane Travers away before he could spill the beans.

Uneasiness rising, I called Ashley's number again.

CHAPTER 44

"COME ON, MAN! YOU CAN HEAR IT RINGING!" ASHLEY raged through gritted teeth. Processing him into the station like a common suspect came as a shock until he realised Pascoe must have directed it as a punishment. His personal belongings were confiscated by the custody officer and were only now being returned after the distinct dressing down – his second for the day – that he got from the resident DCI.

What stung more than the one-way conversation was the absolute knowledge that he deserved it. Yet again, this was his screw up. The opportunity to run his own investigations, almost like a freelance detective, and have the chance of bagging a worthwhile and long overdue arrest or two seemed like a dream job at the start.

Tony called it a paperwork exercise, a crap job intended to do nothing more than show the chief constable for Kent was taking the national audit of unsolved murders seriously. Was that it? Was he never really expected to close any of the old cases?

An hour after arriving at Wingham nick, his possessions were being returned, but in the manner and at the

STEVE HIGGS

speed of a man bored with a task he'd performed ten thousand times before. The custody officer wouldn't allow a detainee to hurry him, even if they *were* being released because they hadn't done anything wrong. That the man before him was a fellow police officer made not the slightest difference.

The phone, which had been ringing on and off for most of the last hour was finally handed over just as it switched to voicemail. Snatching it from the custody officer's hands, Ashley saw the name displayed and the number of missed calls: eighteen!

Punching the screen to call him back, Ashley turned away from the custody officer and pressed the phone to his ear so he could hear.

"Oi! You've to sign for that!" the custody officer warned.

Ashley mouthed a two word reply and started talking the moment the call connected.

"Tony, you're not going to believe what happened," he blurted, stepping outside while the custody officer continued to complain. The rest of his items were still on the desk waiting for him to retrieve them. That included his car keys, so it wasn't as if he was about to abscond.

The custody officer clearly thought so too as he was making no effort to bring Ashley back inside.

Checking left and right to make sure he wasn't being overheard, Ashley was about to give Tony a quick run down on the last few hours' events when his mouth stopped moving.

"What?" Ashley asked. Had he heard that correctly?

Tony repeated what he had just said. "Pascoe is Shane Travers' godfather. That's the connection. That's the reason. We've got him, Ashley, but we need something more. Running to your boss, or mine for that matter, with

258

Shadow of a Lie

nothing more substantial than a connection between the SIO and a prime suspect will get things moving, but if we have a statement from one of the witnesses confirming that he or she was leaned on, coerced, or otherwise instructed by DCI Pascoe to provide either false evidence or to leave out something vital …"

"Like Jane Wallace not seeing the boys with the rug."

"Exactly, Ashley. Jane Wallace came forward to give her statement independently, but what if she talked with DCI Pascoe and he instructed her to omit that part from her statement and never speak of it again?"

"That's a dodgy game to play," Ashley remarked.

Tony agreed. "It sure is, but this is a game called getting away with murder, my boy. Everything about it is dodgy."

Ashley heard Tony release a sigh that sounded like bound up tension leaving his body. "Where are you now?" he asked.

"On the outskirts of Wingham. Where are you?"

"At the nick. I'll come to you."

"No!" Tony snapped. "Is Pascoe at the station?"

Ashley looked across the carpark. The station head was in fifteen minutes ago for sure because Ashley had been giving him a jolly good listening to.

Unsure how to answer, Ashley said, "I think so. I'll check. Why?"

"Because he is watching us. Seven years ago he did something that has probably haunted him ever since, but he will have allowed himself to believe it was in the past and forgotten. Then we started nosing around and now he can feel the noose tightening. He might have breathed a sigh of relief when he heard your boss took us off the case, but now he knows we are still poking around in his business and he's going to do whatever it takes to prevent us getting

STEVE HIGGS

to the truth. I want to know where he is, so we don't run into him."

"Give me two minutes. I'll find out." Ashley ended the call and returned to the bored custody officer where he signed for and retrieved his possessions. Pockets loaded, he made his way deeper into the station and up the stairs to check the DCI's office. The door was open as usual, the desk inside clearly unoccupied.

Ashley stopped, looking around for any sign of the nick's top man, when to his right Constable Blackburn exited the gents' toilet still straightening his uniform.

"Is the boss in?" Ashley asked, hoping he might know.

All he got was a shrug in reply and a grunted, "Boss don't ask my permission to go places."

He checked the DCI's office again, this time grabbing the door frame with both hands to hang through it. Pascoe definitely wasn't there. He wasn't anywhere else upstairs that Ashley could see, and a quick check confirmed he was not in the gents'.

Back downstairs Ashley wandered into the dispatch office in what he hoped was a casual, nonchalant manner. He used his phone to act distracted, feigning sending a text and glancing at the constable with his face glued to a screen and a headset clamped around his skull.

"Hey, um, is the DCI in or out, mate?" he asked, still sounding like it was a casual enquiry.

The constable's eyes never left the screen, his right hand shifting a mouse and clicking before he said, "Out. His car is moving anyway. Oh, in fact, it just stopped."

Concocting a lie on the spot, Ashley said, "He asked me to meet him but forgot to tell me where. Said he had something to show me." Ashley craned his neck around to look at the screen in front of the dispatcher's face. "Where is he, please?"

260

Shadow of a Lie

The constable tapped a key and read from the screen. "Lunsford Lane, Goodnestone. You want me to let him know you're en route?"

"No." Ashley said it too quickly, but the dispatcher showed no sign that he noticed or cared.

Leaving the station, Ashley dug around to get the keys from his pocket and called Tony back.

"He's back in Goodnestone, Tony. I can be there in fifteen."

"Goodnestone? Whereabouts?"

"Lunsford Lane. I don't recall where that is."

The name instantly triggered a memory in Tony's head. He knew it, he just didn't know why. Frowning, he consulted a map on his phone, zooming in and out while at the other end Ashley clambered into his car, got it started, and switched the call over to the car's speaker.

The blood ran out of Tony's face. "Lunsford Lane is where the church is. It's right at the edge of the village, less than fifty yards from where the boys crossed the B2046. If he's there, then he must be checking Craig's grave."

Ashley eased his car out of the carpark and into the road, proceeding in a casual, unhurried manner, but said, "I'm going to blue light it all the way."

CHAPTER 45

ASHLEY WAS GOING TO COME TO ME. THAT WAS GOOD, AND I almost told him to hurry until my brain supplied a better plan.

"No." I blurted. "Go find Jane Wallace. I'll do a drive by to see if I can spot Pascoe. If Wallace admits Pascoe coached her in any way, we will have enough to take this higher. The church, if that is where they buried Craig, will just look like a church and a churchyard. But if he is still there, I'll see if I can spot where he goes. He might lead me right to the grave."

Ashley's voice betrayed his concern. "Tony, you know it was probably Pascoe who shot at you last night, right? Who better to cover their own tracks than the guy leading the investigation?"

Who better indeed?

"Don't worry, I won't approach him. I'll do a drive by the churchyard to see if I can spot him. If he's moved on, I'll go to see Trudy Lawrence again. Now that we know who it was, we can lean on people to admit DCI Pascoe led the cover up. We only need one of them to say it, Ashley. That's all it will take to bring it all down."

262

Shadow of a Lie

Ashley made it apparent he didn't like my plan, but saw the sense in it. We ended the call and sitting in the quiet of my car, I was shocked to find my hand shook when I lifted it to grip my steering wheel.

"Come on, Tony," I huffed at myself. I was just going to do a drive by for goodness sake, but the impact of last night's terror was making itself known. I'd done a great job of ignoring it thus far, pushing it down and distracting myself by focussing on anything but getting chased through the woods by an armed gunman.

A shuddering, slow breath left my body, my head tilted back, and my eyes closed. Clenching my fists, I uttered a bark of determination, snapped my eyes open, and grabbed the steering wheel.

It was time to get this done.

A mile down the road I had to force my hands to relax their strangler's grip on the steering wheel. Had I ever been this tense on the job before? I'd had to chase criminals on foot in the past. Not often, admittedly, but it happened, and I could not remember feeling before the sense of dread that stole through my body now.

I was close to becoming a quivering wreck. Was this the aftereffects of last night? The superintendent wanted me to speak with the appointed psychiatrist, but that was just routine. I had no intention of going. Now I was questioning the wisdom of that decision.

Taking a deep breath and releasing it slowly, I continued to drive, muttering to myself to 'get a grip' and 'man up', the whole way.

The views of fields changed to houses as I came into Goodnestone, my heart rate rising though I told it not to. I was going to do a quick drive by of the church, fully intending to keep my promise not to get any closer. But despite the rising fear, I knew I would do the exact opposite if I saw Pascoe nosing around in the graveyard that wrapped around the ancient building.

That Craig could have ended up in someone else's grave had been one of my first thoughts. There was no evidence to support it, save for the boys' route that day. They crossed the B2046 and came through the woodland behind the church. Reaching it, they had the option to go anywhere in the village, but if they went beyond the church while carrying a body wrapped in a rug, they would have been seen and caught.

Turning my car into Lunsford Lane, I slowed. My heart beating even harder, jacking my pulse up to what had to be a dangerous level. It was making me feel slightly faint, and I was getting annoyed about it.

"Tony, you are a seasoned detective," I snarled at myself. "Get a grip. He's not going to have his gun with him."

The certainty that I was right had virtually no impact on my heart rate, but when I drew level with the graveyard and could find no sign of either the DCI or his car, it began to slow.

Had I taken too long to get here?

I stopped the car for a moment, letting the engine idle in the middle of the road. There was no one else in the street, but chewing my lip and questioning if I ought to just push on to Trudy Lawrence's house, I spotted Pascoe's Audi.

It was down the street, beyond the churchyard, parked out of the way in front of an old, fading BMW. The DCI was wise enough to mask his movements, leaving his car not at the church, but outside the house closest to it.

Heart thumping again, I looked for a spot of my own. I didn't want my car to be too far away from the church. DCI Pascoe might not be all that much younger than me,

Shadow of a Lie

but he would be faster. It still sounded ridiculous that he might try to kill me, but that's precisely what I believed he tried to do last night. Daylight might dissuade him from a second attempt, but I doubted it. If he saw me here, he would know the game was up and his only chance to escape justice would be to eliminate me before I could talk.

I wanted to keep driving, honestly I did, but stubbornness and a refusal to acknowledge the terror welling in my gut forced me from my car. If Pascoe was in the churchyard, I wanted to see precisely where.

CHAPTER 46

CAUTIOUSLY, I MADE MY WAY INTO THE CHURCHYARD, passing under an ancient stone archway leading from the street to an old, winding footpath. It wended its way through the grass past graves to my left and right that were so old the words inscribed into them had worn away.

The footpath led to the church doors, oak things hewn from a tree or trees many hundreds of years ago. I turned left before I reached them, skirting around the church and keeping close to it so I could peer around the corner.

There was no sign of Pascoe yet, but the churchyard extended fifty yards past the back of the church, so there was a lot of ground still to check.

Sidling down the side of the building, I came to the next corner. Peering around it once more, and feeling like a cartoon character with my eyeballs on stalks, I looked and listened for any sign of the DCI.

His car was here, but I couldn't find him. Was he inside the church?

Five minutes later, having walked all the way to the back of the churchyard, and all the way back along the other side, I could only conclude that he was either not

Shadow of a Lie

here, saw me coming and was better at hiding than I was at looking, or he was inside the church itself.

Dismissing the first two possibilities, I accepted the only remaining option and went to the church door. The ball of worry in my gut had grown heavier with the passage of each passing minute, and I genuinely wondered if I might vomit. If Pascoe was inside, he would look up the moment I entered. He would see me, and he would give chase when I ran.

Essentially, at this point, I was gambling that I could cover the hundred-ish yards back to my car and get it started before he could catch me. I didn't like my chances. Nevertheless, my refusal to give in to my fears prevailed.

I gripped the door handle, twisted it, and gave the door a shove.

It was locked.

Standing back, a perplexed expression claiming my features, I glared accusingly at the doors. Had he locked them from the inside? I didn't believe that could be the case, so what did that leave?

Turning around to stare at DCI Pascoe's Audi, there really was only one answer left: the church was never his destination. That wasn't why he came to this part of Goodnestone at all.

So ... what? Where was he? He parked his car in front of the house closest to the church. Was that where he was? He lived in Wingham; I knew that much, so it wasn't his property. Unless he owned more than one, which was a possibility.

Reflecting on my belief the four boys brought Craig's carpet-wrapped body this way, I'd already concluded they couldn't go much further than the church without being seen. The house right next to the church, though. They could go there.

STEVE HIGGS

Drawn to it now, like a piece of steel to a magnet, my feet were moving before I considered telling them to go.

The church dominated the lane, large oak and sycamore trees casting shadows across the front section of the churchyard and spilling over into the street where their autumn leaves filled the gutters and covered the pavement.

There were no houses on the other side of the road, instead the church and the properties to its left and right looked out over scrubland taken over by wild blackberry brambles and gorse bushes. There were tracks through it, worn down by foot traffic where locals walked their dogs or took a shortcut to the village shops. In all, perhaps twenty properties lined the street, each of them a small, detached bungalow except for two which had been built upward into two-storey family homes. I'd seen similar happening all over the county, builders making a killing buying cheap old homes and making them into something new and spectacular.

The first house looked quiet, no sign of life from within. I twisted around to stare at Pascoe's car again. If it was here, then he had to be also.

A path led around the side of the house to a back garden. Did the DCI own the place? I could find that out swiftly enough, but eagerness to spot Pascoe, confirm this was the right place, and slip away unnoticed, drove my feet to move again.

All I had to do was look over the fence separating the back garden from the front. Seconds, that was all I needed.

Except I'm not tall enough.

The six-foot fence sat atop a six-inch concrete plinth to stop it from rotting. I could try jumping to see over, but worried it would make too much noise, I looked around for something to stand on.

A plastic box filled with newspapers waiting to be recy-

Shadow of a Lie

cled provided the extra inches I needed. Carefully, I dumped the contents, upended the box, and placed it silently against the fence, holding my breath the whole time.

There was no sound from the back garden, or from the street in general. Not so much as a radio playing tunes in someone's kitchen. All I could hear was birdsong, the local wildlife oblivious to my perilous situation.

Standing on the flimsy plastic crate and questioning if it could take my weight, I pressed up onto my tiptoes and peered over the fence.

Still no sign of DCI Pascoe. I wanted to catch him in the process of exhuming the body, our investigation and continued doggedness making him so nervous he chose to move Craig to a different location. That was not the case though. The garden was just a garden, disappointingly devoid of macabre grave diggers.

Sighing, I was about to step gingerly back down to the ground when I heard the very unmistakable sound of a shotgun's breech snapping shut.

My eyes flared and my breath caught in the half heart-beat before someone jabbed it painfully into my back, pressing me into the fence to pin me there.

From behind my head came a simple instruction.

"Don't make a sound."

CHAPTER 47

PULLED FROM HER OFFICE TO SPEAK WITH YET ANOTHER police officer, Jane Wallace did nothing to hide the irritation she felt.

"This is starting to feel like harassment," she remarked while crossing the firm's reception area.

Ashley was thankful that Miss Wallace made herself available without making him wait long, but he wasn't sure why she considered a second visit to be so intrusive.

Rather than get into it, he said, "Thank you for seeing me. I'll try not to take up too much of your time."

Since leaving Wingham, Ashley had been running through the questions he wanted to ask. His simple aim was to determine if DCI Pascoe affected the statement she gave in 2016.

Jane sighed impatiently, but with a nod, invited the detective to accompany her into the office proper. She worked for an engineering company in an accounting role, something she neither enjoyed nor despised. Her coworkers were okay, if a little gossipy, and it was an easy commute she could conduct on foot unless it was raining.

She led Ashley to a meeting room where they could sit.

Shadow of a Lie

"I'll be recording this conversation, Miss Wallace. Is that okay?"

She shrugged her indifference.

Once settled into his chair, and with the interviewee in front of him, Ashley took a meandering approach, coming from an angle before going for the jugular if she exposed it.

"Jane, I want to take you back to August 12th of 2016."

"We did this two days ago, and you gave me your card asking that I call you if I remember anything else. I don't remember anything else." She did nothing to hide her irritation.

Ignoring her comment, Ashley said, "You were driving along the B2046 between Wingham and Aylsham at approximately 1712hrs hrs when you were forced to swerve to avoid a teenage boy standing in the road." He read the words directly from his phone where they were saved for easy recall.

"Yes, that's right. We covered this already. Will this take long? I have a lot I need to be doing."

Continuing to ignore her remarks and questions, Ashley persisted.

"That boy you later identified as Timothy Botterill, correct?"

"Yes."

"He was with three other boys who were standing on the western side of the road waiting to cross it."

"Yes, you know all this. The three boys were Daniel French, Andrew Curzon, and Shane Travers, four boys I don't know but whose names are indelibly etched into my brain. What about it?"

"What was on the ground next to them?" Had they been carrying a heavy roll of carpet, Ashley felt confident

STEVE HIGGS

Jane would remember it. Anyone would. Therefore, it had to be on the ground by their feet.

Jane blinked, the question unexpected.

"On the ground? I – I don't recall seeing anything on the ground. What are you asking?"

Ashley watched her face, looking for the subtle cues and clues that might indicate she was lying. There were none. It had been something of a long shot, but worth the try. The boys could have laid the body down out of sight until they were sure the road was clear. Or it was possible Jane never saw it, even though it was visible.

Pushing that to one side, Ashley changed tactic.

"Jane, the investigation has changed." He was going for broke and daring to believe he could get away with it by being right. "We believe the evidence and the witness statements were tampered with by one of the investigating officers."

Jane's eyebrows took a hike up her forehead.

"You mean someone in the police?" Her tone was innocent and filled with genuine surprise.

Ashley didn't want to give her the name he needed to hear. It would be so much more powerful if she said it first. Thinking like a defence lawyer, Ashley believed they would claim he led her, and that she only repeated Pascoe's name if he said it first.

"Jane, this is very important. I need you to answer with complete honesty."

"Of course." She was biting her bottom lip, drawn in by the serious tone Ashley employed.

"At any point during the initial investigation or since, has any police officer asked you to leave out any part of what you witnessed that day?"

Jane tilted her head to one side, the question about as far from what she expected as could be.

Shadow of a Lie

"Asked me to leave something out?" she repeated. "No."

"You're certain," Ashley felt he had to press her.

"Quite certain. I told them exactly what I saw, and they wrote it all down. They recorded it too."

Ashley slumped a little, both physically and emotionally. Jane had seen nothing DCI Pascoe felt a need to tamper with.

With nothing left to ask and a powerful desire to move on to the next potential witness – someone would cave and confirm Pascoe was behind the cover up – he turned off the voice recording function and stood up.

"Thank you, Miss Wallace. I won't take up any more of your time."

"Does that apply to your colleague as well? He's also bugged me twice in this week."

Ashley almost apologised for Tony, only catching himself as the sentence formed.

"My colleague?" To his knowledge, Tony had not spoken with Jane at any point.

"Yes, the tall one."

CHAPTER 48

THE SHOTGUN BARRELS BETWEEN MY SHOULDER BLADES eased a fraction, and I tried to turn my head to confirm I wasn't wrong about who owned the voice. He dug the gun into my skin again almost instantly.

"Keep your eyes forward and open the gate."

I complied. Like I had a choice. Bewildered by the turn of events, I could only assume Beckett was working for Pascoe. However, just like my confusion over Pascoe's motivation until Gary filled in the glaring blank, I had no clue why Beckett would involve himself in diverting the course of justice. Was it money? Did Pascoe have something on him?

Walking through the gate, I looked around again for any sign of the DCI. The pressure pushing me forward lessened once more, and I dared to turn, wanting to face Beckett so I could reason with him. I saw the shotgun butt coming for my face, but there was no time to react.

Stars danced across my vision, my brain disconnecting itself from my body. There was no actual pain, just a numb sensation as the day went dark and the ground came rushing up to claim me.

CHAPTER 49

SITTING IN HIS CAR, ASHLEY COULDN'T FIGURE OUT WHAT he'd just learned. Jane Wallace gave an accurate description of DS Beckett and knew his name. According to her, he'd visited twice in the last three days, the first time only hours after he and Tony appeared on the scene in Wingham.

Why?

He'd asked Jane much the same questions as Ashley, confirming what she recalled about the day, which direction the boys were going, what were they wearing, had she seen them carrying anything?

The natural assumption was that Beckett wasn't happy about having his colleagues' work dug over and tried to make sure the statements given now would correspond to those recorded seven years ago – Beckett didn't want Ashley and Tony to discover something his boss or friends missed.

That was the natural assumption, yet Ashley didn't think it was the right one. Trawling back across the last couple of days, his memory led him to the incident at Andrew Curzon's house. They were interviewing Sarah

STEVE HIGGS

and had just found a corner of her story to pick at. Before they could go any further, Curzon turned up, assaulted Sarah right in front of them. Then Beckett arrived.

He was responding to a report of a disturbance.

But there hadn't been one. They knocked calmly and politely on Sarah's door and though she argued briefly, she let them in. There was no noise that could have caused someone to report an incident until Curzon appeared. Beckett was there less than two minutes later.

Unsettled, Ashley called Wingham nick's dispatch desk.

"Yeah, hi, it's DS Long. Can I get you to check the log for me, please?"

He had to wait, though not for very long, and the answer, when he got it, made his heart stop.

There had been no report of a disturbance. In fact, there hadn't been a single 999 call placed anywhere around the time he and Tony were speaking to Sarah.

Perplexed, and seriously worried about the implications, Ashley tried to call Tony. The message went to voicemail, which spiked Ashley's concern several rungs higher until Tony sent him a text.

"Busy. Can't talk. I'll call you back."

Relaxing, though only a little, Ashley gave himself a minute to calm down and think about what the new information meant.

Pascoe had a direct link to Shane Travers, one of the prime suspects. Now Beckett was acting dodgy, but did that mean he was also involved? What was the likelihood of that? How far did this thing go? How many others were involved? Sarah French vanished after they left her with Beckett. Until now, he'd given it no thought. Suddenly, it seemed like a coincidence too huge to ignore.

Using his laptop to access the Police National Database, he checked for any connection between DCI Pascoe

Shadow of a Lie

and DS Beckett. There was none. Scratching his head, a random notion made him check Beckett's name against the piece of farmland Tony got so excited about.

With a ping, the system delivered the answer and Ashley almost left his chair.

CHAPTER 50

"DS HEATON," WHEEZED A VOICE NEAR MY EAR. "DS Heaton." It was weak and distant, though it also felt close, which confused me.

I flicked my eyes open, and the light hit the inside of my skull like molten lava. Snapping them tight shut, I tried to get my bearings.

"Tony, wake up," wheezed the voice.

My foggy, disoriented brain insisted I knew the voice. I tried to move, discovering instantly that my hands were tied behind my back. Shocked, I opened my eyes again and swivelled around. The pain was instant, but I fought against it, blinking as newsflashes came in from all over my body. It wasn't just my hands that were bound, it was my ankles too.

I could see the plastic tie pressing the fabric of my trousers to my legs. It was tight enough to cut off the circulation to my feet which were already going numb. However, I could still wiggle my toes and feel the inside of my shoes, so I could not have been out for very long.

My hands were likewise secured with a plastic tie, I could feel it with my fingertips. Around my head, a gag

Shadow of a Lie

kept a rag in place. It was stuffed inside my mouth, its presence making me want to vomit. I bit down against the rising bile lest I choke on it.

"DS Heaton," wheezed the voice once more, plaintive and afraid.

I had to roll and twist to get my head pointing the right way, but once I had, my eyes confirmed what my ears already knew. I was listening to DCI Pascoe.

He was bound much the same as me, but had slipped his gag enough that he'd spat out the rag and was mumbling around the side of it.

There was a large knife sticking out of his chest, and his shirt, plus the floor around his body, was slick with blood.

I had been wrong. DCI Pascoe wasn't the one who helped the boys cover their tracks, it was Beckett. With a rush of understanding that felt like putting my brain inside a wind tunnel, I saw it all.

Beckett wasn't connected to the case in 2016, but as a local cop would have known all about it. In many ways, not being part of the investigation would have given him some freedom of movement. He'd spoken with the suspects, probably in the station when no one was watching. I was almost impressed that he coached them well enough to get away with murder. However, while I knew he had done it, I could only speculate regarding his motivation.

For reasons that mystified me, Beckett abused his unexpected power to bury not only Craig's body where it would never be found, but also to bury the evidence linking the boys to it. He helped them get their stories straight, undoubtedly advising them to refuse legal counsel to ensure the boys wouldn't receive conflicting advice.

Pascoe must have known there was something off – he would have listened to the interviews and read the transcripts. He must have seen the same perfectly aligned stories, but for the sake of his godson, he chose not to pursue it.

Until we came snooping.

Prompted by our arrival, he dug back into the case, reopening his own investigation to run parallel to ours, though his was to be completely clandestine. That had to be why he was out in Goodnestone so frequently. It was why I saw him snooping around Mathew Anderson's derelict farm buildings. He was going back over the case, just as we were, trying his damnedest to figure out where Craig's body went. Find it and not only would the whole case reopen in a spectacular way, but a wealth of evidence would surface.

"Sorry about the tyres," DCI Pascoe wheezed at me. "Didn't want you to follow me and figure out what I missed before I could." He was clearly in pain, struggling to breathe and fighting to speak. The knife, a standard kitchen utensil, was buried almost to the hilt in his ribcage, right where his heart would be. The amount of blood pooling around him dictated he was almost certainly lost, but all the while he was conscious he stood a chance. He let his head slump back to the tile. "I always knew that case would come back and bite me."

I wanted to tell him not to talk. That he should save his strength, but all I could do was mumble unintelligible sounds. I was fighting against the gag, using my tongue to force the rag against the cloth holding it in place. If Pascoe could do it, so could I.

Raising his head again, DCI Pascoe nodded his head at the blade.

"That's me done for, Tony. I – I can barely feel my body. There's no time left for me, but there's no sense us both dying. Use the knife to cut your bonds and get free."

Shadow of a Lie

My eyes almost popped out of my head.

"He's waiting until dark," the DCI wheezed, his voice getting fainter all the time. "Then he'll dispose of us both. He can't risk taking us out in the day. When you get free, I think Craig's body is under his shed. I've been looking for somewhere they could have hidden it ever since you arrived. I knew someone helped them. I just never thought it could be Beckett. I mean, why? Regardless, I think we can be sure now that it was him."

By rubbing the side of my face against the floor, I got one corner of the gag to slip down. The effort tore the skin off my ear, but the gag was coming free.

"I always thought they buried the body, but I kept quiet about my suspicions because there is a truth I'm almost too embarrassed to admit." He met my gaze, his eyes begging forgiveness when he said, "I'm godfather to Shane Travers. Did you figure that out?" he posed the question, but wasn't looking to get an answer. Exhausted, he rolled onto his back again, his eyes aimed at the ceiling. "I've only ever told one person the truth of it. I had the case, the biggest case of my life, and who should pop up as a suspect but my own godson." He let out a tired laugh. "If you want to know why I didn't hold up my hand and let someone else take on the case, I'm afraid I just don't have an answer. Not really. I knew my connection to Shane would come out if it ever got to trial and that the truth of it might ruin the prosecution's chances. I couldn't let it go, though. My bosses were watching, so when I didn't say anything straight away, it was already too late." He turned his head to look at me. "Talk about stupid, eh?"

The other side of the gag came free, and I spat out the rag.

Whispering, I begged, "Sir, stop talking. Save your energy."

STEVE HIGGS

"What for?" he croaked. "If I survive, the enquiry that follows will ruin me. It's bad enough that my family will have to live with my shame. I'll not stick around to watch them suffer."

"Sir, you didn't kill anyone. We can still get out of this. I just need to get free."

I shuffled around onto my backside, rolled onto my back, and lifted my knees up to my chest. In a movie I would have then been able to duck my hands under my backside and get them in front of my body. However, either that was a movie trick, or you could only do it if you had abs like Jason Statham. My backside and belly took up altogether too much room for there to be any hope I was going to achieve the effect I wanted.

Rolling over again, I came up onto my knees. From there I could stand and hop. I toppled, righted myself and used a wall for support.

"Detective Sergeant Heaton, I am giving you an order now," wheezed the DCI. "Remove the knife from my chest and use it to cut your bonds. Once free you can bring Beckett to justice and give Craig Chowdry the peace he deserves."

"I'm not doing that, sir."

"Get on with it, man!" he snapped, the effort of it causing a spasm of coughing that ended with an ejection of blood. He slumped, his head rolled back, and he lay still.

"Sir?" I hissed. "Sir?"

If I could manoeuvre myself close enough, I could check his pulse, but I knew there was nothing I could do to revive him. He needed emergency medical help, and he needed it very soon.

Cursing under my breath, I inspected my surroundings for anything I could use. I was in Beckett's utility room. At

Shadow of a Lie

least, that was my best guess. A washer and dryer with an empty laundry basket on top sat against the wall opposite the door. On the adjacent wall, a high shelf held an iron and the little plastic jug to fill it. The iron could make a half decent weapon if I could get my hands free. The other two walls were blank, the room too small to allow Beckett to use them all for storage. There was one door which presumably led back into Beckett's house, so if I could get free and get out, I would still have to run the gauntlet to reach his front door.

Rotating awkwardly on the balls of my feet, I looked back down at DCI Pascoe. His chest had stopped rising and there was little doubt life had left his body.

It horrified me to do so, but seeing no option, I knelt next to his body, shuffled around until I had my back to him and reached out to grip the knife. His blood soaked through my trousers, and I could feel the warm stickiness of it on my hands where I gripped the knife.

I expected it to pull clear with little resistance, yet the vacuum effect sucking against it demanded a good yank to make it move. Sitting back on my haunches, I manoeuvred the blade carefully, twisted to get it between my wrists, and pushed down. I winced against the pain from the plastic tie biting into my skin, but didn't allow it to stop me. The knife didn't slice through as I hoped it would, but a few frantic moments of sawing and grunting did the trick.

With an audible 'snap' the plastic tie separated, and my hands came free. I cut my right pinky finger in the process, blood flowing from a deep cut I refused to acknowledge. In three seconds, my feet were also free, and I put the knife down to pull the gag up over my head.

Rising to my feet, my heart thumping in my chest yet again, I debated whether bursting through the door and

STEVE HIGGS

running would carry a higher probability of escape than carefully, quietly easing it open to sneak out.

Thankfully, I guess, I didn't need to find out because the door opened without me touching it and Beckett came in, his shotgun leading.

"Awake, are we?" he sneered, the business end of what I could now see was a Browning B525 aimed squarely and unwaveringly at my chest. From three feet away, the blast would tear through my vital organs and damned near tear me in half.

I backed up.

"Now, Beckett ..."

"Shut up! You had your chance. You even got kicked off the case, yet you had to keep sniffing around. Pleased with the result, are you? Happy with how things have turned out?" He came forward, stalking across the floor of the small utility room where the tight confines and low ceiling made him seem even bigger than before.

He raised the shotgun to bring it back down on my head. He was going to knock me out again, only this time I imagined he would slit my throat or stab the blade into my heart the way he had with his DCI.

Instinctively, I lifted my arms to protect myself, stepping into his swing so I could catch his weapon, but he anticipated the move, lashing out with a giant leg that caught under my ribs to snatch the breath from my lungs.

Doubled over, I looked up at his face.

Beckett grinned. "Say night, night."

DCI Pascoe screamed in rage. Lying flat on his back with a red halo of blood around his torso, he snatched up the abandoned kitchen knife to prove he wasn't quite as dead as I'd believed. Weak and barely conscious, he nevertheless plunged the blade into the only part of Beckett he could reach – his leg.

Shadow of a Lie

The shot gun went off, the noise deafening at such close quarters. The shot hit the ceiling, most of it going straight through to rain plaster down upon our heads.

Beckett squealed in pain, and I seized my chance. Grabbing the shotgun with both hands, I used the wall behind my body to shove off, driving Beckett back with a terrified scream. I was half blind from the plaster dust in the air, mostly deaf from the ringing in my ears, and convinced I was on the verge of a heart attack the stupid thing was banging so hard in my chest, but I wanted to live, dammit!

No! I wanted to retire! And no six foot five, dirty, psycho cop was going to stop that from happening!

Beckett stumbled backward, his injured leg making it impossible to resist my initial thrust. We fell out of the utility room, slamming into the wall of the hallway outside. He was injured, his shotgun's chamber was empty, and he wouldn't be able to run because there was a knife sticking out of his shin – I could see the glint of metal from the corner of my eye.

He was also three times stronger than me and chose that moment to demonstrate it. It was his back against the wall now, our roles reversed, so with crazed eyes glaring down at me, he pushed the shotgun and me away from his body like he was bench-pressing a toddler.

With all my might, I tried to resist, but any second now he was going to tear the shotgun from my hands and proceed to beat me to death with it.

I kicked the knife.

Beckett howled, and I ran. I had one chance and now that I was out of the utility room, I could see the front door. Dwindling daylight beckoned on the other side and the safety chain, not that a man like Beckett would need one, was dangling free.

STEVE HIGGS

Rage-filled bellows followed me and the sound of the shotgun's breech opening proved enough motivation to make me run even faster.

Covering the twenty yards to the door so swiftly I was a little disappointed not to have travelled back in time, I ripped at the door handle, throwing it wide and tumbling into the dusk beyond. My car was twenty yards away. How long would it take me to cover that distance? How long would it take Beckett to hobble to the door and take aim? How close could he get before I had the car started? I couldn't calculate the numbers, but I knew they were not going in my favour.

Running full pelt, I felt for my keys and a fresh panic arose – they were not there! Beckett must have stripped them from me along with my phone. Looking around, I saw that Pascoe's car was gone. While we were locked in his utility room, Beckett had been cleaning up his mess.

"Heaton!" Beckett roared.

I was outside in the street. There was no chance he could hope to escape justice if he shot me now, but glancing back to see where he was, I learned two things.

Firstly, Beckett was beyond reason. His eyes were two pools of burning hate. He was coming out of his house, the knife still embedded in his right shin and the shotgun held in the crook of his shoulder, ready to fire.

Secondly, I was not alone.

Ashley stepped out from the shade next to the front door, his right leg scything up like a sledgehammer. It kicked the shotgun upward just as it discharged, the shock-wave of the blast less than it had been in the utility room where it seemed to happen inside my chest. All the same, the sound of the blast pummelled me and stopped my heart even as the shot flew harmlessly into the air.

Ashley's leg wasn't done though. With Beckett's arms

Shadow of a Lie

still holding the shotgun raised above his head, Ashley pirouetting neatly off the toe of his left foot to kick the taller man in the face.

Beckett fell back inside his house, my partner following him in. I knew I needed to follow, to give a hand, but my whole body was shaking from the shock of my ordeal, from the adrenalin raging through my body, and from the absolute sense of exhaustion I felt.

I heaved in gulping lumps of air, pushing my legs to make their way back to the house. I had gone barely two steps before Ashley emerged.

"He's out cold," he let me know. "And cuffed. Are you all right? You're covered in blood."

"Pascoe," I managed to croak. "Pascoe is inside. Help him."

Ashley's face formed a quizzical expression, but from the series of questions he undoubtedly wanted to ask, he selected none, choosing instead to dash inside to see for himself.

The door to the house next door opened, a middle-aged woman poking her head out.

"Call the police," I gasped between lungfuls of air. I was still out of breath, but my heart was slowing. "Call the police, please," I repeated when she didn't move.

"I thought I heard a shot. Is everything all right?"

"Yes. The police, please. And an ambulance."

The lady produced her phone from a back pocket, and I walked away believing she would do as I asked. Still heaving air into my lungs, I trudged across Beckett's front lawn, getting halfway to the door when Ashley reappeared. He had blood on his right hand and a bright red mark on the collar of his immaculate shirt.

A sombre expression on his face, Ashley confirmed what I already knew.

"He's dead."

I nodded to accept the news, too little air in my lungs for a verbal response. DCI Pascoe hadn't exactly been innocent, but he was guilty only of foolishness. In the end, he'd tried to figure out who it was that aided the boys in the coverup, and even went so far as to figure it out. That he paid with his life was a terrible thing.

"He died saving me," I told Ashley, a little white lie that wasn't too far from the truth. Had the DCI not put all his final energy into stabbing Beckett, I would likely be lying dead next to him.

I slumped to the grass, my energy spent, but I knew it wasn't over yet. Not by a long shot.

CHAPTER 51

SITTING IN MY CAR, I WAS HANDED A TEA AND ACCEPTED IT gratefully. It was a bit stewed and served with several sugars. Not the way I like it at all, but I wasn't going to complain.

It was cold out now, the temperature dropping in line with the sun setting. Paramedics had checked me out, dressed my cut pinky finger, and gave me a clean bill of health. Apparently, I wasn't having a heart attack earlier, I'm just fat and unhealthy. Those are my words, not theirs.

Sitting in the dark outside Beckett's house, I made a promise to myself that I would lose some weight and start going to the gym. I just had to eat my way through the supply of cakes, biscuits, and other tasty goodies in the house first, then somehow resist buying more.

Beckett had been arrested and taken away. He was going to hospital to have his leg stitched and his broken nose reset – Ashley had kicked him square in the face. Not enough times in my opinion, though I kept that to myself.

The house was completely sealed off, the whole thing considered a crime scene. No one was getting in without a full forensic suit, not that I had any desire to explore inside.

STEVE HIGGS

It hadn't taken them long to find Beckett's gun cabinet, a lockable steel thing from an approved manufacturer. In it they discovered a rifle fitted with a homemade brass catcher, a simple device to ensure spent cases are not left behind. It explained why they found none at the clay pits.

It had been fired recently and was considered likely to be a match if they could find one of the bullets Beckett shot at me the previous evening.

They also found the same grey mud on a set of clothes in his washing machine. He'd stripped but hadn't yet gotten around to turning it on. After failing to kill me, he had to have made his way home, changed into work clothes, and hightailed it back to the clay pits to meet his boss when the inevitable call came in. In the garage they found boots with the same clay and an electric bicycle – silent to aid his escape last night.

They also found his phone and on it the calls placed to Curzon, French, Travers, and Botterill, the first of which occurred within minutes of our arrival in Wingham. He either overheard us speaking to DCI Pascoe or was bright enough to put two and two together. Either way, the trail of evidence was a complete circle. They even found the Post-it note. It was in Beckett's trash. That he had pretended to check my car for it only to steal it instead closed the lid on that mystery too.

Technically, there was nothing keeping me at the scene save for my own morbid curiosity. DCI Pascoe suggested Craig's body might be under Beckett's garden shed, and with that information to hand, the forensics team needed only minutes to confirm he could be right.

There was something dead beneath it leaking telltale gases. Work to carefully excavate the ground commenced almost immediately, the shed literally picked up and moved

Shadow of a Lie

to the other side of the garden by ten officers to expose the dirt beneath.

There was no concrete slab, just a double row of bricks to keep the shed off the ground. This made it easy to explore the exposed dirt. I knew all this from the previous update more than an hour ago and looked up now because Ashley was coming my way again.

Beckoning me when he got to within a couple of yards, Ashley waited for me to wind down my window.

"Come on. You should see for yourself."

I took another swig of the tea, grimacing at the sweetness before levering my door open to dump the rest in the street. The cool night air was bracing without a coat, but I could avoid visibly shivering for as long as this would take.

In the garden, where the shed had once been, a large white tent now covered the space. There were police officers all around it, some in uniform, others not, and moving among them the forensic scientists who would compile and examine the evidence to be found.

Beckoned to stick our heads inside the tent, I needed to do no more than that to know Craig Chowdry had finally been found. Roughly eighteen inches down, they uncovered the rug. Enough of it was exposed for me to see it was rolled around something.

Having seen enough, I withdrew. It had been a long day, and there was still much to do.

CHAPTER 52

WHILE I SPENT THE LAST FEW HOURS SITTING IN MY CAR, officers operating out of Wingham arrested the four boys. Daniel French, Shane Travers, Timothy Botterill and Andrew Curzon had enjoyed a seven-year reprieve on their sentences, but that was over now, and they were waiting for me at the nick.

Weirdly, because they committed the crime as minors, they would not be tried as adults and accordingly, their sentences would be less than they otherwise might.

Travelling back to Wingham, Ashley following behind me, it was now down to us to find out who did what. Did they all take turns stabbing the poor boy? Was it a fight and it went too far? Did Craig bring the knife? All these factors would affect the outcome of the trial that would now follow.

I thought we might argue over who to interview first but we both agreed Shane Travers was still the one most likely to cave. The appointed solicitor was there already by the time we arrived, a different one from last night, Ashley was pleased to find.

We were wrong though. Telling Shane that Craig's

Shadow of a Lie

body had been found wrapped in the rug from his mother's house made him twitchy and nervous, but he refused to answer any questions regarding how it could have arrived beneath Glenn Beckett's garden shed or about what really happened to Craig seven years ago.

Likewise, advising him that Detective Sergeant Beckett was in custody following the murder of DCI Pascoe did nothing to loosen his tongue. He was in freefall, plummeting downward and acting as though he would never reach the ground if he just pretended it wasn't there.

For the most part, he whispered, "No comment," and kept his eyes trained on the ground. He looked and sounded utterly miserable, but no matter how many times I explained that his best bet was to be the first to tell the truth and that if he did, he would be best placed to cut a deal, he refused to talk.

We terminated the interview at four minutes to midnight after a solid eighty minutes of badgering. Ultimately, it would make no difference whether the four boys confessed or not. Forensic evidence would connect them to the body, the rug itself was damning, and we still had DS Beckett to grill.

I doubted Beckett played any part in Craig's death. The reason for the cover up notwithstanding, I believed he would be wise enough to tell us what really happened in 2016.

In a breakroom at the back of Wingham nick, while Shane was being returned to his cell and swapped with Daniel French, Ashley asked, "Do you think perhaps Shane is the one who killed Craig? Like, I mean, the others egged him on, and to prove he was one of them, he went ahead and did it."

I gave it a moment of thought. It would explain why he kept quiet when the pair of us were willing to bet he would

STEVE HIGGS

spill the beans the moment we started on him. It didn't fit though, and I shook my head.

"I think his 'friends' would have dobbed him in. He's not the one the group would protect. I think maybe they all did it. One of them started, either French or Curzon, then they made the others take a turn, involving them all."

Ashley's face pulled into a sickened mask.

"That's pretty grim."

I shrugged. "Kids can be awful. The drive to be part of the group rather than outside it can be powerful. Craig used to be friends with all of them when they were younger. This might not have happened if he'd gone to the same local school instead of the posh private place."

I thought Ashley was going to have a go at me as if I were blaming Craig's parents, but he didn't and moments later we were notified that Daniel French was in the interview room when we were ready.

My body felt heavy. That sluggish feeling you get when you are extra tired and forcing yourself to operate well after you ought to be in bed. There was an argument to leave the interviews until the morning, we had some time to spare, but we also knew there would be a superintendent at Wingham nick by then, there to stand in for DCI Pascoe and control the mess his murder would cause.

This was our case, solved through actual blood, sweat, and tears. If we didn't get a confession tonight, it would likely be taken off our hands simply due to its high-profile nature. By the morning, the story of Craig Chowdry would be all over the news once more. DCI Pascoe's murder making it headline stuff even in a busy news week.

Daniel French looked up when we came in. His eyes were haunted, and his face carried none of the colour from previous encounters.

Ashley could have given him a friendly wave or thrown

Shadow of a Lie

out a comment about how nice it was to see him again so soon, but professional to the core, he made no mention of their earlier altercation, getting through the preliminaries so we could start the interview.

"Approximately two hours ago, a body was found beneath a garden shed belonging to Detective Sergeant Glenn Beckett," Ashley spoke precisely and clearly. "We believe the body to be that of Craig Chowdry."

I watched Daniel's face. A tear formed in the corner of his right eye from which it tracked slowly down his face. He did nothing to stop it or wipe it away.

"The body is wrapped in a rug that we believe was the property of Mrs Judy Travers of twenty-eight Hide Street, Goodnestone." Ashley was laying out what we had, the developments in the old case, and making it abundantly clear Danny and his friends were going away this time.

"Detective Sergeant Beckett is in custody and will be questioned shortly about his involvement in the …"

A knock at the door interrupted the interview. Irked, Ashley paused the recording to answer the door.

There was a young female officer outside. "Sorry, there's a young lady in reception. She claims to have information vital to the Craig Chowdry case."

My eyebrows raised, wondering whether it was Trudy. I almost jumped out of my skin when Daniel French started shouting.

"Sarah! Sarah, tell them nothing! Tell them nothing!"

The solicitor distanced himself, leaning away from his suddenly crazed client and looking shocked when Daniel vaulted the desk. He lunged for the door, and continued to shout at his sister – how he knew it was her in reception I had no idea, but it took both Ashley and me to wrestle him under control.

Well, okay, so it was mostly Ashley and not me, I still

have an injured pinky finger after all, but I was very encouraging to my young partner. The uniformed officer at the door came through it, lending her weight and a further two uniforms joined her, all three required to take the bucking, twisting, deranged Daniel French back to his cell.

He was sobbing all the way, begging his sister to keep quiet and go home.

Confused by the latest turn of events and with the interview very much on hold, Ashley and I went to see if it really was Daniel's little sister.

CHAPTER 53

UNCANNILY, DANIEL WAS RIGHT. THE YOUNG LADY IN reception was indeed his sister, Sarah French. Every bit as pregnant as she had been the last time I saw her, her face was blotchy and red where she had been crying. She looked miserable, as though beaten down by life and whatever terrible secret she had come to deliver.

"Sarah?" I said only her first name, and that was all the prompt she needed to blow my mind away.

"I'm here to confess to the murder of Craig Chowdry."

I almost said, "What?" but Ashley was faster off the mark than me.

Stepping forward he said, "Please come this way, Miss French."

We returned to the interview room, offering Sarah a glass of water or a cup of tea. She settled into a chair on the far side of the table, where she started talking before we could prompt her.

"I'm sorry I didn't come forward sooner," she sobbed, unable to keep her emotions at bay.

Ashley had to convince her to take a drink and a breath so he could set the recorder and get the interview started properly. When he was ready to start, he asked her to explain her story in as much detail as possible.

I kept my mouth shut, ready to listen, though I was expecting her story to be riddled with holes, the young woman here only to muddy the water in the hope it might help her brother.

"I didn't see Trudy that day. I was supposed to, and we really were going to go to Whitstable, but Daniel found the condom wrapper that morning and everything went wrong after that. We had a big fight. I can remember shouting that I got to make the decisions about my body. I was almost fifteen, and he lost his virginity to Cathy Cutmore when he was only thirteen." Sarah paused to take a sip of water and blow her nose. "Sorry," she apologised.

"That's perfectly all right," I encouraged. "Please continue."

"I was still going to see Trudy, I didn't think Danny would do anything stupid, but I heard him on the phone to Andy. I heard Danny say he was going to find Craig and beat him up. We fought again right there and then, and I hit him. My brother, that is. I punched him in the face and gave him a nosebleed, but he shoved me to the floor and left the house, cycling away faster than I could follow."

Sarah blew her nose again, the sound loud in the quiet room. Ashley spoke to the recorder to make it clear what noise a future audience had just heard.

"I didn't know where Danny had gone, so I tried calling Craig. He didn't answer, so I sent him a text and went to his house, scared Danny might go there. Andy was always spoiling for a fight, and Tim isn't much better. As for Shane, well he always did what the others told him, and I know Andy used to hit him if he ever questioned what they were proposing."

"Craig wasn't at home, but he called me while I was

Shadow of a Lie

still close to his house. He was raging about my brother and his friends. He said they attacked him outside the Shop Ryte and threatened to hurt him."

Thus far, Sarah's account tallied with what we knew, and it was interesting to hear it from a different perspective. It was, of course, the first time anyone had heard this version of events.

"Craig arrived back at his house soon enough. He was hopping mad and had a rip in the knee of his trousers. He said Andy hit him and he tore his trousers when he fell over. His leg was bleeding. Craig also said the boys were right behind him and he needed to be ready."

I wanted to ask what 'ready' meant, but knew well enough to stay quiet and let her talk.

"I argued with him, adamant my brother and his friends wouldn't actually do anything. I said we could just go in his house and stay there. That got him even madder. He said I was mad if I thought he was going to hide like a coward. Craig wanted to face them and deal with it once and for all. He went into his parent's kitchen and got a knife. It was a big one, like nine inches long or something," she showed the length with her hands. "I shouted at him to stop being so stupid and he told me I was dumped. He didn't want to go out with me anymore if I couldn't see that he was in the right and my brother was the psycho. He left the house, heading back toward town."

I could see the route in my head. It was a straight line from his house to the place where they found his blood, to the point where the boys crossed the road on their way to Beckett's house.

Sarah continued to explain. "I ran after him, pleading for him to stop, but just like Danny, he shoved me away. I tripped and fell to the ground, and I hurt myself. I guess he felt sorry about it because he came back to check on me.

STEVE HIGGS

He helped me up and when he did, I grabbed the knife. I just wanted to get it off him. I never meant to hurt him." She fell silent, tears flowing down her face. Unable to talk, she sobbed.

Ashley gave her more tissues, and we waited. A minute passed before she was able to talk again.

"Sorry," she sniffed, still barely able to talk.

We encouraged her to continue. I couldn't decide if this was a carefully concocted story or not. She delivered it in a tone and manner that made me believe her. There was more though, so I kept my mouth shut and listened.

"I don't really know how it happened, only that we both had hold of the knife and were fighting to make the other person let go. His feet tangled in mine, and we fell. He went backward, and I landed on top of him. The knife went straight into his chest."

We had to take another break so she could compose herself. When we resumed, she told us how she tried to revive him, panicking and freaking out, certain she had killed him because he had no pulse. By the time her brother and his friends arrived, Craig's colour had changed, and he was going stiff.

According to Sarah, it was Danny's idea to hide the body. He made Shane fetch a rug from his house because his mum's place was closest, and they knew she was at work. Tim went with him.

Sarah finished by saying, "I'm fuzzy about the rest because I kinda folded in on myself. I was freaking out, convinced I was going to jail for the rest of my life. I cannot tell you how good it feels to finally tell the truth."

We had it all on tape, a complete confession that explained everything that happened and why. However, it conveniently removed all blame for Craig's death from the four boys while rendering the death as misadventure rather

Shadow of a Lie

than murder. At face value, Sarah never intended to kill her boyfriend.

Our next task was to pick apart her story, convenient as it seemed, but I had another question first.

"Detective Sergeant Glenn Beckett stepped in to help. He provided a hiding place for Craig's body and coached you all on what to say and what not to say, didn't he?"

Sarah didn't look up, but mumbled, "Yes."

"Why would he do that, Sarah?"

She murmured something too softly for either Ashley or me to make out the words.

"Again, please, Sarah. Loud enough for the recording to hear it."

She drew in a breath, but never took her eyes off the floor when she said, "He's Danny's father."

CHAPTER 54

TWO DAYS AFTER THE EVENTS IN GOODNESTONE, THE STORY
had broken, and the national press was all over it. Ashley
and I both got stern words from our bosses for disobeying
orders, but they were tempered by congratulations for
doggedly running down the solution to Craig Chowdry's
disappearance.

I almost told my boss exactly what he could do with his
congratulations. He wanted to grab a share of the lime-
light shining our way, nothing more. But like so many other
things in my life, the energy to challenge him publicly
escaped me.

Essentially, we got away with our rebellion and the
wrongful arrest charge against Ashley vanished in the blink
of an eye. The fact that it was a cop behind the cover up
allowed us to play up how hard it was to tell anyone what
we were doing and how fast and loose we needed to be
with the rules.

Beckett admitted to everything, his full confession
confirming what Sarah told us and essentially ending the
investigation. Oh, it was going to go to trial, obviously, and
that would drag things out, but the case had been taken off

Shadow of a Lie

our hands, swept up by a new SIO, a detective superintendent this time, who with a proper team at his side would
see DS Beckett went to jail.

Beckett *was* Danny's father, a drunken one-night stand
resulting in an illegitimate son he never told anyone about.
He'd watched from afar, aware of the child, but content to
play no part. However, when Danny's mother died and his
father proved to prefer the bottle to parenting, Beckett
made himself known. Not as his father, not at first. Not
even when he believed Danny killed Craig Chowdry.
Danny and his little sister knew Glenn Beckett as a kindly
local police officer who stopped by the house to help them
out with money or food. He made it seem like it was part
of his job and as they grew, he would have them over to his
house when their father drunk himself into a stupor.

He became someone they could trust. So much so that
when Danny came across Craig's body and his sobbing
sister, he could think of only one person to call. The truth
of his parentage came out much later, when he turned
eighteen and Beckett felt he was old enough to hear it.

Of course, Beckett had no idea it was really Sarah who
stabbed Craig, or that it was an accident. Danny lied to
protect his little sister, fooling the detective into helping to
cover up a crime that never existed. Had they told the
truth, it would all have gone away, a tragedy that would
most likely have recorded a verdict of death by misadventure.

Instead, Beckett was going to jail for murder. The two
counts of attempted murder against me were mere back-
ground noise.

The four boys would probably serve terms behind bars,
but they would not be long ones. Some parts of the press
were even hailing them as heroes - the four plucky
teenagers who put their freedom at risk to save Sarah

STEVE HIGGS

because they didn't know any better. They were guilty of burying Craig's body, but the bulk of that crime would also be carried by Beckett as he was the adult at the time.

There was no blood on them or found on any of their clothes because they didn't kill Craig. With Beckett instructing them, they were very careful to wrap Craig's body in the rug. In contrast, Sarah's clothes were soaked in red, her outfit burned to hide the evidence, not that anyone ever looked at her as a suspect.

Jane Wallace almost caught the boys with the body. Had she come along the road a minute earlier or later, she would have seen the roll of carpet with Craig's feet sticking out from one end.

Shane *had* been trying to tell me the truth the night I almost got shot. He was spotted leaving the Post-it note and got his black eyes courtesy of Andrew Curzon, just as I suspected. Danny then told Beckett, who forced Shane to go through with the meeting. Shane escaped on Andrew's dirt bike, the four boys relying on Beckett to make sure I was dead and that the evidence wouldn't link back to them.

Had he succeeded in his attempt to kill me, one could only assume he would have gone after Ashley next.

Prompted into action by our arrival, DCI Pascoe was doing what he ought to have done seven years ago – trying to figure out who helped the boys. I believe he had narrowed it down to Beckett and was looking into his holdings. That was why he was at Mathew Anderson's – he *is* Beckett's uncle, a fact Ashley discovered after his second meeting with Jane Wallace. Pascoe must have been eliminating possible sites where Craig might have been interred. The search led him to Beckett's house.

He'd sent Beckett off on an errand that afternoon, getting him out of the area so Pascoe could snoop around,

Shadow of a Lie

but the house was fitted with one of those camera door-bells which alerted Beckett that his boss was at his house.

I had arrived just a few minutes later.

At the nick in Herne Bay to meet with Ashley, I was still refusing to take my sick days in favour of pursuing the next case. I'm not sure I could accurately articulate what had changed in me, but I ate fruit for breakfast this morning, and didn't have anything to drink last night.

The murder of Michelle Canet beckoned, a fresh case for us to sink our teeth into and Ashley had a secondary investigation he felt worthy of our efforts at the same time – that of a known white racist murdered more than a decade ago. However, my hopes that he might have put the Bruce Denton case behind him were dashed when he brought it up again.

Raised aloft by solving Craig Chowdry's murder, he was more confident than ever that we could crack it together. I gave him the same response as before – that it was unsolvable and a waste of his time, yet I could see how badly he wanted to take it on.

I was left with the impression he wanted to solve it for me, to give me closure or something. He didn't understand how investigating my old case would deliver precisely the opposite.

For more than two decades, I pursued new evidence mercilessly. At the weekends, after work, between cases ... whenever I could, I went back to Bruce Denton's murder and tried to find that which might open the door to identify the killer. I had lost a key piece of evidence, but it couldn't be the only clue out there.

The people connected to the case: the victim's neighbours, work colleagues, parents, and more got used to my regular visits. In some cases, my appearances were welcomed; his parents were happy I wasn't letting the case

STEVE HIGGS

go, but others came to resent my pestering. The same questions over and over again, asking if they remembered anything new, confirming what they heard and saw on that fateful day and the period leading up to it.

Complaints found my boss, and he came to find me, but I refused to stop investigating even when I was barred from bothering some of those who might conceivably yield pertinent information.

It wore me down, but I knew I couldn't let it go, not if there was a chance someone would remember something. If that happened, I had to be the one to hear it first.

However, as the years went by, I came to accept the case would never be solved and that the killer would never be found. This was good, because I didn't need to solve the case. I didn't need to work out who snuck into his house to bludgeon him to death. There was never any doubt in my mind who was behind it.

I knew for certain who was responsible because I killed Bruce Denton.

I fake the mental anguish and emotional turmoil, and if I do say so myself, I am quite good at it. At least, no one questions it, and they never have. That is not to say I don't feel stress whenever the name 'Bruce Denton' arises.

The piece of vital evidence I lost was a camcorder. It belonged to a kid a few doors along the street from Bruce Denton's house. Given it as an eighteenth birthday present, he was shooting footage of his motorbike and managed to capture Bruce walking into his house with a woman. A blonde woman. We found blonde hair on Bruce's pillows, but no one knew the identity of the mystery woman. She didn't come forward, and I knew she never would.

The video evidence might have led us to her, and I could not allow that. I continued to pursue the case for all those years specifically to be certain I would be there to

Shadow of a Lie

intercept and control any new information if it ever arose. Witnesses living in his street reported seeing a man sitting in his car in the days before Bruce's murder, but the descriptions they gave conflicted due to my selection of disguises and the car they claimed he was in didn't match either because I took cars from the impound.

My caution, combined with a clearheaded approach, reduced the potential evidence to almost nothing. What little there was came about through chance – not something I could protect against, yet by being the man leading the investigation, I got to control it. Some statements made their way into the bin and the one piece of evidence I knew could sink me – the camcorder – went somewhere it would never be found.

Worrying whether I would ever be caught used to keep me awake at night. It still does occasionally, but not very often anymore. It wasn't as if any new evidence was about to come to light.

EPILOGUE

THE LETTER OF PERMISSION TO DIG A TEST PIT FINALLY arrived two months before the team assembled on the edge of the bog at Monkton Nature Reserve. The fight to obtain it, just for a series of test pits, was never supposed to become a mission for the person behind it, but that's what it turned into.

George David was twenty-nine when he wrote the first letter, tasked with it at the time by his professor, a man named Derek Holcombe. He got no answer, but knowing he was expected to be persistent, he wrote again and again. He made phone calls and waded through layers of bureaucracy to finally arrive at someone who would make a decision.

The decision was no.

Monkton Nature Reserve covers a wide swathe of land from Herne Bay out towards the Kent Peninsular and the seaside towns of Margate and Broadstairs, the latter made famous by Dickens when he wrote *Bleak House*. Settlements existed on the land more than four thousand years ago and it was to explore and hopefully untap the potentially rich

Shadow of a Lie

historical pickings they would find there that drove George to continue trying.

Professor Holcombe retired as all people do, dying just eighteen months later from bowel cancer, a disease he knew about when he chose to end his time at Canterbury University.

New professors came and went, George David serving them all as a research assistant, though he got no glory for the papers they eventually submitted using his hard work. He didn't mind so much; it was how the system worked and without the right letters behind his name, no one would ever read the works even if he did publish them himself.

Listening to a local radio station as he drove to the site, the newsreader told him all about a teenage boy who went missing seven years ago only to be found the previous day.

He parked his car, a tired and faded blue Land Rover three series, next to a Ford Fiesta. The Fiesta belonged to Nancy Beswick, one of the archaeology students taking part in the dig. George, twice divorced, was quite aware of Nancy's physical attributes, not that he harboured any thoughts of making a move. It would be highly unethical for a start since he worked for the faculty, but more because he felt certain she would laugh in his face.

Like the other students, who ranged in age but were all in their twenties, she was almost thirty years his junior.

There were other cars parked at the edge of the road, right next to a gate that led into the field where they would dig their test pits. The grass on the verge, in need of a cut and wet with dew this early in the morning, showed where others had already walked. Removing a pair of wellington boots from the boot of his car, George rechecked the equipment in his bag and set off across the field toward the

STEVE HIGGS

people he could already see gathered under a small copse of trees.

There were raised groundworks to his left, a clear sign of human inhabitation many centuries before, and he found a sense of anticipation, the same he got every time he embarked upon a new dig. Sometimes there was nothing of worth to be found, yet he held great hope for this site. After all, it would be a cruel irony to have struggled for so long to obtain permission for the excavations only to then find there was nothing here.

By noon that day, the test pits were almost dug, not that he had picked up a shovel himself. That came down to the students and, shockingly, to the professor who was in his late thirties, single, and clearly someone who went to the gym. It was warm for October, and the professor had elected to remove his shirt – clearly so he could show off his physique, not because the temperature demanded it.

George noted that Nancy couldn't keep her eyes off him, and she wasn't the only one. Any thoughts of removing his own shirt were quickly quashed; George hadn't seen the inside of a gym since he left school and was less than athletic even then.

Distracting himself by taking a walk to visit the other test pits, George wandered across the field.

On the far edge of their dig, right next to the road, the final test pit in the series was in a bog. The whole area was a natural wetland, the water table rising in the prevailing centuries since humans inhabited it. It was the rarity of the wetland in this part of the world that created so much contest to their application to dig. Diverse wildlife, some found nowhere else in Britain, carried protected status, but the boggy nature of the ground was known to help preserve some artefacts and that made it especially attractive to the archaeologists too.

Shadow of a Lie

Drawing near to the furthest test pit, George could hear the guys there arguing about something. Sam Riddell and Carl Brady were not generally given to emotional outbursts and, in fact, were paired together and given the dirtiest job because it was expected they would give the task their best without complaining.

"What's going on, chaps?" George spoke up to announce his presence since neither was looking his way. "Everything okay?"

Standing in the hole, Sam shot his head around to look at the approaching research assistant. George only got a brief glance from Carl.

"It's contaminated," Sam remarked, his attention back on the hole.

George felt his eyebrows knit together, questions forming. Carl crouched, almost vanishing from sight as he ducked into the hole.

Where the land sloped down on this side of the field, the water table was higher, and their test pit was filled with dark, muddy water. The contents of the hole were spread out in a series of examination trays, but George could see nothing to provide a clue to Sam's statement.

That changed a moment later when Carl pulled a large object from the water. It was coated in mud which dripped and plopped back into the water around the two students. They were filthy, their wetsuits and fishing waders just as dirty as everything around them.

If they minded, they were yet to complain, but George was too focused on the object in Carl's hands to care about their happiness or comfort. It was big, that was the first thought that struck his mind. A tingle of excitement rippled through him. What had they found? It looked bulky and heavy; was it a bronze artefact? Some kind of

STEVE HIGGS

stone carving that would relate to a deity the ancient settlers worshipped?

Carl hefted it into the nearest examination tray, flicking mud from his hands while complaining.

"This mud is the worst. I dropped this stupid thing the first time."

George wasn't listening. He needed to know what it was. Coming down to one knee, the water on the ground immediately soaking his jeans, he reached out to tentatively touch the object. There was something odd about it, something about the sound it made when it touched the surface of the tray that wasn't … right.

"It's a plastic bag," announced Carl, clambering back out of the hole. "So unless the ancient Britons were also time travellers, this has been added afterward."

Both men voiced their intention to get lunch, stripping off their soaking outer layers a few feet away while George stared at the find. The wet mud was slowly flowing away from the smooth surface of the plastic to confirm Carl wasn't wrong.

George's top lip twitched in annoyance. It wouldn't ruin the dig, but it would mar their results and call into question what they found elsewhere. Years of petitioning only to find the site was contaminated.

About to turn away, he stopped when curiosity demanded he see what was in the bag. Beneath the mud the plastic was clear, so he used the remains of a bottle of spring water in his pocket to chase away that which still clung to it.

Two things were revealed almost instantly. Firstly, the object inside the bag was a camcorder. Quite what a piece of eighties hardware could be doing so far from civilisation was anyone's guess. The second thing George noticed made his heart thump.

Shadow of a Lie

Along the top edge of the bag ran a blue bar about an inch thick. Below it in bold letters he read the legend 'Evidence Bag'. Beneath that were boxes of information. The writing on them was surprisingly intact.

"DS T Heaton," he read, his eyebrows scrunched together as he squinted at the next box. "June 19th, 1993?" The thing was thirty years old!

Now that the mud was mostly gone, he could see the inside had suffered only minimal seepage over the three decades since it found its way into the bog. Incredibly, the bag had done what it was supposed to do – preserve the contents. The camcorder looked dry inside the sealed container.

George David had no idea how the evidence bag could have arrived in the bog at the edge of a field so far from the nearest town, but knew there and then he was going to have to call the police.

The End

AUTHOR'S NOTE:

Dear Reader,

Thank you for reading all the way to the end and beyond. Unless you elected to read this bit first, in which case, please go to the start and I'll see you back here in a few hours.

This story came about in 2019 when I thought it would be a good idea to enter a short story writing competition. This is, of course, not a short story, but an expanded tale developed from that original idea.

Needless to say, I did not win the short story competition, but when I finally returned to it in 2023, I discovered it was not all that well written. This does not come as a surprise to me. I have written almost one hundred books now, my skills developing through practice.

There will be books to follow this one, Ashley and Tony returning to explore another case and then another as they work through both the list of unsolved murders and Tony's last few weeks before retirement. There is, however, a very definite end point coming. If you read the book before arriving here, you will understand why I cannot write more about it without ruining the shocking events to come.

Author's Note:

I'm typing out this final note at the start of July with the rain pattering against the window just a few feet in front of my face. Yesterday, I was on holiday with my wife and children, tomorrow I will probably be painting walls in the freshly plastered playroom. Life as an author is like that – different every day, though I spend much of it immersed in my own little imaginary world.

Take care.

Steve Higgs

WHAT'S NEXT FOR THE COLD CASE TASK FORCE?

Sometimes, the hardest truth is the one we hide from ourselves.

Detective Sergeant Tony Heaton has been living a lie for thirty years.

Plagued by his failure to solve a brutal slaying in a peaceful seaside town, Tony is weeks from retirement when a new piece of evidence comes to light.

He knows the case better than anyone on the planet, and is perfectly positioned to dive straight back in.

But DS Heaton doesn't need to solve the case. He already knows who the killer is, so as those around him sift the truth from the lies, he must work to stay one step ahead.

The truth must stay hidden, even if that means lying to himself.

FREE BOOKS AND MORE

Want to see what else I have written? Go to my website.
https://stevehiggsbooks.com/

Or sign up to my newsletter where you will get sneak peaks, exclusive giveaways, behind the scenes content, and more. Plus, you'll be notified of Fan Pricing events when they occur and get exclusive offers from other authors because all UF writers are automatically friends.

Click the link or copy it carefully into your web browser.
https://stevehiggsbooks.com/newsletter/

Prefer social media? Join my thriving Facebook community.

Want to join the inner circle where you can keep up to date with everything? This is a free group on Facebook where you can hang out with likeminded individuals and enjoy discussing my books. There is cake too (but only if you bring it).

https://www.facebook.com/groups/1151907108277718

Printed in Great Britain
by Amazon